M000298418

LAST LIGHT

LAST LIGHT

Catherine Ross

This first world edition published in Great Britain 2005 by
SEVERN HOUSE PUBLISHERS LTD of
9–15 High Street, Sutton, Surrey SM1 1DF.
This first world edition published in the USA 2005 by
SEVERN HOUSE PUBLISHERS INC of
595 Madison Avenue, New York, N.Y. 10022.

Copyright © 2005 by Catherine Ross.

All rights reserved.
The moral right of the author has been asserted.

British Library Cataloguing in Publication Data

Ross, Catherine
    Last light
    1. Female friendship - Fiction
    2. World War, 1939-1945 - England - Lincolnshire - Fiction
    I. Title
    823.9'14 [F]

    ISBN 0-7278-6254-5

Except where actual historical events and characters are being
described for the storyline of this novel, all situations in this
publication are fictitious and any resemblance to living persons
is purely coincidental.

Typeset by Palimpsest Book Production Ltd.,
Polmont, Stirlingshire, Scotland.
Printed and bound in Great Britain by
MPG Books Ltd., Bodmin, Cornwall.

Dawn

2004

The key ring in the ignition chimed like a tiny warning bell as she swept the Jaguar out of the Channel Tunnel. Accelerating up the incline, she glanced down at the key ring – the stubby spent Messerschmitt bullet captured in its silvery Duralumin cage. It was her talisman, her keeper of memories. It had been all these years.

She turned her eyes back to the road, fought her way through the sudden surge of accelerating traffic, then headed south down the motorway, speeding over the long concrete bridges, the glistening arrow of the road.

The sun had risen clear of morning cloud. It twinkled between the spring leaves of the poplars. Miles on and the poplar trees became plane trees. Then pine forests climbed low hills, turning, further along the route, into dense forests above closely packed valleys threaded with rushing streams. Resistance country. She thought of Gabby.

Around midday, she left the main route, following a minor road to the south-east. Soon she was in rolling fields of pasture and grain. The sun shone on a slow-moving curve of river. She let down the windows. A light wind ruffled her hair. She breathed in the sweet scents of France – fertile earth, spring flowers, wine, resin – but not pleasurably, wishing she hadn't come. Not sure that, even after all these years, she could cope. Not on her own. She drew in a deep steadying breath. Six months ago, they had found the bodies, or rather what fragments of them remained.

Burned, crushed, buried, concreted over, forgotten, because sixty years ago the French had wanted to forget. They wanted to forget the war, the occupation, the brutality, the torture, the shame of the collaborators and the gallantry of the Resistance.

3

The rubble of the infamous Gestapo house in the infamous square was swept away a couple of years after World War Two ended; the site was concreted over, then a block of cheap utilitarian flats was built on the concrete. But now times had changed. Remembrance had become the order of the day. The finding of the bodies had coincided with a surge of pride in France's history and in the bravery of the Resistance, and – more potent still – with European Union grants being handed out for the rebuilding of towns and cities in their original character. The square at d'Orages was one of them. Last year when the already decaying concrete flats were bulldozed away and the ground excavated, they had discovered human remains and, nearby, pieces of the exploded Lancaster bomber.

Some of the bodies had been identified by shards of human bone, by teeth, by crumbling fragments of clothing, the aircrew by their identification discs. The tortured bodies of the Resistance workers were beyond separation.

The remains had been decently and swiftly buried. But now the time had come for a plaque and a ceremony to honour them. It was all over now. Other wars had thrown up their war crimes and their war criminals. World War Two's crimes had been forgiven. It was the courage that had to be remembered.

World War Two's enemies being now our friends, the dais in the square at d'Orages would be decorated with the flags of Germany as well as France and Britain. The brass bands would play *Deutschland Über Alles* as well as *God Save the Queen* and the *Marseillaise*. A German priest would assist the Bishop of Lincoln, in whose bishopric had lain Holmfirth-on-the-Moor, the thunder of whose bombers had nightly rocked the Germans' beautiful triple-towered cathedral, a landmark for all aircraft, hostile as well as friendly.

And because the discovery of the remains had come when the British government felt it expedient to bang the European Union drum, the Foreign Secretary had indicated that he might be present, and the Defence Ministry had assiduously traced Holmfirth's surviving personnel with a pressing invitation to attend.

4

She should have refused. But there were so few of them left. Had he been alive, her husband would certainly have gone. And he would have wanted her to go, wouldn't have let her refuse. But she was old now and alone. Holmfirth belonged to her vanished youth.

Yet Holmfirth had changed all their lives, the women's as well as the men's: made them confront life and death. They had grown up too swiftly and fiercely, like newly hatched creatures in some atomic accelerator; and not just because of that one desperate raid at last light.

THE HEAT OF THE DAY

1943

One

The tannoy woke her. A hissing, indrawn, doom-laden breath half-smothered in weird atmospheric cracklings from the amplifier immediately above her head. Had she been dreaming? Of school of all places: the same narrow bed, the same bare floor, the unrelieved darkness.

Now she was aware of the scrubby blanket under her chin, the two thick identification discs strung around her neck, the red one proof against fire, the green against water, the hardness of the three biscuits that made up the mattress, the throbbing ache of her vaccinated arm, the stifling, threatening atmosphere all around.

The indrawn breath exploded into a harsh nasal voice. 'An aircraft has crashed on the runway. All available personnel are to turn out with torches and search for the body of the pilot.'

Immediately, her own breathing was suspended. She felt icy cold and sick with panic. She clutched the blanket protectively closer under her chin and lay absolutely still.

'I repeat,' the inescapable voice rasped round the small downstairs room of what had once been an RAF married quarter, the tone more hectoring now. 'All available personnel on to the airfield immediately. Search for the body of the pilot.'

Search for the body of the pilot! Her limbs shook. Her teeth chattered. Search for a body! It couldn't mean her. She was hardly personnel yet, surely. She was still Carole Kemp, aircraftwoman second class, with two weeks' terrible initial square-bashing and a pathetically short course in MT driving behind her, and still, despite the blue uniform, a nineteen-year-old only a year out of school.

She didn't know the geography of the airfield. She had only arrived earlier that night.

9

She had never set foot on an operational station before, had never seen a dead body; wouldn't know where to begin to look for one, wouldn't want to find one. Didn't know anything about death – or life come to that. Had never seen a man's naked body.

Hadn't known the so-called facts of life until three weeks ago on that fearsome training course, when, following a lecture on poison gases and a period testing their masks in the decontamination centre, an RAF doctor had given them a talk on venereal diseases, and so that they would better understand that area of their anatomy, had drawn diagrams on the blackboard. Diagrams that her father, a Methodist minister, would have forbidden her to see and at which one of the more faint-hearted girls was sick into her handkerchief.

The tannoy crackled again. The disembodied voice snarled menacingly now, as if he had X-ray eyes and could see through the blacked-out, taped-up windows to where she was trying to lie doggo.

'This is an order. I repeat, this is an order. All personnel are to search for the body of the pilot.'

The voice had an effect. Above, now, someone thumped out of bed. There were two other girls upstairs in this small terraced house built flimsily in the thirties for the families of other ranks. The two girls had arrived last night at the railway station dragging their kitbags and cases along the dark platform. But before they had time to speak, an RAF corporal had appeared, waving a torch, shouting 'Holmfirth! Let's have you! Get cracking!'

The black shape of a three-ton Daimler had materialized. Outside the station, its tailboard rattled down. The corporal shoved the three girls up into the interior, which smelled of dust and new wood and spilled oil. They had squatted among crates of spares, and drums that gurgled as the corporal accelerated away into the darkness. The Daimler swung round corners, up a gentle slope, through the fretted blackness of a pine wood, and finally, reluctantly slowed for the pillbox, the red and white pole and the duty service policeman marking the entrance to RAF Holmfirth-on-the-Moor.

Holmfirth was a vast township built on the Lincolnshire flatlands, its gaunt hangars, its barrack blocks, its workshops solid against a misty sky. To the left of the road stood the

10

stalks of the lead-in lights with their shielded lamps; as the RAF policeman raised the gate pole, black bat shapes with red glowing exhausts swooped and roared over the truck. They had arrived at an operational station. She should have been warned.

Then through the gate, and into the guardroom, where a group of SPs (service police) clustered around a glowing stove, eyeing the girls expertly from head to foot, while a corporal SP examined their identity cards. Then they were swept on again into the truck and over to the deserted cavern of the cookhouse. Plates of baked beans on greasy fried bread were dropped in front of them, eaten in silence, plates washed in the huge vat of dirty water at the cookhouse exit; and then they were consigned to this married quarter, unfurnished except for metal lockers and iron bedsteads.

They had seen nothing but the guardroom and the cookhouse, the dark roadways, the lead-in lights, and the swooping aircraft. Now one of those aircraft, those black shapes, had crashed. But surely they couldn't want her to look for the body of the pilot. She huddled deeper down, wincing because her left arm was puffy and sore where the same doctor who had drawn the diagrams had supervised the mass giving of injections and vaccinations, economically using the same needle throughout.

Now the thumps above were turning into the heavy sound of a kitbag being dragged across the bare boards, the screech of a metal locker being opened. She heard the voices of Bunty the buxom blonde with the kewpie-doll face, and Gabriella, the tall tight-lipped girl who wore on her sleeve the propeller of a leading aircraftwoman and an R/T operator's flash, and who had told them nothing about herself except that she was half-French.

Then came the clatter of clumsy issue shoes on the bare treads of the stairs. Down came Bunty, fully dressed in uniform, her tie neatly knotted, her respirator slung, wearing her steel helmet instead of her issue cap and yet, with the curl of yellow hair pulled forward from under the helmet, looking more than ever like a celluloid doll.

'Come on, Carole! Get cracking! You heard what the man said! Dress yourself!'

'No!'

11

'Gabriella's nearly ready! Raise yourself! Get up!'

'They don't mean us!'

''Course they do! I've bin in longer than you, sprog! Everybody means *everybody*!'

Bunty leaned forward, grabbed a handful of hairy blanket and whipped the whole lot back.

'Ooh! You're wearing a nightie! Naughty girl! You're supposed to wear your issue pyjamas.'

'They tickle!'

'You'll get more than a tickle if they catch you in that! Take it off! Come on! Get dressed.'

As Carole began reluctantly to swing her feet on to the floor, Gabriella descended into the room. Even at three o'clock in the morning, with circles under her dark-brown eyes, she walked erect and with an elegant dignity. She brandished a small torch.

'Is your kit in the locker?'

'Yes.'

She glided over. The green metal door squeaked open. The new scrubby battledress top and trousers were flung at her, followed by a blue shirt and loose collar, then a pair of thick navy-blue directoire knickers.

Gabriella held up a bright pink bust bodice, the size of twin parachutes, twisting the garment by a disparaging finger.

'Jeezus wept!' Bunty exclaimed, snatching the bodice, holding it against her own well-developed bust and giggling wildly. 'It's too big even for me! Didn't stores have your size?'

'No.'

'You could make do with half.'

'Just put it on,' Gabriella said briskly. 'Shoes?'

'By the bed.'

'Don't bother about your tie. You'll have to have your respirator though. And your tin hat!'

Gabriella detached the steel helmet from Carole's respirator and plonked it on her head.

'Right! That's it! Off we go! Mind the blackout!'

'Don't look so worried,' Bunty whispered to Carole. 'They'll have found the poor sod by now!'

But to nail that comforting lie, the tannoy burst out as they turned the doorknob. 'The east–west runway has been searched.

12

Personnel now proceed to the area between the runways and the aprons.'

'Wherever that might be!' Bunty muttered.

Out in the moist autumn-scented darkness, it all seemed detached from reality. Out there, nearly two thousand people lived and worked. Somewhere out there, a young man, maybe no older than they were, maybe piloting one of those dark shapes that had flown over them a few hours ago, had died.

Instinctively, they slowed their pace, aware that they moved in an unmarked, unknown and threatening landscape, simultaneously overwhelmed by the need to find, yet the fear to find.

'We don't know where to begin!' Carole slowed her pace further. 'We don't know the layout! We don't even know where the aprons and runways are!'

'It'll be thataway!' Bunty took her arm. 'Near the lead-in lights.'

Of the three, she was the one who came closest to enjoying the drama, the feeling of being where the action was.

Encouragingly, she whispered breathily to the others, 'I'm not scared of dead bodies! They're nothing to be afraid of! It's the living ones you gotta watch.'

Their footsteps echoed. They looked about them uneasily. Strangely, there was no sound of aircraft engines.

'They'll have suspended flying,' Gabriella said authoritatively, 'until they find him.'

'Or what's left of the poor clot!' Bunty sighed.

It was a deceptively, beguilingly, beautiful night. Above a misted horizon arched a starlit sky, fingered in the east by blue-white searchlights unmenacing and unhurried. The two rows of married quarters were to the south of the airfield; most of them looked as yet unoccupied, the narrow road between them deserted, echoing to their steps. But once out of that little backwater, past an enormous ARP water tank and on to the main airfield road, some of the two thousand inhabitants came into shadowy view.

Here was subdued noise and urgency. Uniformed figures were hurrying towards what must be the main runways. A Bedford truck lumbered past them, its gears crashing noisily, its lights baffled into slits, its rear filled with airmen.

Catching a brief sight of the three girls, the airmen stood up, waving and wolf-whistling. A fire engine screamed past

13

it then. Followed by a skidding ambulance. Maybe they had found him. Maybe they could now go back to what, even after a few short hours, had become a sort of home.

But no. As they approached the gaunt outlines of the hangars, a sergeant with an SP armband stepped out of the shadows and barked at them, 'Airwomen! Over here! At the double!'

He let his bullseye lantern flick over them. Then he handed each of them a stick and a whistle.

'We're out of torches. Use what you've got.'

Dispassionately and crisply, he directed them to search the area beyond this first hangar, Number One, moving then in a line along the side of the north–south runway towards dispersal. He waved his arm in the rough direction. All they could see in the pale starlight was a vast area of coarse bumpy grass that stretched from the sharp black shadow of the hangar towards a black shiny strip that was the runway. Carole hung back. Her still ill-fitting issue shoes pinched her toes, her arm hurt, she felt sick with apprehension.

'Come on!' The other two grasped an arm apiece and marched her forward to the corner of the hangar.

A small door cut into the main door was open. Through it, they could glimpse overalled and goggled men at the top of high gantries, working on a stripped-down airframe, sending showers of brilliant blue sparks up into the iron rafters.

Bunty lingered in the doorway, dropped Carole's arm, put her fingers to her little kewpie-doll mouth and whistled piercingly. Then she ran ahead of the other two, laughing into the darkness of the scrubby wasteland.

Here there were sweet night smells of crushed grass and wild thyme and damp earth. But, as they picked their way forward, their nostrils were filled with a pungent mixture of petrol and scorching smothering those scents, and another smell too awful to identify.

'Come on, you two!' Bunty called, cheered by the sight of the men in the hangar. 'Give me the torch! Get one each side of me! I'm not scared! My mum used to lay out bodies. I used to watch her. Now walk slowly. Keep your eyes skinned.' Bunty assumed an unlikely command, flicking the feeble torch beam right and left, while the other two inched forward, trying

14

hard to concentrate on their view of the tussocky decaying grass, the clumps of thistles, parting them dutifully with their sticks, trying to find the pilot, but just as fervently hoping that they wouldn't.

The ground was uneven, full of hillocks and holes, soggy, smelly patches of bog, and thickets of sharp-thorned bushes that could easily hide a man's body. In the wavering light, they assumed strange, menacing and mysterious shapes. A cold wet wind was blowing, rustling the tough dead bramble leaves like someone stirring, trying to get out.

'Like I said, I'm not scared of dead bodies!' Bunty repeated, though much less certainly now. 'Sometimes my mum used to let me help her make them look nice.' She sighed heavily. 'But some, of course, you couldn't.'

'Shut up!' Gabriella said, without rancour. 'We need to concentrate. What's that over there?'

She wobbled her torch beam to the right. But it was just a clump of thistles. Carole began counting the paces as she took them. She sneaked a glance at the luminous figures on her watch. Nearly half an hour had gone by.

'Surely they'll have found him by now?'

'They're still searching.' Gabriella pointed to little pinpoints of light, dancing like fireflies away over on the other side of the airfield.

The wind had swept the sky clean of the last trails of mist. Starlight glistened on the moist black runway and, suddenly silhouetted, the rearing outline of a broken aircraft appeared, its gaunt structure now being furred in thick white foam. A dead dinosaur with midget figures moving hastily, purposefully around it. Thin ribs of baffled torchlight danced. Distant voices shouted. A camouflaged vehicle raced down the runway, a red cross painted on its side. It turned off, screeched to a halt beside the skeleton, its striped headlights momentarily throwing up faces and figures in sharp relief.

Here the air was full of the acrid smell of smouldering, and here the ground rose in small shallow curves like the tumuli the fifth form had visited on their geographical expedition last year.

'Dispersal air-raid shelters under here,' Bunty told them knowledgeably. 'For the ground crew working on the sites.

15

Not that they use them for that.' She giggled shrilly. 'For couples. For fun and games.'

'Let's have a rest.' Carole tottered towards the slope of one of the mounds. She flung herself down, pulling the bulky respirator off her shoulders. It slid a little away from her down the slippery grass. She stretched her arm to retrieve it. The respirator had come to rest against another object. A round leather ball. A picture came into her mind of the dispersal crews playing a game of football while they waited for the aircraft to return.

The picture shattered as her fingers felt the ball further. A sticky ball. A burst broken leather ball, covered with red jam and porridge. Then she saw, in that pale starlight, that the ball wasn't a ball. It was a leather-helmeted human head.

The whole airfield shimmered around her, swelled and shrank. She let out an ugly sound that was half a scream and half a long-drawn-out animal howl. The other two girls bounded over to her, and then stopped a pace short. In Bunty's hand, the torch wobbled unsteadily. She covered the bulb with her hand. The light through her fingers shone stripily crimson.

'Don't look!' Carole shrieked. 'Don't shine the torch.'

'We have to look!' Gabriella assumed an icy command. She snatched the torch from Bunty's hand and shone it steadily on the pilot's head. Carole heard her sharp indrawn breath, but she said nothing.

'Jeezus Christ!' Bunty wailed and wept. 'Jeezus bloody Christ!'

They all subsided to the ground, covering their faces with their hands, banging the heels of their heavy shoes into the ground, like children in a tantrum. Then they put their whistles to their wet weeping formless mouths and blew with all the force of their lungs, as if trying to blow the whole damned bloody cruel war away.

Help came. Dozens of men eventually solidified out of nowhere, clumping in their boots, breathing heavily and noisily. Lights flashed. A stretcher appeared, very white in the darkness, covered in a thick red blanket, disappeared again. A few minutes later, other men rushed up, shouting that they'd found the rest of the poor clot, at least more or less the rest.

The tide of busyness swept past the three girls as if they

16

were surplus pieces of background in a play. They sat for a while in silence, shivering, unable to move. Suddenly the night had become unbearably cold, so they struggled to their feet and staggered drunkenly back towards the hangar.

The same sergeant SP held out his hand wordlessly for the sticks and the whistles.

'She found him!' Bunty told the sergeant proudly, nodding towards Carole.

He looked unimpressed. 'Good-o.' He frowned. 'All of him?'

They shook their heads wordlessly and moved off.

Clouds had again blanketed the stars, and a light drizzle was turning into rain. They held up their faces to it. Gradually, the rain, the night air, the comradeship of walking together began to revive them all.

'I brought some Camp coffee with me,' Bunty said. 'If the electric's on in the kitchen we could make us a cup of black.'

They began to stride out more briskly, revived by the prospect.

They reached the big ARP tank, and turned with relief into the married quarter road.

Halfway down, a large figure suddenly loomed ahead; a figure at first unidentifiable under the big camouflage ground-sheet, which doubled as a macintosh. Then, above the greens and browns of the groundsheet, they spied a well-worn WAAF cap, its owner obviously of some seniority.

The figure barred their way. A baffled torch shone stripily on each of them in turn from head to foot. It came to rest on Carole. A sharp accusing stripe of light pointed threatening as a dagger at her throat.

The groundsheet visibly swelled like a giant toad. Out of it came a rasping voice, a woman's, but very low on the vocal register, almost a man's. A voice laden with authority.

A corner of the groundsheet was flicked back so that they could see that authority – three chevrons, surmounted by a crown. The WAAF flight sergeant, almost as powerful a being as the WAAF Queen Bee herself.

'Airwoman, what's your name?'

'Kemp.'

'Kemp what?'

'Carole Kemp.'

The groundsheet swelled again.

'I don't want your first name, you silly bitch. As far as I'm concerned you haven't got one. Kemp, Flight Sergeant! That's what I want! Say it!'

'Kemp, Flight Sergeant.'

'What's your number, Kemp?'

'Two-zero-five-zero-three-seven-three.'

'Two-zero-five-zero-three-seven-three what? You forgot it again! Say it!'

'Two-zero-five-zero-three-seven-three, Flight Sergeant.'

From under the groundsheet the flight sergeant brought out a notebook, then a pencil. She licked the stub of the pencil. 'Kemp, you're on a charge!'

'What for?'

'Don't you bloody well ask me what for! I'll give you what for! I've a good mind to put you on another charge for that! You're improperly dressed, airwoman, that's what for! Where's your bloody tie? And you . . .'

'We were in ever such a hurry, Flight Sergeant!' Bunty put in quickly and pacificatorily. 'We went out to look for the airman.'

'I've no bloody doubt you went looking for an airman! That's all you girls ever bloody do! That's what you joined up for!'

'For the pilot of the aircraft that crashed, Flight Sergeant. Like we were told to do!'

'Don't you argue with me! And don't you use that insolent tone neither. I know exactly what you mean, you stupid bitch. Name and number! You're on a charge too!'

'What for?'

'What for, Flight Sergeant! And don't bloody ask what for! For insolence and insubordination, that's what it's bloody for!'

Gabriella gathered herself together, so that she was as tall, though not as mountainous, as the groundsheeted figure.

This time in a deliberately insolent tone, she asked, 'Would you mind moderating your language, Flight Sergeant.'

And then, as she had intended, they were all three on a charge together.

Two

Flight Officer Hermione Caldbeck heard airwomen's charges every other morning at 0900 hours, so the three girls did not have long to wait for summary justice.

Charge-hearing was a start to the day that Flight Officer Caldbeck enjoyed. It had a delicious touch of theatre, and the theatre was second only to hunting in her interests. A lively and very popular socialite, she had been persuaded, or rather challenged, to join the Women's Auxiliary Air Force in what she called a moment of alcohol-induced madness. To wit, her twenty-first birthday party two years ago on the family estate near Coleraine. One of the house guests had been an air vice-marshal, rather keen to ingratiate himself with her father, Sir Randolph Caldbeck. Over his umpteenth champagne, the air vice-marshal had promised her a quickly arranged commission and his sympathetic fatherly eye over her new career, if she dared to accept his challenge and join up.

She had dared. The social scene in Ulster had become a desert, drained of its suitable young men. She was young and beautiful and she relished a challenge. The air vice-marshal had been as good as his word. Her time in the ranks had mercifully been of the briefest. She had sailed through the amusing OCTU at Windermere, housed in the Old England Hotel, marching around the lakeside roads, behaving like officers and gentlemen in the bar. Once commissioned, her rise in rank had been meteoric.

The air vice-marshal had visited her twice when she was an assistant section officer at Waddington, frequently when she was a section officer at Air Ministry and three times here at Holmfirth where she had been appointed WAAF commanding officer. The air vice-marshal's eye was less fatherly, more predatory, each time.

Holmfirth was a good posting. It was further from London than she would have liked, but family friends still owned and occupied Holmfirth Manor, only a few miles from the airfield, and being the Queen Bee was bliss.

Hermione was well aware that she was a very attractive young woman. Slim, small-boned, with big brown eyes, a delicate nose, and black hair cut into a Cleopatra fringe – wherever she went, she was the lodestar. Last night she had graced a superb party at Holmfirth Manor, had met several handsome types, a brigadier, a submarine skipper, stayed till the early hours. So she had missed the crash on the airfield, the third in a fortnight. Squadron 777 was in the process of re-forming, and its wing commander, though a dreamboat, drove his men hard.

As Flight Officer Caldbeck walked smartly from the WAAF officers' wing of the mess to her office nearby in station headquarters, eyes turned. Not just to give her the salute, but frankly to undress her. However impeccably Gieves had tailored her barathea uniform, however fine the grey lisle stockings (silk forbidden), however fetching the cap from under which the black fringe, the half curl of hair on to her cheekbones, enticingly escaped, nothing could do justice to the pocket Venus that was beneath.

Arriving at station headquarters, pushing open the swing doors, flicking a glance at the board showing Holmfirth's state of readiness, she returned the salute of the policeman on duty and wished him good morning with a smile she knew would make his day and disturb his night.

Opening her office door, she drew in its smell of polished linoleum and leather and documents, its sense of order and control. She drew out her leather-cushioned chair and waited with amused contempt for the knock on the other door, which gave on to the orderly room.

It sounded at once.

'Come!' Flight Officer Caldbeck commanded, settling herself in the chair behind the vast desk.

In the flight sergeant marched.

Flight Sergeant Bertha Grimble was the subject of numerous amusing anecdotes with which Hermione regaled her friends and fellow officers. Grimble was built like a wrestler and was naturally nicknamed Big Bertha, after the First World War heavy gun.

She had been an overlooker in a Bradford woollen mill, and had apparently put the fear of God in all the weavers young and old. From under her well-worn WAAF cap (she had been among the early recruits in 1939) only a whisker of mouse-coloured hair escaped. Her face was heavy-jowled, the skin grey and grainy with lack of sunshine. Her pebbly eyes only softened when they looked at her commanding officer, Hermione Caldbeck. It was, Hermione sometimes remarked, like having a devoted bloodhound that only barked in a ghastly Bradford accent.

'Good morning, ma'am!' The flight sergeant brought her polished shoes noisily together, smiled a terrible piano-key smile (some hostile dentist had lumbered her with the most lamentable false teeth) and gave a salute so smart that it made her arm quiver like an arrow in an oak.

'I've put the charge sheet on your desk, ma'am. Three offenders, ma'am.'

Flight Officer Caldbeck pulled her cap forward to a more severe angle, pushed her hair out of sight, and inclined her head for Grimble to approach.

Immediately, Big Bertha stumped over to stand beside her commanding officer. She smelled strongly of carbolic soap, Brasso and shoe polish, and underlying these sharper smells, an oily lanolin odour, which Hermione identified as the legacy of all those years in the woollen mill.

Grimble bent over her flight officer. She seemed to sniff in the scent of expensive bath oil which still clung to Hermione as she pushed the copy of *King's Regulations* closer to her folded leather gloves, both necessary accoutrements for charge-hearing.

Then, drawing a deep breath, Bertha Grimble pointed to the charge sheet and the entries thereon.

'There, ma'am! One airwoman on charge for being improperly dressed. The other two for insubordination. Can't have that, eh, ma'am?'

'Certainly not!' Hermione smiled at her warmly. Here in Bertha Grimble she truly had the iron fist over which she could gracefully drape herself as the beautiful velvet glove. She felt certain that the airwomen and the airmen, and of course all the officers, adored her. She treated the airwomen as decently as her family treated their servants in Coleraine. She spoke kindly to them when the need arose, and she often smiled when she returned a particularly good salute. She was the Queen Bee and she behaved accordingly.

'When did these airwomen arrive, Flight Sergeant?'

'Last night. Nine thirty train.'

'Not taken them long to offend then?'

'No, ma'am. They don't break 'em in properly at Bridgnorth. Not these days. They go in as rookies in civvies and they come out as rookies in uniform. They don't give 'em what for!'

'Well, no doubt you will, Flight Sergeant!' Hermione lifted her gloves and playfully flicked the flight sergeant's arm. A gesture which always brought a smile to the grey face. 'Well, wheel them in!'

The smile had vanished and had been replaced by a stern scowl by the time the flight sergeant flung open the door from the corridor.

Outside, Carole and Bunty stood with their escorts, airwomen of the same rank, as required by *King's Regulations*. Being the lowest of the low – airwoman second class – two headquarters runners were sufficient These were girls whose duty it was to act like human carrier pigeons whisking messages from one section to another. They were girls without a trade, humble in general, instantly obedient; their uniforms immaculate.

An LACW had been hastily summoned from accounts to act as Gabriella's escort. All three escorts wore their hats as symbol of their virtue. The offenders, as dictated by *King's Regulations*, were bareheaded.

'Escort and accused. Aa–a–a–ten–shun!'

As number-one accused, Carole came to attention as smartly as her swollen arm would allow.

'That's a sloppy attention, Kemp! How you passed your

22

square-bashing I will never know! What've you got for arms? A couple of bananas? Here!'

Flight Sergeant Grimble fiercely grasped the swollen arm. 'Hold that rigid as a bar! Fingers curled. What're you screwing up your face for, airwoman?'

'Nothing, Flight Sergeant!'

'Better not! I don't like dumb saucy!'

'No, Flight Sergeant.'

'And look at those buttons!'

'They're new!'

'They're new what?'

'They're new, Flight Sergeant.'

'I know they're bloody new! Haven't you heard of Brasso, Kemp? You gotta work on 'em! Know what work is, Kemp?'

'Yes, Flight Sergeant.'

The flight sergeant gave a loud disbelieving snort and shook her head.

'What ma'am'll say I do not know! She's always like a new pin. And so should you be! Okeydoke! Let's get cracking. Lee–eft turn!'

They turned.

'Forward . . . wait for it . . . ma–arch.'

Flight Sergeant Grimble stood in the doorway of the Queen Bee's office as they passed her, the ghost of a pleasurable smile touching her thin lips. She looked across at her commanding officer sitting behind her desk as pretty as a picture; then she returned her gaze, severe now, to the airwomen.

'Ri–ight wheel!'

She watched them march round in front of ma'am's desk.

'Halt!' She called at exactly the right second. 'Le–eft turn!'

That brought ma'am, the escort and accused eyeball to eyeball across the polished desk.

'Ma'am!' Bertha stamped over. She saluted. 'Escort and accused present and correct.'

'The witness, Flight Sergeant?'

'I am the witness, ma'am. I am the witnesses.'

'In all three cases, Flight Sergeant?'

'Yes, ma'am.'

'Very good.'

Flight Officer Caldbeck turned her eyes to the accused, a rather gauche-looking, quite pretty girl with flushed cheeks and unblinking grey eyes. These now regarded her with an extraordinary expression, almost like loathing. Slightly discommoded, she began to read from the charge sheet.

'Two-zero-five-zero-three-seven-three, Aircraftwoman Second Class Kemp. Is that your number, rank and name?'

'Yes, ma'am.'

'You are charged that on the 15th October 1943 at zero-two-fifty hours . . .' Flight Officer Caldbeck broke off and turned her eyes up to the flight sergeant. 'What on earth was she doing out and about at that time in the morning, Flight Sergeant? Is there a further charge?'

'No, ma'am! They all went out to look for the airman!' She gave Hermione a disbelieving smirk. 'Or so they say!'

'Very well.' Hermione returned her gaze to the charge sheet. 'Contrary to *King's Regulations* –' she laid a reverent hand on her copy – 'para one hundred, clause ten, you were improperly dressed, in that you were not wearing your uniform tie. Are you willing to accept my judgement and punishment or do you wish to opt for a court martial?'

Carole stared at her, wide-eyed and disbelieving. I have strayed through Alice's looking glass, she thought. In a moment, this Queen Bee is going to become the Queen in Wonderland. It would be off with her head, not just off with her hat.

'Airwoman, answer your commanding officer!' roared the flight sergeant. 'And take that impudent look off your face! Ma'am asked you a question!'

Carole drew a deep breath.

'I accept, ma'am.'

'And how do you plead, Kemp? Are you guilty or not guilty?'

'Well, I didn't have a tie on, but we were in a hurry because—'

'Guilty as charged, she's saying, ma'am. She wasn't wearing a tie. There is no argument. She's just trying to plead extenuating circumstances.'

'Very well, I shall enter the plea of guilty. Flight Sergeant, your witness account please.'

Big Bertha stepped in front of the desk, turned, stamped and saluted, and began her highly coloured account with relish. Carole didn't listen. She almost wished herself back making cakes for harvest festival at Austwick. Her father, thin, ascetic-looking and wispy-haired, would be writing his sermon, her mother, decades his junior, making plaits of bread.

'Thank you, Flight Sergeant! Very concisely and clearly given.'

The flight officer turned to the guilty airwoman. 'I must say . . .' She looked down at the charge sheet to find the miscreant's name. 'Kemp . . . I must say that this is a frightfully bad show. On your first night here!'

'We were in a hurry! We . . .'

'Don't address ma'am unless she asks you a question!'

'In a hurry you say, Kemp?' Hermione frowned. 'Hurry is never an excuse. What is your trade?'

'MT driver.'

'MT driver, ma'am.'

'Well, there you are, Kemp! I don't have to say more! That is exactly my point! You will be a very poor driver if you allow yourself that excuse, won't you?'

'I suppose so, ma'am.'

'No suppose about it, Kemp. You can't scamp your appearance or your job or flout the rules, simply because you're in a hurry. Can you?'

'No, ma'am.'

'It might be a tie you forget to put on today, but a handbrake tomorrow.'

Carole said nothing and tried not to look too mutinous.

'Mightn't it, Kemp?'

'I hope not, ma'am.'

'Don't contradict your commanding officer, airwoman!'

'Well, I sincerely hope not too, Kemp.' Hermione shook her head doubtfully. 'Have you reported to your section yet?'

'No, ma'am. I'm reporting after this!'

'When you do, tell the officer in charge, Flying Officer Wright, that you have been found guilty and awarded seven days confined to camp.'

'With extra duties, ma'am?' Big Bertha prompted greedily.

25

'Of course with extra duties. Dismiss.'

Marched out into the comparative sanity of the corridor, Carole was handed back her hat.

She was wearing it at an exaggeratedly jaunty angle when she reported twenty minutes later to the MT Section, a derelict-looking straggle of buildings between the hangars and stores. Dodging around two-ton Dennis trucks, Commer vans, rescue vehicles, and various camouflaged cars on the oily forecourt, she found a shack that clearly housed the offices. She stepped through the open doorway. Inside was another door with the name Flying Officer Wright, Officer in Charge MT painted on a once white board.

Carole knocked. There was no response. She knocked again, louder this time. Still no response. She cautiously turned the knob.

'Bugger off!' a voice called as she slowly pushed open the door. 'Go on, whoever you are! I'm busy. I have no transport available. Bugger off! Scarper!' Then, as the man lounging behind the desk with his feet resting on it caught sight of her, he swung his legs hastily off the desk top. A deliberately wolfish smile spread across his pale face.

'Well, well, well!' He stroked the end of his carefully waxed RAF moustache. 'What have we here? Another lamb to the slaughter I do believe. Come into my parlour, my dear.' He beckoned her forward with both hands.

She advanced to the front of the desk and saluted. 'ACW2 Kemp, sir!'

As she stood rigidly to attention, he hauled himself to his feet, came unsteadily from behind his desk, and walked unhurriedly round her, his bloodshot eyes surveying her from head to toe. He smelled of whisky and aftershave.

'And very nice too.'

'Reporting for duty, sir.'

'I gathered that. I'm not just a handsome face, y'know!'

Carole unbuttoned the top pocket of her tunic, brought out her posting document and her 1250 and handed them to him.

He took them from her, tossed them on the desk without looking at them.

'What's your first name, darling?'

'Carole, sir.'

'Nice. Very nice. Suits you. Sounds like joy bells. Well, you can ring my bell any time, Carole!'

'I also have to tell you, sir, that I have been up on a charge this morning.'

'Have you, bejabers!' He looked delighted, admiring even.

'And I was found guilty and given seven days confined to camp.'

He clicked his tongue and twirled the ends of his moustache. 'So, you're a bit of a naughty girl?'

'Not really, sir.'

'Pity. Well, we don't bother with charges in this section. A smack on the hand. Or some other place.' He slapped his own thin rump. 'That sufficeth.' He grinned.

Carole said nothing.

'So, where were you posted from, my dear?'

'MT training school at Blackpool.'

'So, no experience!' He clicked his tongue. 'Ah, well! Not to worry! Soon lick you into shape. What did you drive in Civvy Street?'

'A Morris van.'

He resumed his seat behind the desk and sat back, elbows on the arms of his chair, his fingers together. He smiled reminiscingly.

'I used to sell Morris Cowleys. The most successful salesman in the south-west – that was me. Made a fortune. Didn't keep it. The old problem. You know what I mean?'

'No, sir.'

'A woman. Took me for all I had. Mind you, she hasn't made me hate women. I love 'em. And I know how to treat 'em. You ask my girls. You won't come to any harm with me. Wright in name and right in nature. That's me. But watch out for my flight sergeant. I'm going to ring for Chiefie Tordoff now!'

Flying Officer Wright banged the button of a buzzer on his desk. Its sound echoed down the hut.

'He'll show you round. But Tom's a right bastard! A real brute. One for the women too. If he gives you any trouble let me know. Got a real harem complex.'

After the most perfunctory of knocks, in came Flight
Sergeant Tom Tordoff, as if he owned the place, a big raw-
boned Geordie in a greasy boiler suit, his dark hair flicked
forward over a frowning forehead. He seemed to fill the room.
He brought with him a smell of sump oil and cigarettes, and
it was clear he was the real master of the section.

This time she was examined with steely grey eyes that clearly
found her wanting.

'Take her in tow, will you, Flight. Show her the ropes.'

The flight sergeant jerked his head for her to follow him.
He had scarcely closed the door behind them when he issued
Flying Officer Wright's warning, only in reverse.

'If Wright gives you any grief, chases you round the desk,
makes you stop in the woods on a late trip, just tell me. I'll
sort him out. And you need to watch out for the aircrew.
They're like him. Oversexed bastards. Ground crew aren't
much better. Just less pushy. Beware of all officers. The only
man on the camp you can trust, apart from me, is the padre.'

Carole, as a daughter of the manse, nodded respectfully.

'No, hinny! Not for what you think! Not because he's a
man of God! Hell, no! But because he doesn't like little girls.
He doesn't fancy them! D'you read me?'

She didn't exactly. But she nodded. In fact she wondered
if he liked big bosomy ones, or if it was because he was faith-
fully married.

'Is he married?'

'The padre? Don't be daft.'

He led the way down the corridor to a room with a notice
painted on: Drivers' Pool. He opened the door on to a long
room thick with cigarette smoke. The wooden walls were
decorated with dozens of curling pin-ups of Betty Grable and
Mae West and Jane from the *Daily Mirror*. Two girls were
lounging beside a glowing coke stove, reading old movie magazines and sipping strong brown tea out of tin mugs. Further
over, beyond a desk littered with papers, a group of men were
playing darts.

'This is Carole,' Chiefie shouted and shoved her forward.
'Our new sprog. Over there is Judy.' He pointed to a girl with
a delicate heart-shaped face under a mound of frizzy auburn

hair, who lifted up a heavily stained enamel teapot from the hearth and called in a Cockney accent, 'Wanna cuppa, ducks?'

'She wouldn't drink that muck. Carole's a wee lady. And over there's a big lady. Fenny. Fenella something or other. Double-barrelled. Can't spell it.'

A very tall girl with a long nose and an apologetic expression stood up, dusted the biscuit crumbs off her battledress, and held out her hand. 'Welcome to the madhouse.' She spoke in what Carole's mother would have called a cut-glass accent.

'And over here are the lads!' Flight Sergeant Tordoff pointed to the darts players. 'Kevin, Buster and Archie.' The three men put down their darts and lifted their hands. 'Three of the biggest bastards I've ever come across.'

They smiled back at him as if it were a compliment, which it probably was.

'The others are on duty. Or should be! Stuffing themselves at the cookhouse, I bet! Don't trust any of 'em.'

The men had resumed their darts and the girls had picked up their magazines, when Chiefie spoke again. 'One more thing, playmates!' He put his hand on Carole's shoulder.

'This young sprog is on extra duties and seven days CC. She's made a bit of a record. Not twenty-four hours on the station and she's been on a charge. How about that?'

There was an immediate titter of approval and an enthusiastic round of clapping.

'Well done, my dear!' Fenella called.

'You'll be into all the rackets in no time.' Judy laughed approvingly.

'And she don't mean tennis!' Kevin shouted.

'That's enough of that! We don't run rackets in this section!'

Everyone laughed disbelievingly. Buster held his nose and pulled an imaginary lavatory chain. 'Big one, Chiefie!'

'Hey, you lot! You're giving the kid the wrong impression, you know.' He put his hand on Carole's arm. 'We'll leave this bunch. Take a look at the yard. Then I might give you a bit of dual on one of the heavies.'

'Aye . . . aye . . . aye!' the drivers called after them as they walked out into the cooler, fresher air of the yard.

'Take no notice, hinny! They're ignorant bastards. Here

we go! Mind that oil! They're some careless buggers round here.'

They picked their way carefully among huge lorries and vans drawn up on the forecourt like beached whales. Chiefie stopped to kick a pair of legs protruding from under a low-loader.

'That's Bert! Best mechanic we've got! Don't bother to come out, Bert!' he called as the legs wriggled. 'Just showing a new sprog the ropes. You get cracking. We're crying out for that low-loader with the bloody Brylcreems pranging their kites. Another Cat Three waiting when you've got her moving.'

He walked on a pace and then called to the legs. 'The kid's name's Carole. Wet behind the ears. Easy on the eye.'

Chiefie smiled down at her kindly. 'No offence meant.'

She nodded.

'None taken I hope?'

'No. None.' She ventured a smile. 'I'm glad about the easy on the eye bit.'

'Don't let it go to your head. Handsome is as handsome does!' He pointed to a line of vans. 'Three nice little Hillmans here. I'll start you off on one of them most likely. Trouble is the runs are mostly with officers. Can be dangerous for a kid. On the other hand, I might try you with the Commer. Rations and personnel. Ambulance and fire you'll have to build up to. Likewise the bomb trolley. Then, of course, there's God's car.'

'The padre's?'

''Course not! The station commander's. He is God. See the little flag. See the klaxon. You gotta be very good on and off duty to drive that!' He stroked the immaculate bonnet lovingly as he passed it. 'And last but not least, the ten-tonners. My beauties.'

He stopped in front of the first of three monsters, a well-worn six-ton Dennis lorry, with huge wheels and a snarling visage – anything but beautiful.

'Lovely, isn't she?'

Carole eyed the monster warily and said nothing.

'Well, up you go, kiddo! Into the passenger seat. Want a leg up?'

'No thanks.'

'When we get round the peri track, I'll let you drive her, if you're good. She has her days. Can be a bitch if she feels like it.'

He went round the front of the lorry and swung himself up beside her.

'Comfy?'

She settled herself into the scuffed leather seat. The cab stank of petrol and grease and cigarette smoke.

'Yes, thanks.'

'Nice lot of leg room, eh?' He touched her legs to make sure they were comfortable. 'And very nice legs too, under all that, I reckon.'

He adjusted the mirrors, flicked the little rubber gremlin that hung over the windscreen and switched on.

The Dennis's engine roared.

Pressing the accelerator pedal, he said, 'She takes a bit of warming up. You have to show her who's master. Double declutch. You soon get used to it.' He released the brake. 'Hang on to your hat, canny lass, and keep your knees together.'

The engine settled sweetly. Speedily, but surprisingly smoothly, they swept out of the MT yard and turned left towards the hangars and the runways.

'Stores on your left, kiddo! Flying Officer Meakin in charge. Meek and Mild we call him. But he isn't. Willing to do business though. We do a lot of business with him. One litre of petrol equals one new shirt on clothing parade. That sort of thing. Drives a hard bargain.'

'Is she difficult to steer?' Carole watched him pull round the wheel.

'So-so. Bit heavy for a girl. Responsive though. See that tall building? That's the decontam. Just beyond's the padre's office and the chapel. Church parade every other Sunday. I can put you on duty if you don't want to go.'

'Do you go?'

'Christ, no! Now watch me change gear. Nothing to it really. Hangars One, Two and Three ahead!' He pointed. 'They're working on a Cat Two in Number One. That means repairable on site. And there's a Cat Three waiting to be carted off when the low-loader's mended. It's all go. So, tell me what you did before you joined up, kiddo.'

'For the last six months I've been driving a delivery van.'

'The Morris?'

'Yes. For my uncle. He's got a newspaper business.'

'Like it?'

'No. But at least I learned to drive.'

'And before that? No, don't tell me. It was school, wasn't it?'

'Yes.'

'Christ! My drivers get greener every day.' He trod harder on the accelerator as they whipped past the hangars. He gripped the wheel, savouring the speed and power. 'Now here we go! The open road!'

He swept the lorry over the apron and on to the perimeter track. The wide expanse of the airfield opened up to them – flat, peaceful-looking, the tussocky grass still quite green. It smelled countrified and sweet. A whole world away from last night. That awful smell, the darkness, the shouts, the howl of klaxons, the dancing torches, the leather-helmeted head. The head. She clenched her fists.

'Pray there's no aircraft decides to land, kid!'

Chiefie leaned forward, craned his neck to the left and the right. 'It looks OK. And flying control isn't erupting. That's it over there! We can't go as fast as we'd like because these big ones have inhibitors. Now watch me carefully, and when we get over to dispersal we might change seats.'

He trod harder on the accelerator. The rough grassland between the runways whipped by. The runways were empty, harmless as country lanes. Beyond the grassland, the buildings of the airfield, the water tower on its high stilts, the rectangular brick bulk of station headquarters, the concrete workshops, moved smoothly round as on a turntable. And behind them, the distant village of Holmfirth, a conical church spire, a huddle of houses, some grand mansion on a rise, a narrow belt of woodland. It was almost as if the helmeted head had never existed, nor the pilot who had tried to land on that harmless lane of a runway.

'Watch my feet as well as my hand, kid.'

'I am doing.'

'You're not concentrating!'

'I'm trying to.'

He grunted. Then, after a moment, broken only by the steady roar of the engine. 'Well, here we are, pet. C Dispersal. Want to have a go?'

'Yes, please.'

Chiefie switched off the engine, turned, looked at her. 'Are you always as pale as that?'

She shrugged.

'Not scared, are you?'

'No!'

'Right then! I need to ask you a question, sprog. A technical one. What must you do if you park any vehicle for longer than an hour?'

'Take off the distributor head.'

'Good. Know why?'

'In case a German parachutist lands.'

'That's what they say! A British black marketeer, more like. Well, come on, you've passed your oral. Let's get cracking. I'll get out and you can wriggle over.'

Chiefie jumped down and hauled himself up again into the passenger seat. 'Check she's in neutral. Start her up. Get your hand right round that gear! It won't bite! Off we go!'

The ten-tonner was a brute. Smelly, raucous, unwilling to accelerate and heavy to steer.

'She prefers men drivers,' Chiefie said smugly. 'Firm hands. These ten-tonners are like carthorses. My dad used to drive a coal cart in Newcastle. Loved his horses.' He sighed. 'But you're doing all right! Better than I thought!' He whistled to himself, alternately scanning the perimeter track, and studying her absorbed profile.

'Right! Slow down! Stop here! Good! Nice stop! This is D Dispersal!'

She looked around at the rickety corrugated-iron buildings. Peewits rose from the grass beyond. A pigeon flew out of the roof of the first hut. Brambles had crept over the step.

'Not used at the moment. What you might call deserted! A lonely place! Not a soul in sight.'

Suddenly he shoved back his battered cap, seized her round the shoulders, and pulled her towards him. His big streaked face loomed over her. 'Give us a kiss, hinny!'

'No!' She shoved fiercely at his chest. 'No!'

'Come on! Just a wee one!'

'Get lost!' She squirmed her head and shoulders away and kicked out at his legs.

'Ouch! I'm your section flight sergeant, don't forget!'

'So?'

'So I can do you favours! Or do you down!'

She managed to jab him with her elbow. 'I don't give a damn!'

'Phew! That's swearing, kiddo! You wash your mouth out!' He shook his head, slapped his hands on his knees and began to laugh, a deep, amused, unfeigned laugh. 'OK, kid. You'll do. Now remember! Be like that with the Brylcreem boys! They'll all try it on!'

Suddenly she realized he was teasing her, or worse, trying to teach her the facts of an MT driver's life, like removing the distributor head when you parked, and that made her feel humiliated and angrier still.

The key was still in the ignition. She started up the engine, crashed clumsily into gear, noisily shoving the clutch down twice, then hauled off the handbrake and trod fiercely on the accelerator.

The whole vehicle juddered in protest and then jerked wildly forward. She heard Chiefie's shocked indrawn breath like music in her ears. She pressed harder on the accelerator. She was getting the measure of this brute, of both brutes. The six-tonner went much better at speed. It was like a carthorse that has spied a green meadow. The engine roared throatily and steadily, the big tyres sang. Carole began to enjoy herself.

'Stop now, hinny!' Chiefie called in an altered tone. 'There's a good girl.' He spoke as if to a toddler who has grabbed a valuable fragile object, or a carthorse that has suddenly run amok. 'Easy does it, darling! Whoa there, whoa! You've had your joke! I've had mine! Quits, kid!' He held up both hands in surrender. 'Quits,' he repeated. 'We'll be getting into traffic soon!'

Their wild dash round the perimeter track had brought them full circle towards the technical area of workshops, equipment and maintenance.

But, now launched, Carole found it difficult to stop. Her clammy hands stuck to the wheel. Her foot seemed welded to the accelerator pedal. But, with an effort of will, she wrenched it off, and pressed on the brake.

Too late. Out of the road leading from the workshops and on to the perimeter track shot a gleaming Humber saloon. Carole swerved wildly, but the great grinding lorry was heavy to turn and reluctant to relinquish its momentum. It caught the bumper of the Humber and swung it round like a toy. There were squeals of brakes, a graunching of torn metal. Then silence.

Beside her, Chiefie sat stunned, turned to stone, incapable of words.

Not so the driver of the Humber. Out of the torn vehicle leapt a young man with startling red hair and a rage to match. His forage cap was shoved to the back of his head. He advanced menacingly on the six-tonner, wrenched open the driver's door.

'Get out!' he shouted.

Carole looked down into bright-blue angry eyes, a flushed and furious face. She saw the three rings of a wing commander on his epaulette.

'Out!'

She jumped down on to the tarmac feeling life couldn't possibly get worse.

Then, like a divine intervention, the air-raid siren sounded. It echoed from a dozen tannoy boxes.

'Enemy aircraft in the vicinity. Take cover!'

Undeterred, the wing commander shouted at her, 'You're on a charge, woman! I'll deal with you later!' He glowered at Chiefie. 'As for you! I'll have your bloody balls!'

Then he ran back to his damaged Humber, got in, managed to start it up, and sped off round towards flying control like a bat out of hell.

Three

In a different mood, Gabriella was walking from station head-quarters towards flying control when the alert sounded. She hardly heard it, or the desynchronized growl of the Heinkel, or the distant crump beyond the village of bombs. She was already miles away.

Not for the charge itself, but what had followed had been like the opening of a door, letting her glimpse a new, more challenging and frightening life.

Gabriella had been given the same punishment as Carole and Bunty. Seven days confined to camp with extra duties. Confinement to camp meant little to her. She had nowhere to go anyway. If anything, the punishment was welcome. It cemented her friendship with the other two girls in the house. In comparison to her, they were both pitifully young and knew so little of life. Not that she knew very much herself. Though, beside them, at twenty-three she felt immensely old. But she liked and trusted them. She had been glad to be with them until she was marched through that door to the Queen Bee's office.

This was the first time she had been on a charge. The petti-ness of this present one, and the ludicrous administration of RAF justice, appalled her. So did the complacent, vividly pretty, very spoiled young Queen Bee and the grovelling of the flight sergeant.

But the Queen Bee had surprised her. As she carefully blot-ted the entry of the punishment awarded to Gabriella on the charge sheet, she had come straight to the point. 'Flight Sergeant,' she had said, smiling brightly, 'I want a further word with this airwoman in private. You can march out her escort.'

'What about me, ma'am? Won't you need me? To take notes, ma'am. Be a witness. Fill in what's what?'

'No, thank you, Flight.' Another dazzling smile. 'What I have to discuss is strictly confidential. You may dismiss.'

As soon as the flight sergeant's offended steps had faded, the flight officer turned to Gabriella.

'You may stand at ease, Willoughby.'

Gabriella had stood at ease, with her feet apart, hands clasped behind her back, wondering what on earth was going to be said.

'So, you are French, Willoughby?'

'Half-French, ma'am. I was born in France. My mother was French.'

'Where is she now?'

'She was killed in the Blitz, ma'am.'

Flight Officer Caldbeck made a dutiful little motion with her shoulders of passing sympathy.

'But you lived in France.'

'Intermittently. Our home was in Ealing. After my father died, we stayed for a while with distant relatives in France.'

'And when was that? When did he die?'

'Fifteen years ago, ma'am. He was gassed in the First World War. He died of emphysema.'

'Any brothers or sisters?'

'No, ma'am.'

'Any attachments?'

'No, ma'am.'

'And, of course, you speak French?'

'Yes, ma'am.'

'Fluently?'

'Yes.'

'And you were working as a telephonist.'

'Among other things, ma'am.'

'Splendid!' Flight Officer Caldbeck wrote busily.

In the pause, Gabriella asked quietly, 'May I know what all this is about, ma'am?'

'No, Willoughby, you may not. However –' she drew in her breath – 'I can tell you a little.' She lowered her voice. 'I have received a signal from the DWAAF herself.' She looked

37

up to see if Gabriella was suitably impressed. 'From the very top. From the director herself. She has been asked to supply this information by the war cabinet. It is immensely important. And utterly confidential. You realize that?'

'Yes, ma'am.'

'All WAAF commanding officers, such as myself –' she pressed her hand on her bosom – 'are asked to supply a list of French-speaking officers and airwomen.'

'Why, ma'am?'

'Ah! That, I am not allowed to tell you. However, I am allowed to ask if you will volunteer for your name to go on that list?'

'Even though I don't know its purpose, ma'am?'

'Its purpose would be for special duties.'

'And those are?'

'I can't say. Except that they might involve service overseas. And perhaps some added danger.'

'Might that service be in France?'

'Yes, Willoughby.'

'Then I would like my name to go forward, ma'am.'

'Would you like a little time to consider?'

'No, thank you, ma'am.'

'Very well.' The Queen Bee looked at her watch. 'Is there anything else you want to ask me? I can't promise to answer. But you may ask.'

'Have you any idea of the work, ma'am?'

'No, Willoughby. And even if I had, I couldn't tell you. It might simply be translating documents, liaising with the Free French. It might be . . . well, anything.'

'I understand, ma'am.'

'Splendid. You can report to your section now. It all sounds very exciting. Very worthwhile. I only wish my French were slightly better. *Mais je parle français seulement un peu*,' she added in an excruciatingly bad accent. But it was, she felt, a nice democratic touch.

'Attention, Willoughby! Left turn. Quick march. Close the door behind you.'

The door of flying control was deliberately made so that it was difficult to open. By the time Gabriella had struggled with it and closed the door behind her, the all clear was sounding, and the sky was silent.

The inside of this stuffy concrete box smelled of Camp coffee, chalk, sweat and cigarette smoke. But there was a relaxed and friendly welcome, which Gabriella found surprising and touching.

'Come along in, dear girl.' The officer in charge squinted at her over his half-moon spectacles and beckoned languidly from behind his desk. He looked every inch the schoolmaster he had been. In his late thirties, already balding, he played along with the role of venerable sage which the young aircrew had thrust upon him. The other three occupants of the room looked round, regarding her with friendly interest.

'Business is brisk, Gabriella,' the flight lieutenant said, 'so we are very glad to have you. Yes, I know your name already! It was on the signal. Mine's Archie Birdsall. Always known as Beaky.'

He shook her hand, then waved towards a stocky girl with her fair hair cut in a page-boy bob, sitting at the wireless set. 'Jan. Married to a Navy type. She's our morse wizard.'

The girl got up, gave her a gap-toothed smile and stretched out to shake Gabriella's hand.

'Next to her,' Beaky went on, 'Linda, the best-loved voice on the station. Our R/T queen.'

'Hi, Gabriella!' A chubby red-faced girl waved from behind her set.

'And over there, about to do the decent thing and make you a cup of coffee, is Jimmy, our wireless mech. A genius, no less.' Beaky pulled out a chair. 'Now come over here and sit down. Till our laddies get airborne you can tell me all about yourself.'

Gabriella eased herself past the wireless and R/T sets and the controllers' dais and slid into the chair. She was just about to confess to Beaky that she had been put on a charge and given seven days confined to camp when the door was flung open.

In burst a tousled red-haired pilot in his mid-twenties with the three rings of a wing commander on his battledress epaulettes. His battered cap was perched on the back of his

39

head as if thrust up by the eruption of red hair beneath. Vivid blue eyes flamed as they alighted on Gabriella and Beaky.

'Coffee, sir?' Beaky rose politely from his chair and spoke placatingly. He beckoned to Jimmy. 'Coffee for the wing commander as well, if you please. You like it with milk, don't you, sir?'

'Coffee! That's all you lazy bastards ever think about! As for you girls . . .' He slid into a chair, put his feet on the table, pushed off his cap and lobbed it skilfully across the table on to a wall hook, eyeing Gabriella with undiminished hostility. 'Whose side are you girls on, I ask myself?'

Before she had time to answer, Beaky intervened smoothly, 'Gabriella, this is Wing Commander Jonathan Scott, our much respected squadron commander. Known as Red. No one can think why.'

The wing commander laughed almost apologetically, his anger apparently forgotten.

'And this is LACW Willoughby, our much needed new R/T operator.'

Wing Commander Scott graciously swung his feet to the floor, stood up, grasped her hand and smiled with surprising sweetness. 'Welcome to the madhouse.' Then his face clouded as he remembered his anger. 'I hope you do a damned sight better job than the young sprog I've just met.'

'What went wrong with that meeting?' Beaky asked, sitting himself down again, putting his fingertips together like a head-master about to listen to the report from a frustrated prefect.

'It wasn't a bloody meeting. It was an encounter. She foisted herself on me!' The wing commander snorted, breathing fiercely on the embers of his anger.

'Dear me, sir. The girl who can foist herself on you is a . . .'

'A clueless clot, Beaky.'

'So how did you meet, sir?'

'Via our respective vehicles.' The wing commander spoke weightily.

'Oh, dear. I can guess. Your Humber! You had a collision!'

'A collision? I never have a collision! She collided with me! A bloody little schoolgirl. Only arrived last night! This morning, driving a ten-tonner like a maniac. Pranged my wing!'

'Good heavens, sir! That's outrageous! Was there much damage?'

'Enough to get her guts for garters! And Chiefie Tordoff's.'

He dipped two fingers into the top pocket of his battledress and brought out a folded form, which he waved threateningly. 'I have the charge form here! I shall throw the book at the pair of them. Have them court-martialled.'

'Quite right!' Beaky winked at Gabriella. 'You do that, sir!'

'No, don't.' Gabriella intervened sharply, despite Beaky's wink. 'That would be awful. She only arrived last night. And she's already been on one charge.'

The wing commander turned narrowed eyes on her. 'Well, there you are! You've proved my point.'

'She was only on a charge for not wearing a tie, sir!' Gabriella said icily, with heavy emphasis on the sir. 'A tie,' she repeated loudly. 'When we went out to search in the middle of the night! And you, sir, are not even wearing one now! In broad daylight! On duty!'

'Portia in person! God help me! He turned up the collar of his battledress and pretended to cower. 'God save me from clever women!'

'Oh, he will, sir!' Gabriella blurted before she had time to consider. 'Any woman with half a brain would steer . . .'

'That's enough, Gabriella! Personal remarks are not permitted in this section. Even under provocation. Even under extreme provocation. You were saying, sir?'

'I was saying I shall demand courts martial. I shall take Flight Sergeant Tordoff and little Miss Melting Eyes to the cleaners.'

Again, Mr Birdsall winked at Gabriella. This time she winked back. She smiled broadly. *Melting Eyes* and *courts martial* somehow didn't go together.

Then the teleprinter began clacking. The wing commander was transformed. He jumped to his feet, walked over to read the flimsy as it emerged.

'What will he do about the charge?' Gabriella whispered in Beaky's ear.

'Sweet Fanny Adams, dear. He'll threaten. But he'll not harm a hair of Miss Melting Eyes' head.' He looked

41

momentarily rueful. 'At least not in that way.' He glanced over at the wing commander.

But the wing commander wasn't listening. He was studying the paper in his hand.

'Le Creusot,' he muttered. 'A pinpoint. And about time too.'

Until she heard the name Le Creusot, Bunty thought that despite the charge and Flight Sergeant Grimble, she had landed on easy street. She accepted that easy street probably had its dark places and dark encounters, like charges and flight sergeants, but apparently Le Creusot was another, far darker than the others.

Mildly indignant about her punishment, but in no way depressed by it, Bunty had reported as instructed to the office of the sergeant in charge of the officers' mess. On an RAF station, the officers' mess was the place to be. Her mother had always said, 'If you want to get on, go where the money is.' And in wartime, with all the rationing and shortages, a girl might adapt that wisdom to go where the good food and comforts and dishy men were. So the officers' mess was that place.

This mess at Holmfirth was a peacetime building – solid red brick with a fine wide entrance (sandbagged, of course, for safety) and long windows taped up against bomb blast. Polished wood doors on the inside, big curved polished wood bar in the hall. A thick red patterned carpet on the floors, and, peeping through the glass doors into the dining room where some officers were still eating their breakfast, a spread of food. Ham, fruits, sizzling dishes of sausages and bacon, never seen these days in Civvy Street. And the whole place packed to the roof with lovely young men, real pin-ups, handsome as film stars. What girl would want more? If this sort of life came with a snobby Queen Bee and a horrible flight sergeant, it just went to show that you got nothing for nothing.

The sergeant in charge of the officers' mess staff was a man. And the grapevine said it was best to have a man as your section boss. Men were a soft touch compared to women. A sign on the door of the mess office said Sergeant Freddie Fisher NCO i/c officers' mess.

When Bunty knocked, a soft friendly voice bade her enter. When she did, she saw a thin little chap with a long neck and a big Adam's apple.

'Come in! There's a comfortable chair over there. Sit down.' He sizzled his S's and had a nice way with him. Her mother, who liked tough meaty men, would have said he was a pouf. Being a pouf simply meant to Bunty that he wouldn't try it on.

When she had sat down, he perched himself like a friendly gnome on a corner of his desk and asked for her first name.

He dismissed the information about the charge with an airy wave and the opinion that Big Bertha was a sadist, whatever that might mean.

'But now, Bunty, let's talk about you. Where do you come to us from?'

'RAF Heywood.'

He wrinkled up his thin nose. 'A maintenance unit. Deadly boring. You'll find it better here. An operational station. Less bullshit. More fun.'

'Good.'

'Your duties will be just the same. You'll have four officers to look after. Keep their rooms clean. Take them their morning tea, despatch their laundry. Press their uniforms, clean their buttons and shoes and generally make yourself useful. Don't be familiar. And don't let them get familiar!'

'No, Sergeant. I won't.'

'They'll try it on. They always do. But remember, no dating is allowed between officers and other ranks. Dating is a chargeable offence. That's the rule throughout the RAF. It's all in *Station Standing Orders*.'

'I'll remember that, Sergeant!'

'And no jumping into bed with them either!'

'As if I would, Sergeant!'

'No! Of course not! But some girls do. However, I'm a good judge of character. You may look fluffy. But I can see you're a nice girl. Nice or not, I have to give this warning to all my boys and girls.' He sighed. 'That was why your predecessor had to leave. Clause eleven.'

'Preggy?'

43

'Afraid so. Clause eleven is the one clause everyone knows, isn't it? The baby's father wasn't one of our chaps, though. A Yank, she said. From Granton base just up the road.'

'Was she very upset?'

'She was. She didn't want to go home. And her parents didn't want to have her. What will the neighbours say? That sort of thing. But maybe the Yank will come up trumps and marry her. She was very fond of him. He gave her lovely presents! Silk stockings, chocolates.'

There was a moment's silence while they both mentally examined the odds on a marriage. They found the odds pretty low and sighed.

Then Sergeant Fisher said briskly, 'And that brings me to another warning.' He folded his arms across his chest, making his narrow shoulders look narrower still. 'Don't get fond of your four young men. They're good kids. But they'll not be with us for long. You'll not get one for keeps.'

'Is the squadron getting posted soon then, Sergeant?'

'No, luvvie.' He drew a thin finger across his huge Adam's apple. 'The chop. That's what most of them'll be getting. Half of these lovely lads will be dead come the spring.'

'That's awful, Sarge.'

'Well, you can work it out. Seven men to every kite. A couple or more shot down every few nights. It leaves a lot of empty chairs.'

Bunty's eyes filled with tears at the thought.

'You've to make up your mind never to get upset. Meantime, I'll show you their rooms. Look after your chaps while you've got them.'

Her chaps were, luckily, not in their rooms when Sergeant Fisher led her along the polished linoleum corridor to the living quarters and opened the door of room number seven, which had a card with names on it, but which she didn't get the time to read.

'Playing squash, I would guess,' Sergeant Fisher said, raising his little sandy eyebrows at the disorder.

'Looks as if they've had a practice here first.' Bunty tried to crack a joke to regain her spirits. She had tried to thrust last night to the back of her mind. But it had been horrible.

44

As she had told her new friends and housemates, Carole and Gabriella, she was used to seeing dead bodies, because her mother worked at the undertaker's and they got a free flat as part of her perks. But what Bunty wasn't used to was people she knew dying. Aircrew she regarded as the sort of lusty young men you saw on recruiting posters: handsome, clean-limbed, joyful and brave. The posters depicted them with a young girl in WAAF uniform like herself, gazing up adoringly at them above the caption, 'Serve in the WAAF With the Men Who Fly.' It was that poster which had finally made her join up at twenty before she was called up. That and her mum suddenly wanting to get married to her horrible undertaker employer. He was going to sell his house and move into the flat, and as her mother said, three is never company.

'Well, Bunty, see what you can sort out before they get back. You'll find cleaning stuff in the cupboard outside, and a spare overall. Get your own overalls tomorrow from stores. The names of your bods are on the doors. Pilot Officer Stafford and Pilot Officer Berenger in this mucky room. Next door, in number eight, it's Pilot Officers Dutton and Bladowski.'

'Come again, Sarge. Blad what?'

'Bladowski. A Pole. Mad as a hatter. All Poles are mad, bad, sad. And randy, of course. Well, I'll let you get a move on. The gen is there'll be an op tonight. Rumoured to be a hairy one.'

A hairy op. Two times seven men not returning of a night put the officers' mess in a more sober light. But she would make the best of it, Bunty thought, picking up old newspapers, folding them and putting them in a neat pile, retrieving dirty socks and stuffing them in the linen basket, one with a big hole which she must remember to darn, polishing the linoleum round the red patterned rugs, scrutinizing the photographs on the painted walls.

That was PO Berenger's mother, she would guess, and his father in a dog collar. Carole's father wore a dog collar in the photo she'd shown them, but he looked years older than this chap. No sign of PO Berenger having a wife, but beside PO Stafford's bed there was a picture of a girl with her arms round the neck of a big black and white sheepdog, shadowy parents in the background, the girl his sister most likely. In the next room, there was no photograph by PO Bladowski's bed. No personal possessions. The Pole's space was finickily neat, his bed made, the white counterpane without a wrinkle, his shoes already polished and in a straight line.

PO Dutton's space made up for it. Everything tossed around: shirts, collars, books, packs of cigarettes, papers. Only one large photograph graced his portion of the bedroom wall, that of a very beautiful middle-aged woman. PO Dutton's mother, surely. Her eyes seemed to implore from the photograph, *Look after him.*

There was writing on the photograph. Bunty leaned forward to read it. Yes. It read, 'To Crispin on his nineteenth birthday, from his loving mother.'

Crispin. That was a name all right. The horrible undertaker would have had a laugh at that one, all right. He liked to jeer at unusual names.

Bunty could imagine exactly what Crispin would look like. She imagined him as she polished the floor vigorously, as if the harder she polished, the brighter the floor, the more likely were her chaps to survive. Crispin would be tall, with long straight legs, slim, fair-haired and aristocratic. Then she got to her feet, turned round as the door opened, and there he was, exactly as she had imagined him.

'I'm Crispin Dutton,' he said, holding his squash racquet under one arm and extending his hand. 'Are you our new slave?'

'Yes, sir. I'm Bunty.'

'Nice name.'

'So is yours,' she lied.

'No it's not, Bunty. It's bloody awful. Usually I'm called Chris.'

He was wearing a shirt and white shorts and those long legs were tanned. His face was flushed and his eyes bright. Too bright, scarily – maybe even scared – bright.

'Good game, sir?'

'Bang on.'

'Did you win?'

'But of course.' He whacked the air with his racquet. Then

he glanced round and smiled. 'You've made the room look really nice, Bunty.'

'Thank you, sir.'

'Well, I'm off for a shower. Then it's all systems go. Having a crack at Hitler tonight.'

Someone banged on the half-open door and called, 'Have you heard the gen, Chris? It's le Creusot!'

PO Dutton half turned and, after a momentary pause, just long enough to swallow, called back 'Yep. I heard. Wizzo, eh?'

His tone was relaxed and confident. But when he turned, Bunty knew she had been right about his eyes. Scared bright all right. That's what le Creusot had done to him.

PO Dutton was shit-scared.

Bunty was shit-scared herself that night as the wind moaned in the disused chimney of the married quarter. There had apparently been a last-minute delay in the le Creusot operation, which had been called at the worst possible moment, after the aircraft had been bombed up, the crews briefed and out at dispersals. So, it was not until the early hours that the aircraft eventually took off.

She had hidden her head under the blanket while the metal windows and lockers and iron bedsteads vibrated and her precious tin of Nivea face cream and her alarm clock tinkled nervously together.

Bunty counted as the bomb-laden aircraft staggered over their roof into the squally night sky – one . . . two . . . three . . . four . . . five – then she couldn't count because other aircraft from the north seemed to be joining in, squadron after squadron gathering like flocks of birds. The sky above was filled with the most all-embracing engine roar, as if the heavens were a metal sheet that giant hands were shaking and banging to make perpetual thunder.

Bunty ventured to murmur, 'Are you awake, Gabby?'

Gabriella didn't answer. Gabriella also lay still, listening and counting the successful take-off of Holmfirth's heavily laden contribution to the night's operation. She had remained all afternoon and evening in flying control. Beaky had

47

suggested she stay as a supernumerary to familiarize herself with the workings of the section. She had spent the time watching the R/T and wireless operators, chalking the aircraft and crew entries on the board, making tea and coffee, chatting with Jan about Jan's husband and the stress of being a submariner, and picking up what useful gen she could from Jim, the mechanical genius. All the time pushing to the back of her mind her recent conversation with the Queen Bee. The thought of what it might open up for her was simultaneously too exciting and too daunting to think about at the moment. Meanwhile she watched and listened carefully.

The night's le Creusot operation was to involve only six Lancasters from Holmfirth, but their role was to be disproportionately significant: its importance had drawn the sting from the red-haired wing commander's anger, transforming him into a cool, capable but, in a subdued way, a gratified leader.

The six Holmfirth Lancasters would be breaking away from the main force to go in low and pinpoint the important Schneider works at le Creusot. Pinpoint bombing was, she knew, regarded as very hazardous. But, as the wing commander had cheerfully remarked to Beaky over a mug of black coffee, you had a good chance of the bombs landing where they ought, and not on some wretched suburb.

So reasonable had been his mood, that when he stood up to leave, she had ventured to suggest, 'You won't put her on a charge, will you? The driver, sir?'

He looked at her bemused. 'What are you talking about, girl?'

'The WAAF truck driver, sir. Your Humber.'

'Oh Christ, that!' He reached for his cap and set it on the back of his head. He blinked as if trying to recall something that had happened a long time ago. Then he dipped two fingers into the breast pocket of his battledress, and brought out what she assumed was the threatened charge sheet. He screwed it up and lobbed it into the wastepaper basket. 'Satisfied?'

'Yes, thank you, sir.'

'But tell Miss Melting Eyes this is her last chance. If she does that again, I won't scrub the charge.'

'I'll tell her, sir.'

When the door closed behind him, something in his expression made her walk over to the wastepaper basket, take out the screwed-up piece of paper and smooth it out. It wasn't a charge sheet at all. It was a mess laundry bill. As she tossed it back again, she saw to her chagrin that Beaky was watching her. He shook his head chidingly. 'Don't tell me you were taken in by all his sound and fury?'

'We–ell, a bit, I suppose.'

'I told you he wouldn't, didn't I?'

'You did.' She sighed, thinking if she had guessed what her future work was going to be correctly, she must judge people better than this. Other people's lives as well as her own might depend on her judgement.

'The Wingco doesn't put bods on charges. He gets what he wants without. He's a natural disciplinarian. Anyway, he's clearly sweet on your friend. But don't tell her yet. He doesn't stay sweet on any girl for long. Just tell her she's off the hook.'

Carole had made down her bed and was about to climb into it when Gabby returned to the billet. She greeted the news with gratitude and relief.

'And Chiefie? Is he off the hook too?'

'I imagine so. Was he very angry?'

'I'll say! With me. Not the Wingco. Luckily the air-raid warning went and we had to get the lorry back to MT. Then Chiefie made me go down the shelter till the all clear. He wasn't worried about the charge.' She sighed. 'I didn't want another one quite so soon.'

'Well, remember the FFI tomorrow. We're all on it. If you forget that, you will be on another charge.'

Carole tried out one of Chiefie's expletives and clambered into bed. It was ages before she drifted off, and even after the planes had gone, she woke at every sound of an engine. But these weren't aircraft engines, just heavy vehicles trundling along the main camp road. And when all three alarm clocks shrilled in number five married quarter, the sky was still quiet. The bombers had not returned.

'Shouldn't they be back by now?' Bunty asked Gabriella,

the only one who might have an inkling, as they slung their respirators, straightened their caps and rushed out to join other shadowy figures forming up in the glimmering first light for the morning parade.

'Probably another hour yet,' Gabby whispered. 'I don't really know.'

'Silence!' Flight Sergeant Grimble bellowed. 'No talking on parade! Squa–ad . . . Att–en–shun! Ri–ight dress!'

She marched up and down, bestowing a scowl on each airwoman, a specially ferocious one for Gabby, the secret of whose conversation with the Queen Bee she had been unable to discover. She pointed to insufficiently bright buttons, to escaping wisps of hair, flicked a badly tied tie. Then she ended up with a roar. 'You're the sloppiest lot I've ever seen. I'm letting you off now 'cos I don't want you late for your FFI.'

The dreaded letters stood for the innocent enough words, Free From Infection.

The end of establishing such freedom was totally desirable but the means were not, because in such a motley township as an RAF station, infection often struck in the most personal and embarrassing of places.

Carole, Gabby and Bunty ate their breakfast; a slice of fried bread which, when pricked with a fork, oozed yellow globules of fat, a thin dark-brown evil-looking sausage, a slice of white bread, a tiny square of margarine and a dob of raspberry jam, all mixed up on the same plate.

'The pips in the raspberry jam are little splinters of wood,' Bunty informed them. 'Honest! They have people making them and putting them in. The catering girls at Heywood told me. It's just red jelly and wood splinters and they can stick in your bowels.'

But, like the other two, she wolfed the food down. Then they put their plates on a stack and sluiced their irons (their knives, forks and spoons) in a great steaming wooden vat of filthy water at the door and formed up to be marched to sick quarters.

Assembling in the waiting room there, they were told to

50

strip down to their knickers, then line up in the corridor outside the treatments room.

'Get in the corporal's queue when we go in,' Bunty whispered. 'The sergeant's a real cow. My sergeant, Fisher, knows all about her. They're both in the sergeants' mess. The corporal's supposed to be all right, though.'

Two by two, the girls were admitted to the treatments room, where they formed two more queues, one for the sergeant, the other for the corporal. There was no choice. They were directed by a medical orderly, who handed each girl a packet of sanitary towels, with the instruction to be economical with them and not use them for make-up. Gabby raised her eyebrows at Carole. They had both landed in the sergeant's queue. Bunty waved to them from the comparative safety of the corporal's.

The inspection was being loosely supervised by a bespectacled grey-haired medical officer, Doc Malone, a two-ringer brought in for the duration, clearly uncomfortable with his lot. He was walking up and down and avoiding looking at the girls in their various states of undress. Carole tried not to look at the girl in front of her having her head examined for lice, her ears poked, now her mouth, her teeth being exclaimed over with disgust, then a wooden spatula being thrust half down her throat.

At the order, 'Knickers down,' Carole shut her eyes.

But there was no need to be so tactful. Suddenly everyone was alert and looking upwards and outwards, craning their necks to see through the taped-up windows. The first throb of engines sounded far away, then swelled nearer and nearer. The frames of the windows began to rattle. The bombers were returning.

'All right! Don't hang about.' The sergeant beckoned. 'Let's be having you.'

Heavy fingers began parting and thumping through Carole's hair. The worst moments were when the fingers paused. Had a louse hopped on to her in that crowded train? The talk in Bridgnorth had been of lice that could jump on to you from yards away and form happy families within days.

Carole could hear the bombers clearly now. Soon their squadron would turn into the circuit; the ground crews would be counting them in. In a moment they might glimpse the aircraft in the sky beyond the taped-up windows. She hoped the fiery wing commander would be one of them.

'Stand up, airwoman.' The jungle patrol had retreated. No lice or nits, thank God. 'Well, you look OK waist upwards. Drop your knickers.'

Fixing her embarrassed eyes on the window, while the sergeant bent down and peered, Carole was the first to see it. A great spurt of blood-red light against the grey overcast sky. A Verey light fired off by one of the returning bombers. It described a melting red arc against the cloud, signalling a casualty on board.

Four

The casualty was on board PO Dutton's aircraft. He had returned with his rear gunner dead, and Rob, his mid-upper gunner, shot through the neck. Blood everywhere. The doctor and the ambulance arrived quickly and carted him straight off to hospital in Lincoln. The emergency dressing Chris had put on was soaked black with dried blood. He looked ghastly.

Bunty saw the ambulance disappearing towards the gates as she hurried out of sick quarters. The rumour was already circulating that it was PO Dutton's aircraft, and she was sure that he would need her. She'd only just met him but she felt she knew him already. It must be a ghastly business to come home with a casualty among your crew, to try to keep the poor chap alive and avoid flak and fighters at the same time, and she knew Chris would take it hard.

She delayed only to make a short detour to gather some Michaelmas daisies, which she had spotted surviving in a back garden of one of the married quarters. She slipped a little bunch of them into her respirator, hurried to the officers' mess and was just tiptoeing past the open door of the mess office when Sergeant Fisher called out to her.

'Bunty! What on earth are you doing here? You're not on duty till sixteen hundred hours.'

'I know, Sarge! But there's one or two things I need to sort out.'

He gave her what her mother would have called an old-fashioned look but he didn't ask her exactly what.

'Anyway,' she said loudly and defensively, 'I'm supposed to be on extra duties, aren't I?'

Sergeant Fisher didn't deign to reply. He just raised his little fluffy mouse eyebrows, sighed heavily and got on with his accounts.

Bunty donned her overall. She collected a box of cleaning materials from the cupboard and let herself quietly into room eight.

Her opposite number on the shift, a young batman nick-named Tubby, had taken down the blackout and tidied up a bit. But that was all. He hadn't given the room a real clean, put a sparkling finish on it, or made it look welcoming.

Bunty immediately set about repairing that omission. She brushed the rug, she polished the linoleum and the locker, the windows and the mirror. She gave special reverent attention to Mrs Dutton's photo frame and then she set the Michaelmas daisies in a tooth glass beside it.

Lastly she stood in front of the sparkling mirror and repaired her own make-up. She had her lovely Tangye orange lipstick in her pocket and she was just outlining her cupid's bow, when PO Dutton staggered in. He looked a wreck: face drained of colour except for his red puffy eyes, which made him look as if he'd been crying.

But it wasn't just that he looked so awful that got to her. He looked so angry too. Angry with her.

'What the hell are you doing in here?'

'Cleaning up, sir.'

'I don't want you cleaning up. I don't want you in here! Get out! I want some rest. Go, damn you! Go!'

He jerked his head towards the door. Then, as she moved towards it, he saw the Michaelmas daisies. His mouth contorted as if he was going to be sick. He seized the flowers in a furious fist and thrust them at her fiercely. 'And take these with you! Off! Off! Off!'

He slammed the door behind her. She stood leaning for a moment against the doorjamb, unable to move. Then the door opened again. Out came her box of cleaning materials. 'Are you still here? Go. Get lost!'

He slammed the door again. She still stood where she was, transfixed. Through the thin panels of the door, she heard him fling himself on his bed and, just as she began to walk slowly away down the corridor, the sound of sobbing.

54

This time when she retraced her steps past the open door of the mess office, Sergeant Fisher called her in.

'Come and sit down, duckie.' He pulled out a chair, but avoided looking at her. 'I've been thinking, if you're so keen to do those extra duties, you can help me put these mess bills into their envelopes.'

He handed her a pile of bills and a packet of envelopes, poured a mug of tea from the never empty metal pot and set it in front of her. 'Make sure you put the bills in the right envelopes.'

'I will, Sarge.'

After a few minutes silence, broken only by the rustle of paper and footsteps along the corridor outside, the sergeant murmured, still without looking at her, 'Mr Dutton's had a very rough trip. But he did well.'

'How d'you know, Sarge?'

'I get to know everything here. The Wingco told me. He'd just come back from debriefing.'

Bunty sipped her tea. 'Mr Dutton looked awful. Really awful. Like he'd seen a ghost or just struggled back from the North Pole.'

'So he had, in a way. One gunner dead, the other nearly bleeding to death. Not to mention the damage to the aircraft.'

'Awful!' Bunty moaned. 'That's why I thought I might be able to help him.'

'Well, you can't. Get that into your head! Now, when you've finished stuffing those bills in the right envelopes, go and get yourself a wad at the NAAFI. When you come back for your fourteen-hundred-hours duty, you can clean the bathrooms.'

'Thanks a million, Sarge!'

'Leave Mr Dutton's room, and, like I told you, leave Mr Dutton alone too. Keep your distance. Let him keep his. Otherwise, you're asking for trouble. There will be plenty more nights like last night.'

So there were. An aircraft was lost the following night, another two the night after. Then the squadron was stood down for eight days.

But throughout the following week, when they were back on the battle order, the losses mounted. And then in November came one memorable long-haul operation over the Alps to

Milan, led by the wing commander and with all available aircraft on the battle order.

The occupants of number five married quarter saw them take off at last light: Bunty from the window of the mess office, Gabriella from flying control and Carole from the driving seat of the ration lorry, the only vehicle that she was allowed to drive.

Chiefie had not yet forgiven her for the collision with the Wingco's car. Though the damage to the Humber had been swiftly repaired and the clean and polished car delivered back to him with a complimentary tankful of MT petrol as a sweetener, Chiefie insisted that Carole should remain in the doghouse.

That evening when she returned the ration lorry to the MT section, Chiefie asked her derisively if she had waved the Brylcreem boys goodbye.

'No. But I saw them take off.'

'You bet you did! Which one d'you fancy? No, don't tell me! It's the Wingco, isn't it?'

'Hardly.'

'It would be hardly, pet! Very hardly. He's a bastard!'

'Aren't all men?'

'Oh, hear her! Who's getting the cheeky one! You wouldn't have said that three weeks ago!'

'I'm a quick learner.'

'I had thought of letting you meet them in. But I won't now.'

'I'm not on again till eight in the morning, so you couldn't. They'll be in before that.'

'Five hundred hours. What're you doing tonight?'

'It's domestic evening. I'll be cleaning the billet and laying out my kit.'

'You girls live the life of Riley. Well, don't forget to sluice out the ration lorry before you go. And don't stay awake listening for the Brylcreems.'

Returning to the married quarter, pushing open the door of her downstairs room, Carole saw a bulky kitbag and a small suitcase beside the hitherto empty bed along the wall opposite hers. She was about to go over and examine the name painted on the kitbag, when a wispy, prim-looking woman of about thirty, with her thin brown hair in a tight roll, came downstairs, still fussily drying her hands on a towel, and remarking by way of greeting, 'You get so dirty on them trains.' The newcomer sighed, then flicked the towel over her shoulder, held out a small, well-scrubbed hand and introduced herself. 'Two-zero-six-zero-seven-eight Carter, Edith. ACW1. Equipment assistant.'

'And I'm Carole. Carole Kemp. ACW2. MT driver. Where were you posted from, Edith?'

'Melksham. Where they train the cooks. Or not, as the case might be.'

'Like it?'

'Had to. Hobson's choice.' She looked around the bare room. 'How many are in here?'

'Just two others. Upstairs. But I expect we'll get more.'

'I don't think so.' Edith shook her head. 'I was told I'd be sharing with three.' Carole didn't ask from where she had got her information, but Edith volunteered it. 'I was told by Arnold.' She lifted her left hand, her fingers spread to show the gold band on her third finger. 'Arnold's my husband.'

Carole smiled. Bunty would be pleased. Bunty often bemoaned the fact that there wasn't a married woman among them to tell them what marriage was all about. Sex, in other words.

'Is Arnold already on the station?'

'No. Not actually on. Not in that way.' Edith shook her head. 'Arnold's passed on.' Edith smiled pityingly at Carole's astonishment. Then she explained. 'Arnold comes through to me. Not all the time, of course. When something important happens. Like me being posted and such like.'

Then Edith sat on her bed, dragged her kitbag closer, pulled the strings open and from its depths extracted an elliptical piece of wood, which Carole at first thought was an easel. Luckily, before she had been foolish enough to ask if Edith painted, she saw her stroke the piece of wood reverently. 'He comes through on this. My Ouija board. Heard of them?'

'No. Never.'

'Well, they're wonderful. Arnold speaks to me on this. When I need him. So it's very precious. I don't want the others touching it.'

'No. Of course not.'

'What are the other two called?'

'Bunty and Gabriella. Bunty's a batwoman. Gabriella's R/T.'

'Is she toffee-nosed? Her in R/T?'

'Far from it.'

'Usually they are. The R/T girls. It's a well-known fact.'

'Gabriella isn't. You'll get on with her.'

Edith looked doubtful.

'What did you do before you joined up?' Carole asked.

'I served in the draper's shop at Edenbridge.'

'Where's that?'

'Kent. I was born there. That's where I met my Arnold. He was in gents' shoes, and I was in haberdashery. Buttons, beads, ribbons, feathers, suchlike. Now, where can I put this to be safe?'

They decided on the top shelf of her metal locker.

'You'd better push it out of sight, otherwise ma'am might haul it out. It's domestic evening. I'm told ma'am often checks the lockers as well as our kit.'

'I don't mind about the kit. Mine's in apple-pie order. I love sewing.'

'I hate it,' Carole opened her locker and brought out her uniform clothes, preparatory to checking them for holes and tears, and missing buttons or name tapes.

'Well, I'll stitch on your shirt buttons, mend your stockings, clean your brass buttons, if you clean the bed spaces.'

The division of labour worked satisfactorily for an hour. The downstairs room was filled with the smell of floor polish and Brasso. While to the accompaniment of buttons being clicked in and out of the button stick, Edith told her how Arnold, who was the most perfect of men, had been sent with the BEF to France the day after the wedding and had been killed on the beach at Dunkirk.

Suddenly, the loudspeaker set in the room crackled, hideously reminiscent of that crackling in the middle of the night three weeks ago. The tannoy voice burst out, 'Enemy aircraft in the vicinity. All personnel not on essential duty, take cover. I repeat, take cover.'

The desynchronized beat of a German aircraft sounded almost directly overhead, and then, as it began to fade away towards the east, the rattle of machine-gun fire, the explosion of ack-ack guns.

Carole, still on her knees polishing the floor, half rose.

'It won't be anything much,' Edith said equably, not stirring herself, even shaking out a few more drops of Brasso on to her cloth, 'Arnold would have said.'

And, to give credence to her assurance, as Carole got to her feet, the all clear sounded.

Carole woke at the first sound of the returning aircraft, a faint vibration in the south-east, grazing the pearly silence of first light. She held her breath and listened, willing the aircraft to a safe landing.

Edith stirred in her sleep, but didn't wake.

Upstairs, Bunty threw off her blankets, scrambled out of bed, drew back the blackout and pressed her face to the taped-up window. The sound had swelled to a great deep-throated roar, filling the whole sky, shaking the earth, rattling the windows, making her heart hammer, but she could see nothing except the soft haloes of the landing lights.

If the runway lights had been switched on, it meant the boys were about to land. Pray God it was all of them, and that they got down safely. If she strained her eyes, she could just glimpse black bat shapes slowly circling, the glow of a Lancaster's exhausts.

As she watched, a green light soared into the sky. The green Very, permission for the first of the bombers to land.

Gabriella stood on the balcony holding the Very pistol and watched the Lancaster line up, hover and then swoop down to a smooth landing. O-Orange, the Wingco's aircraft. It was followed by three more Lancasters, the fourth with what looked like a great cannon hole in its fuselage. The fifth aircraft, D-Dog, came in fast, as if desperate to land. It raced down the runway and went bumping on, over the rough ground, slewed, fell on its port wing. There was a soft crump. A tiny lick of flame. Then the fire engines and the ambulance were screeching along the perimeter track. She stared transfixed till Beaky came out and took the pistol from her. When she stepped inside, Jim was chalking up the arrivals on the blackboard.

The R/T was full of urgent voices. Gradually the gabble died down. The roar in the sky now was of overflying bombers returning northward to their bases in Yorkshire. No more, it seemed, for the Holmfirth circuit. Gabriella looked at the board.

Below D-Dog, entered as crashed on landing, there was an empty box.

A-Able, skippered by Flight Sergeant Jennings, a New Zealander with a crew of officers and with already one tour under his belt, had not returned.

Gabriella sat herself at the R/T set and tried to call him.

'A-Able, this is White Knight, are you receiving me?'

But her set was full of the crackle of static, great surging waves of sound like the sea, and the howling of gremlins. Not a single human voice.

After a while, over her shoulder, she asked Beaky, 'Shall I send out a Darkie?'

He nodded gravely. 'Yes, do that.'

It was the last hope, but still no one answered.

'So the Brylcreem boys took a bit of a pasting,' Flight Sergeant Tordoff greeted Carole at eight that morning. 'Listened for them coming back, did you?'

'No,' she lied, 'I slept like a log.'

'Surprised the racket didn't wake you. Three damaged. Two came in with dead men on board. One Lanc lost. One overshot. Didn't go up in smoke luckily, but the second pilot bought it.'

Carole shook her head wordlessly.

'However, the Wingco came back all right. To answer your unasked question.'

'I'm not really interested.'

In reply, Chiefie made his usual derisive gesture.

'Did PO Dutton get back?'

'Yep.' Chiefie grimaced. 'Not sweet on him as well, are you?'

'No. I'm not sweet on anyone. It's just that my friend Bunty bats for him.'

'And she takes a motherly interest in him?'

'That's right.'

Chiefie raised his eyebrows then rubbed his hands together and said, 'Well, back to business. I want you to clean out the Hillman vans. Then I've a cushy job for you.'

She looked at him warily.

'It is, you know. Really cushy. Scout's honour!'

'Tell me.'

'Collect a load from the officers' mess and deliver same to stores. Here's the six-five-eight. Take Hillman three-five-two. No collisions mind, that's a nearly new van.'

He still hadn't quite forgiven her. He hadn't let her come within spitting distance of the heavies, and even the fact that the Wingco had let the matter drop only, Chiefie insisted, made it worse, because his generosity was due to some reprehensible attraction between the pair of them.

'What sort of load, Flight Sergeant?'

'Oh, not a heavy load, pet. Clothing mostly. Shouldn't take long.'

Although it was only halfway through the morning, a party was in full swing at the officers' mess. Shouts, laughter and snatches of incredibly bawdy songs leaked out through the front windows of the handsome neo-Georgian building as Carole drove round to the rear.

Last night they had lost seven members. Six from Flight Sergeant Jennings' crew had been flying officers, the RAF in its anachronistic way not seeing any inconsistency in NCOs giving orders to officers in the air; the pilot killed in the crash landing was a flight lieutenant. So, the dead men were being sent on their way with the traditional thrash – a beer swilling session which had begun not long after debriefing was over. A similar party was taking place in the sergeants' mess.

Parking her van neatly at the back of the officers' mess, Carole entered the building by the back door, as her lowly rank demanded, and made her way through the kitchens to the corridor leading past the noisy crowded hall bar. She slipped quietly past the groups of aircrew to the mess office.

Sergeant Fisher's dejected voice bade her enter.

'Good morning, duckie. Though not really a good morning. Don't tell me you're the driver for this lot?'

He was standing unhappily in the midst of piles of clothing and little cardboard boxes labelled *Personal Effects*.

Carole nodded.

Sergeant Fisher eyed her sympathetically. 'I hate this more

61

than anything else. It's my least favourite job. I don't suppose you're going to like it much either.' He sighed. 'Where've you got your van parked?'

'Just outside, at the back.'

'Well, here it all is then. The missing men's personal effects. Have to get them down to stores. I don't like doing it. Seems as if we can't wait to throw them out. But we have to get their rooms ready for the next lot of poor sods.' He shook his head lugubriously. 'It brings it home to you. Would you like a cup of tea before we begin?'

'No, thanks. I'd rather get it over with.'

'Well, we have to check them over first. So let's get cracking!' Sergeant Fisher produced a long sheet of paper with the missing men's names on it, and printed with the items that should be handed in.

Sergeant Fisher walked from pile to pile intoning the names, checking the items, doing his best to humanize the whole cold-blooded ritual by little kindly remarks about the deceased. 'Phil was a jolly sort of bloke, always good for a laugh . . . Sam was a very clever young lad, could've stayed at university, but he said he wanted to do his bit . . . and Ian, the best bod at walking on the ceiling; you can still see some of his prints . . . a lovely pianist, another Victor Sylvester . . .'

It was like a bizarre but intimate funeral service conducted to the background of the bawdy blasphemous songs, the crash of breaking glass and the irreverent laughter from the aircrew in the hall bar. And, at every pile, Sergeant Fisher ended his brief eulogy with, 'I hate doing this. I really do.'

Then he gave a final heavy sigh, leaned on his desk and signed the forms with a flourish. 'There you are, duckie! There's not much really! They didn't own a lot of personal things. They all travelled pretty light.' He opened the door to a large cupboard at the back of the office, and dragged out a porter's trolley. 'There we go!' He began swinging the bundles on board. 'They're expecting you in stores. I've given them a tinkle. The wheels are a bit wobbly, but they'll get you to the van.'

He stood in the mess office doorway to wave her off. 'I'd come and give you a hand, but I daren't leave this place unmanned. They're a wild lot and drunk as newts. They'll be getting really daft in a moment, doing the hokey-cokey, shooting the glasses and wrecking the joint.'

As Carole pushed the squeaking wayward trolley down the corridor, the tempo in the bar was hotting up. More uniformed bodies than ever were crammed into the hall, the shouts were more raucous, the laughter more shrill.

As she reached the bar, fearful that someone would turn and see their comrade's effects being carted away, she was relieved to see that a chug-a-lug competition had now begun, so they all had their backs to the corridor They were chanting, 'Drink, chug-a-lug, chug-a-lug', their faces raised to the officer standing on the bar who was trying to down as many pints as he could in one gulp.

She pushed on. She didn't look sideways. She tried not to look at her load either. One of the effects boxes was open at the top. An alarm clock with a Mickey Mouse face stuck jauntily out. The same clock which had no doubt roused its owner last night to go on that fatal op.

She couldn't bear to think about it. Then, just as she was almost clear of the bar, a figure holding a brimming tankard stepped abruptly backwards as he raised the tankard to his lips.

With horror, Carole recognized the red hair. Her hands shook. The intractable trolley responded to her violent jerk by going into its own uncontrollable sideways wobble. The sharp metal corner caught the wing commander on the ankle.

He let out a whoop of pain that turned into an angry roar as beer cascaded down his uniform. Choking, he turned and grabbed her by the shoulder. 'You! You!' His angry eyes widened in recognition. 'Christ! I don't believe this! You've done it again! God Almighty! You're out to get me, aren't you?' And, putting on a Yankee accent, 'Who're you working for, sister?'

At the sound of his voice the other men turned. The man on top of the bar jumped down, belching loudly. The rest of them all stared at her then doubled up with laughter, as if pleased, like children at a party, to have a new diversion. If any of them saw her load, it appeared to be a matter of complete indifference.

'Here, my girl!' The wing commander shoved her aside. 'Let me! I'll take over. You're not fit to be in charge of this vehicle either! Move over. I'm requisitioning it. You're relieved of your command.'

'No! No!' She gripped the handles of the trolley till her knuckles were white, and set her mouth pugnaciously. It was all terribly wrong that he should push that load of dead men's clothes. Nothing would induce her to let go.

She drew a deep breath. With what dignity she could muster, she said hoarsely, 'I'm sorry I hurt your ankle. I hope it isn't painful!'

'Painful! Painful? It's killing me.'

'I'm sorry.'

'I reckon you've broken it. Budge over.'

'No!'

'That's an order!'

'No!'

For answer, he simply grabbed her wrists, twisted them and spun her round. Her fingers uncurled. With a sudden surprising movement, he flung her bodily over his shoulder in a fireman's lift. The drunken aircrew shouted and stamped and whistled their approval. Then, using one hand to keep her legs from kicking, he guided the trolley with the other, while behind them the boozers from the bar, like children following the Pied Piper, stamped down the corridor after them, cheering and singing.

Pummelling his shoulders with her fists, trying to kick, hissing, 'Put me down!' suddenly she gave up, lapsed into stony acceptance. His feet crunched over the gravel of the mess car park. He marched up to her Hillman van, stopped, smacked her bottom hard, and swung her down.

Quite politely he asked, 'Want me to load that lot?'

'No, thank you.' She also spoke quietly. Her anger and embarrassment had drained away. She had begun to think sadly, This is how they do it. How they can carry on night after night. This is how they face the awfulness that no one else can really know.

The awfulness, or the official word for it, was the subject of a squadron meeting held three days later in operations.

The Battle of the Ruhr was ending. The even more dangerous Battle of Berlin was about to begin. Air Chief Marshal Harris had been told by the Casablanca Conference that his primary object must be 'The progressive destruction of the German military industrial and economic system, and the undermining of the morale of the German people to a point where their armed resistance is fatally weakened.'

But the raids were getting tougher, the German Luftwaffe stronger. They were putting up a stiff resistance to Bomber Command, as witnessed by the casualties at Holmfirth and other RAF stations. The ack-ack and fighters had been particularly active over Dusseldorf. Chris Dutton had been coned in the searchlights over the target, hit by cannon fire and lost most of his hydraulic fluid. Most of the crews had similar horror stories to tell at debriefing.

Now standing in front of the blackboard on which was pinned the map of Europe with its little black swastika flags showing German occupation from Norway to the Mediterranean, the red-haired wing commander pointed to a tape fixed from Denmark to some distance south-east of Paris.

'The Kammhuber Line, gentlemen . . . and ladies.' He smiled at the WAAF intelligence officer and Gabriella, as if pleased with himself for remembering to acknowledge their presence, and then addressing the assembled aircrew, 'I don't have to tell you about Kammhuber. It comes up at almost every debriefing. The dazzle from the radar-controlled searchlights, the strength and accuracy of the flak. Once they light on you, the flak is automatic. The night fighters also are radar directed. You're caught. All too bloody *Heil Hitler* and efficient.'

The aircrew groaned and laughed comfortably.

'And now the good news!'

'Will it be?' Gabriella whispered to Beaky.

He shrugged. 'Who knows?'

'We'll be taking delivery of two new Lancasters equipped with H2S, the radar scanner, which, as I don't have to tell you, gives a picture of the ground below. In three months, we hope to have all our aircraft equipped with Oboe, Gee and H2S. And, best of all, we'll be doing pinpoint bombing on selected targets.'

He paused while the aircrew cheered. Like a flock of lambs, Beaky whispered to Gabriella, baa-ing with delight when they saw the sign to the slaughterhouse.

'The squadron will be stood down next week, but you're all going to be hard at it. Circuits and bumps, cross countries and blind bombing exercises. Flight Lieutenant Birdsall will have a word with you now. Right, Beaky, over to you!'

As Beaky rose, the Wingco jumped down from the dais and took the empty chair beside Gabriella.

'Are you settling in, Portia?'

She was surprised, interested, pleased and yet alarmed that he remembered their conversation about Carole's collision with his Humber.

'The name's Gabby, sir. And yes, thank you. I'm settling in.'

'Like it?'

'Some of it.'

'Let me guess. You like the work but not the bullshit.'

Gabby nodded.

He sat for several minutes in silence, listening to Beaky's precise talk. Then he asked, 'Did your young friend tell you? She had another go at me?'

'She did mention something.'

'Something.' He raised his vivid blue eyes to heaven. 'She nearly chopped my leg off.'

'Really?'

'Yes, really. She's a menace to shipping that one.'

'It was an accident, sir.'

'That's what she said before, Portia. This was a second offence. I had to deal summarily with her.'

'No court martial, sir?'

He smiled. 'I might still hold that over her.' Then his smile faded. His whole expression changed. He folded his arms over his chest, a frown of concentration on his young/old face. His intent, assessing gaze travelled from the speaker to each and every face in his audience. On the surface, the men all looked relaxed, eager, uninhibited, undaunted by any peril to come, raring to go. But underneath . . . ?

'Well done, as usual, Beaky!' The Wingco said when F/Lt Birdsall jumped down from the dais and returned to claim his seat.

As the Wingco began to walk away, he said over his shoulder to Gabriella, his blue eyes indulgent, 'You might tell that infant femme fatale from me, I haven't forgotten!'

Nor had Gabriella been forgotten. Four days after the squadron had been stood down from operations, and in the consequent temporary lull, there came a signal for LACW Willoughby to report three days later for an Air Ministry interview.

The days of the stand down were not idle.

Flight Sergeant Grimble seized the opportunity to get the WAAF on to what she called top line discipline-wise.

Another FFI was laid on for those who had escaped it the first time round. Kit inspections were promulgated on Daily Routine Orders. Extra parades, physical training and route marches round the Lincolnshire country lanes were organized; these extras culminating in Big Bertha's special delight, gas drill. Usually the NCOs in charge of sections were co-operative in making excuses to get the girls off these parades. But Carole was still in Chiefie's doghouse. 'No, pet. I am not getting you off PT. I don't want to put too many of my vehicles at risk. Anyway, it'll do you good, and it does us blokes a power of good to see you all in your blackouts.'

They saw them all right. When the shivering airwomen were assembled on the grass between the hangars and dispersal, clad, despite the bitter north-east wind, in their cotton shirts and navy-blue knickers, the hangar doorways immediately became full of airmen with nothing better to do than cheer them on and wolf-whistle like hooligans.

There was no audience for the gas drill. The girls had to don yellow, brown and green camouflaged gas capes made of some stiff, shiny, odd-smelling substance that gave them the appearance of over-smoked kippers. Wearing the service gas masks, they became big wheezing prehistoric monsters of the deep, and if anyone hadn't used her demisting ointment properly, blind as bats.

At the same time, they had to chant the mantra for poison-gas recognition. 'Phosgene smells like musty hay, mustard smells of rotten eggs . . .'

As an added refinement, Big Bertha required that, finally, they had their masks tested 'for real' by sitting in the decontamination unit while one of the noxious gases was pumped in. The more their eyes watered, the more they coughed and spluttered, the more did Big Bertha congratulate herself and them.

'Good thing you've got me to see these masks are tested! Otherwise, if the Jerries drop gas, you lot'd be up the spout!'

Bunty managed to escape the gas drill entirely. Sergeant Fisher was a brilliant defender of his staff's right to escape such discomforts. Numerous telephone calls to Flight Sergeant Grimble and buying her a few pints in the sergeants' mess secured Bunty's release.

The excuse that Bunty was needed for extra duties at the officers' mess was not entirely false, though Sergeant Fisher hadn't known that then. He simply hated all WAAF NCOs and delighted in confounding their ridiculous efforts to be, as he saw it, military men.

He rightly suspected that Bunty gave that little bit extra attention to her boys, but Bunty hoped Sergeant Fisher was still unaware that Chris was moving into the area of needing her for far more.

That Düsseldorf operation had taken as much out of him as the overshoot. Losing your hydraulic fluid could mean that, even if you struggled home, you couldn't get your wheels down, so it could be curtains.

At first, like he did with the overshoot, Chris wouldn't let her near him, was really quite nasty. But she'd not let him get her down. She kept smiling, and on the evening after gas drill, when Chris wasn't flying, she'd brought him a nice cup of after-dinner coffee, and Chris had begun talking.

He'd made her sit down on Mr Bladowski's bed and, waving the cup of coffee, had said, 'Every time I drink coffee now, I remember emptying our flasks to replace the hydraulic fluid.'

Then out it all came. He told her all about being coned and how shit-scared they'd been, and said there was nothing on earth like that huge blue light in your eyes pinning you to the sky like a dead moth. And then all the ack-ack coming up at you, the bangs, the crashes, reckoning every one was your last.

He had wept.

'Did the coffee work?' Bunty prompted.

'Well, there wasn't enough of it. So then we peed.'

'You never!'

'Yes, we did. But there wasn't enough of that! We tried and tried!'

'Oh, Lordy Lord!' Bunty burst out laughing.

And then Chris laughed too.

'I wish I'd been a fly on the wall!'

She didn't, of course. She'd have been shit-scared. But she wanted him to see the funny side. 'What a lark. You rude lads! All trying to pee like mad!'

'And we couldn't! Not at first! We'd all had a leak before we got over the target! But we squeezed out just enough!'

'What a carry-on!' She giggled. 'Talk about coming in on a wing and a prayer!' She hummed the tune. 'Anyway, you got home! I thought about you.'

She leaned across and patted his hand. From her silver photograph frame, the posh-looking lady seemed to eye her approvingly.

'You said one for me, did you?'

She flushed at his derisive tone. 'Nothing wrong with that, is there?'

'Of course not.' He smiled sweetly. 'I'm touched.'

'And you're a good skipper. They all say that. And you've got a good crew.'

'The best!'

'With good kidneys.'

They both laughed again. And on that happier note, she tiptoed along to the mess kitchen, heated some milk, put in a generous splash of Sergeant Fisher's special brandy and literally tucked Chris into bed. His roommate PO Bladowski wasn't around. But then he was hardly ever in his room. Poles were very different from the British apparently. According to the grapevine, they couldn't do without it. They were always off into Lincoln womanizing.

PO Dutton had a good night's sleep. He was just waking up when she came back on duty next morning, so she fetched him a cup of tea. PO Bladowski's bed had not been slept in.

'I'm on a cross country at ten thirty,' Chris told her, looking gloomy again.

69

'That should be right up your street. Clever pilot like you. With such a bang-on crew.'

But Bunty noticed his hand was unsteady as he lifted the teacup to his lips, and it rattled in the saucer when he put it down. She wished she could do something to help him, maybe put in another shot of Sarge's brandy, or say something really reassuring. But she couldn't think of anything. She didn't see him go off, but she did hear the sound of aircraft engines starting up, and there were several Lancasters in the circuit that morning.

Then in the afternoon, after stripping the beds, when she was standing in the corridor with the great square laundry basket on wheels, sorting through the sheets and counterpanes, Chris suddenly emerged from the bar. He was grinning all over his flushed face.

As he came somewhat unsteadily up the corridor, he stopped to whisper in her ear that he had successfully done his cross country, that the Wingco had congratulated him and his crew and bought them a round of beer. Chris just couldn't wait to tell the good news to someone . . . anyone.

'No more than I expected, Chris. Like I told you, you're a fine pi—' Bunty began. But Chris wasn't listening. He was pushing past the laundry basket to hail one of the navigators who was just coming out of the bar. He too was a recipient of the Wingco's largesse, weaving a drunken progress from the bar to his room.

'How about a game of squash?' Chris said. 'Right now? Wizzo! Be with you in two ticks.'

He didn't even say goodbye to her. He didn't need her. Not at the moment anyway.

She was still gazing wistfully after Chris when Sergeant Fisher approached. He was carrying a clipboard and looking important.

'I'm checking dilapidations for stores,' he told Bunty in his prissy manner. 'Kindly get rid of that hulking great laundry basket. Stop mooning after Mr Dutton and man the telephone in my office for a while.'

When Sergeant Fisher returned with his list of dilapidations, he again took up the theme of Mr Dutton.

'You're not forgetting that little talk I gave you, are you, Bunty?'

'Which one, Sarge?'

'You know perfectly well, Bunty. Don't be tiresome.' The sergeant tightened his soft little mouth. Even though he was so nice, he could be quite severe. 'About getting too thick with the officers you do for.'

'No, Sarge. I'm not forgetting.'

'You seem to spend a lot of time chatting up Mr Dutton.'

'He needs to chat to me, Sarge.'

'Why?'

'He just does.'

'If he has problems, he can tell the padre.'

'Oh, the padre!' she exclaimed scornfully. She had seen quite a bit of the padre around the mess, daintily drinking coffee in the ante-room, sipping a pre-dinner sherry in the bar.

'Oh, he's a lovely looking fellah. Looks ever so clean and holy. But I don't think Chris, I mean Mr Dutton, could ever talk to him.'

'He can talk to his chums then. To his crew.'

'Oh, no. Least of all them!'

'Why not?'

'You know what it's like, Sarge! He has to keep up their spirits. Be the skipper!'

'If you want my opinion, they need their spirits kept up about him. I smell a rat!'

'What d'you mean by that, Sergeant?'

He leaned across the desk. 'I smell a case of LMF.'

'That's a terrible thing to say!' Bunty exclaimed with vehemence born of her own anxiety. Her cheeks flamed.

She had only heard the expression LMF a few days ago in conversation with Gabriella, who, having been longer in the service, knew about these things. Gabriella had told her that, in aircrew parlance, the letters stood for Last Minute Funk, but in official language for Lack of Moral Fibre. Both terms were horrible and disgraceful to pin on brave young men who had been to hell and back and who just couldn't take any more of the awfulness of operations. But those letters were dreaded by the crews, Gabriella had said, more than death itself.

'LMF's a dreadful thing! A dreadful thing to put on anyone!'

'Don't bite my head off, duckie. We all know that! And far

71

be it from me to cast a stone! LMF's a bloody disgrace! A disgrace to the powers that be. But if he's got it, he's got it.'

'You make it sound like an infectious disease.'

'And so it is, duckie! That's the whole point. If you've got it, you have to be isolated. The powers that be know it spreads.'

'PO Dutton has not got it,' Bunty enunciated with indignant clarity.

'You don't know the symptoms. I do. I've seen cases before.'

'Well, he isn't one of them!'

'Suit yourself. Don't say I didn't warn you. I'm willing to bet!'

'I can't bear any more!' Bunty jumped to her feet. 'How can you talk like that? When you're safely on the ground?'

'And he'd be better safely on the ground! So would his crew!' Sergeant Fisher's thin nose became more pinched than ever in his anger. 'I'll tell you one thing! I'm not getting you off any more parades if you use your time mooning around Mr Dutton. The squadron'll be back on ops in thirty-six hours' time. Then what's Mr Dutton going to do?'

'He'll manage.'

'And I'm to be Queen of the May!'

Bunty wished she could think of something devastating in reply but she couldn't. 'Is that all then, Sarge?' She asked as he noisily pulled open a drawer in the filing cabinet and began riffling through the files as if she was no more than a grease spot on the floor.

'Yes, thank you, Bunty. You might as well go back to your billet. Start getting your kit in order for all those kit inspections I'm not going to get you off.'

She didn't know if he was joking or not. But she didn't care. She was much more worried about Chris and the awful thought that he might have LMF.

Instead of walking straight back to the married quarters, she cut across the station and along the perimeter track to flying control in the faint hope that the battle order might be known.

Bunty intended to make the excuse that she had come to tell Gabriella something, though she knew perfectly well that Gabriella had got up early that morning to go to the Air Ministry for some interview or other.

72

Five

Gabriella was at that moment leaving the impressive portals of Adastral House in Kingsway. Her interview, on the other hand, had been remarkably unimpressive, informal in fact. The interviewing panel had consisted of three people, a bald-headed civil-service type with an emollient manner who acted as chairman. A moustached army colonel and a youngish, dark-eyed, dark-haired woman with an intense manner who spoke English with a French accent.

They had made her feel immediately at home, and better still, made her feel an individual, a person – a welcome change after being just a number in the WAAF. The chairman had asked her if she smoked, and passed a silver cigarette box over the desk, but she had declined and no one had lit up.

The chairman had then begun by asking her simple questions about her educational background and her parents.

'When was your mother killed?'

The question was asked in a neutral matter-of-fact tone. She replied in the same flat matter-of-fact tone. 'Two years ago. She'd taken a job as cook at the Café de Paris.'

'Yes, I remember the Café de Paris getting it.' The chairman nodded. 'A direct hit. Snake Hips Johnson was playing.'

All three nodded.

'And you worked for a while with the BBC?' the dark-haired woman asked.

'Translating?'

'Yes.'

'Do you remember a man called Bancroft?'

'Head of the European division. I remember him vaguely. We never spoke. I was too low down the scale.'

73

And then they showed they had a good deal more knowledge about her than they let on.

'After your father died, you made several trips back to France?'

'To stay with my grandmother, yes.'

'At St Bartolomy?'

'Yes.'

'Did you have friends there?'

'Quite a few.'

'Can you remember their names?'

'The local doctor. Pierre Latour. His wife and family. I knew their daughter quite well. And the curé, Father Bernarde. Most of the shopkeepers . . . the baker . . . Jacques . . . Jacques . . . Manoire, I think his name was.' Gabby screwed up her eyes, trying to remember the life which, for years, she had been trying to forget. 'There was a big farm on the road to La Rochelle. I helped at the harvest. The boys let me ride their horses.'

Gabby's voice trailed away. She wondered if any of them could be alive and still living there. Under what conditions? Under Nazi occupation? She daren't speculate.

Then the questioning was taken up by the dark-haired woman, without warning in rapid French. Gabby answered in French. The woman spoke with a slight Bourbonnais accent, but Gabby had no difficulty in answering her.

'*Sprechen Sie Deutsch?*' the colonel asked her.

She shook her head. 'Not enough to get by. But I could work on it. I took it in school certificate.'

'What grade did you get?'

'Distinction.'

How well, the colonel went on to ask, did she know her area of France, and how well the rest?

'Within twenty miles of St Bartholomy, very well. Within forty miles, quite well. The rest not so well.'

'And now,' the chairman said, 'we shall have coffee and tell you something of what this is about.'

It was much as she had guessed. Selected French and German-speaking servicemen and women were to be dropped in both Occupied and Unoccupied France to make contact with and assist the Resistance.

How appealing – or on the other hand, how daunting – would Gabriella find that?

'I can't think of anything I would like to do more.'

He had smiled, not entirely approvingly, at her enthusiasm, and asked if she had any questions.

She smiled back. 'Will you answer them?'

'Probably not. But ask them anyway.'

From their meagre answers, she had learned that, if selected, she would do her training in England in an unnamed area that bore some similarity to where she might be dropped. She would learn map reading, disguise, tracking, burglary, self-defence. How to handle a revolver, a knife, a rope. How to survive, how to be innovative, how to service and repair radios, how to drop by parachute. Meanwhile she was to work on her R/T and W/T skills, improve her German, tell no one. There were many hurdles to be surmounted. This meeting was just the first of them.

They ushered her out without telling her whether or not she had surmounted that first hurdle.

They bade her 'good afternoon' rather than 'au revoir', which she would have found more encouraging.

Making her way down the sandbagged steps of Adastral House and walking in the gathering darkness towards Charing Cross, Gabriella stopped at the Lyons Corner House, feeling suddenly hungry. She had been provided with a paper bag of her travelling rations for the journey. Spam sandwiches, two slices of butterless bread imprisoning a thin slice of the tinned shiny pink meat known as baby's bottom. She had fed the sandwiches to the seagulls along the Embankment.

The blackouts were going up over the windows of the Corner House but she could glimpse a three-piece orchestra of thin elderly ladies in shiny pastel dresses, playing vigorously. Couples, mostly in uniform, were dancing in the centre of the floor. The famous Lyons 'nippies', in their black dresses, little white aprons and frilly caps, wove in and out of the surrounding tables with their trays of tea and little cakes.

Gabriella pushed open the doors and went in.

The noise of tinkling teacups, spoons, rattling trays, shrill music, talk and laughter burst on her like a sugar bomb. The air smelled of warm toast, melting margarine, cheap perfume and hot tea.

Gabby found a small unoccupied table in a quiet corner. She ordered tea and a toasted teacake. With a sigh of relief she slid her respirator off her shoulder, unbuttoned her great-coat, and, for the first time that day, relaxed. She wanted to sit somewhere quietly to digest what she had just been told, to ponder those things that she had guessed without being told, and to assess her chances of being accepted.

But London always evoked mixed memories. Even the music ground out by the gallant ladies, who would keep going no matter what the night might hold, evoked memories of her mother: of her delight at getting the job at the Café de Paris, her pleasure when the famous Snake Hips Johnson had complimented her on her crême brulée – ersatz, of course, because of the rationing – made of dried eggs and skimmed milk. That dreadful night, two years ago now, when she heard that the Café de Paris had suffered a direct hit.

Then, as Gabriella glanced around the crowded café, she became aware that someone was watching her intently. Two tables away, a young man, a civilian, wearing dark glasses, tall, broad-shouldered, with hair close-cropped like a soldier.

The nippy put down her tray. The toasted teacake smelled hot and delicious and there was a thin square of margarine to accompany it. Gabby spread it like a miser. The tea smelled fragrant. She poured it carefully, tried to make the most of this little journey into civilization. But the man's stare bothered her. He was no one she knew. She avoided looking in his direction. But she could feel his eyes on her.

Finally, she drained her cup, opened her respirator, took out her wallet, put down the money for the bill, buttoned her great-coat, slung her respirator and went out thankfully from the bright lights into the anonymous darkness. She put on her cap and stood for a moment blinking her eyes.

The blackout always seemed worse in London than on an RAF station. The great buildings cast their own angular shadows. The slitted baffles over the headlamps of passing vehicles seemed to dazzle rather than illuminate. The only help to pedestrians was the white paint edging the pavements.

When her sight was adjusted, she began walking towards the underground. She crossed the road, dodging cars and buses and trucks. The underground entrance was down a side street. She had almost reached it when she became aware of footsteps behind her, hurrying footsteps, almost catching her up. She half turned.

A rough hand seized the strap of her respirator. She tried to seize it back. But the man pulled the respirator off her shoulder, tore it open, snatched her wallet, gave her a great shove which sent her reeling, and was about to make off, when she spun round, grabbed his arm, hung on, lifted her knee and shoved it hard into his groin. He groaned loudly, swore, dropped the wallet, and ran. As he disappeared into the darkness, she leaned against the wall, choking and breathless. An elderly man, carrying a briefcase and a small civilian gas mask, stopped and asked if he could be of assistance. Gabby thanked him and shook her head, too angry to speak and too suspicious.

She felt momentarily shocked by the episode. London, she knew, was full of pickpockets and bag snatchers, making the most of the blackout. But she suspected that this was no ordinary bag snatcher. When he involuntarily yelped in pain and swore, his swearing was in Savoyard French.

Number five married quarter, when Gabby returned to it, was shrouded in sleep and darkness. Carole was on duty, but Bunty had made down her bed for her and left a chocolate biscuit nicked from the officers' mess on the bolster, beside a note which read, 'Mr Dutton's on this op. Wake me when you hear them coming back.'

It was around five when the first uncertain hum of engines echoed through the overcast sky. Bunty was instantly awake when Gabriella touched her shoulder. 'Is it them?'

'Yes.'

'Have you started counting?'

'Not yet.'

'How did you get on in London?'

'All right. Difficult to know really. Journey back was awful. No heating. Stopped at every station.'

77

'If they accept you, will you get posted?' And, before Gabriella had time to answer: 'That's one in the circuit now, isn't it?'

'Yes. And another.'

'They're coming quite fast now.'

'Good sign. I've counted six. Some of them might be going round though, doing another circuit.'

At that point Edith came stumping upstairs carrying a tin tray with three mugs of tea, and a pile of sliced bread and margarine.

'The cup that cheers,' she announced. From the pocket of her dressing gown she brought out a knife and a jar of Marmite. They sat on Bunty's bed, listening and chewing abstractedly.

'These don't seem to be turning into the circuit.' Gabby looked up at the ceiling, above which the sky echoed to the sound of bombers higher in the sky droning northwards.

'Twelve went,' Bunty said.

'How do you know?'

'Just do.'

'We'll know how many are back when Carole comes,' Edith said. She was surprised at herself for how she had fallen into the ways of this little house and how well she had been accepted by the other three. 'She's one of the crew pick-up drivers.'

'Lucky her,' Bunty sighed fervently.

Sitting at the wheel of the open Commer truck, Carole would not have echoed that sentiment. Despite her leather gauntlets, her hands felt frozen, and her feet like lumps of ice. Her teeth were chattering, though more with apprehension than cold. Not for herself, for the crews. In the privileged position of being able to count the bombers as they returned, she would rather have been almost anywhere in the world. It was a dark night and a cold sea mist was rolling in over the wolds. What wind there was blew in from the east. It smelled of salt and sodden earth, diesel and high-octane fuel. Only intermittent lights showed on the blacked-out airfield, most of them with an immediate purpose – the ambulance, the fire engines, the CO's car, the padre's, the bomb trolleys ready to cart away any unused bombs, the shielded glow of the runway lamps, the green of a Very light pistol and, far away, searchlights fingering the overcast sky, meaning enemy aircraft somewhere around; intermittently a quick crack of light from the dispersal hut behind her as a flight mechanic opened the door to see if their aircraft had landed yet.

Scanning the sky, she could just distinguish the dark shapes of the returning Lancasters flicking in and out of the clouds, now visible, now invisible, insubstantial as black moths round the runway lights. But the noise of their engines was deafening, harsh, desperate to land. The first one lining up with the runway now, coming in fast, a little uncertainly, wobbling from side to side, wheels banging down with a heavy crump, tyres smoking. She could smell the burned rubber through her half-open window, saw the fire engine move closer. But the Lancaster bounced on, settling, then running fast along the runway, turning off to B Dispersal. Seven men, with luck, safely home for tonight.

But not yet the crews she was to transport.

The green Very light soared up again. Another Lancaster lined up. She could see the glow of its throttled-back exhausts reflected on the cloud. She got out and let down her tailboard ready for the crews to scramble aboard. Above her, more dark shapes moved among the clouds. She began to feel more comfortable, beginning to enjoy the sight of the grey clouds suddenly solidifying into a black aircraft, watching its steep descent and safe landfall. Still her crews had not arrived – no clumsy, jacketed, booted figures appearing.

Suddenly all the runway lights went out, turning the whole airfield into a well of darkness.

'How can they land now?' she asked of the empty truck, then, shoving her head out of the side window, asked it of the empty wet tarmac in front of dispersal.

In answer, the harsh aircraft sound diminished as if they were turning away, the sound immediately replaced by the rattle of machine-gun fire. Little flashes burst in the sky immediately ahead of her in the wetness of the cloud, liquid like a child's painting. And then a shape emerged, smaller, leaner, faster than the Lancasters, but seeming to line up with the dark runway ahead of it.

A bemused, uncomprehending spectator, she saw the aircraft sweep down – but not to land.

Instead to level out low, and scream at hedge height down the length of the runway, red bursts of fire blossoming from its wings. Then the flash and crump of bombs.

Simultaneously, a distant but urgent voice over the tannoy was calling, 'Enemy aircraft! Take cover! All personnel not on essential duty take cover! Take cover!'

Whistles sounded. Somewhere on the other side of the airfield, orange flames flickered up, a great billowing sheet lit the sky. Shocked, petrified, powerless to move, Carole watched the black shape turn, and, as if it had just spotted her, sweep roaring over the truck. She could almost have reached up and touched its spurting, rattling underbelly. There was the snap of breaking glass and a whoosh of rushing air.

Glass tinkled inside the cabin. A round jagged hole appeared in the passenger windscreen. She stared at it numbly, only beginning to tremble as an impatient hand wrenched open the driver's door.

'You stupid bitch! I might've known. Sitting like a bloody rabbit!' Hauling her out of the cab by the strap of her respirator and the collar of her battledress, F/Sgt Tordoff frogmarched her across the wet grass down the slippery concrete steps to the dispersal shelter. There was no one else there. It stank of urine.

'What about them?' She jerked her head towards the dispersal hut. Her teeth were still chattering. It was hard to breathe, never mind get the words out. 'The crews aren't taking shelter.'

'They're on essential duty.'

'So am I.'

'You were, sprog. You're not now. The rest of the aircraft aren't coming.'

'Why?'

'They're diverted to Coningsby on account of our Jerry visitors. Control didn't want those bloody MEs jumping on the backs of the Lancs as they landed. So I reckoned I'd come and tell you. Thought I'd find you doing something bloody daft!'

'Thanks.'

'For what?'

'For doing that.'

'I wasn't thinking of you, sprog. I was minding my truck.'

She smiled tentatively. 'So was I.'

'That's my job, kiddo. Next time, mind yourself. Get out pretty damned quick. If you can't get to the shelter get under the truck. Understand?'

'Yes.'

'Here. Take a swig of this.' He unscrewed a greasy leather covered hip flask and handed it to her. 'A good swig.'

She put it to her lips and took a modest sip. The whisky scalded her throat. She almost gagged. But she was determined not to choke. She took another mouthful, gratefully feeling the sudden warmth course through her.

'Here! Have a fag as well!' Chiefie felt in his battledress pockets and brought out a squashy packet of Woodbines. He handed her one. 'It'll calm your nerves.'

'My nerves are calm.'

''Course they are. That's why you're shaking.' He struck a match, shielding it with his hand, a steady hand, bringing it close, studying her face.

After a moment, 'Was that your first drink and your first fag, sprog?'

'No, of course not.'

Then the tannoy announced: 'All clear. I repeat, all clear.'

Thankfully she crushed out the nauseating cigarette on the floor of the shelter and got stiffly to her feet.

'Well.' Chiefie stood up. 'Better see what the damage is, I suppose. Get the lads working on it.'

She followed him back to the truck. The night sky was clearing. An intermittent moon shone on the deserted runway. There was no more aircraft noise, just the sound of a fire engine and repair vehicles hurtling round the perimeter track.

'Christ!' Chiefie touched the bullet hole in the windscreen, then peered inside the cab, 'That was close! Wonder where the bullet went. There! I see it! Into the back of the passenger seat! Fifteen inches thataway and you'd have had it! That's one of your nine lives gone, pussycat!'

The following afternoon, when she reported for duty, Chiefie handed her a small package. 'Just something the metalworker wallahs knocked up. Don't bother to open it now. Get cracking. I've put you on the ration lorry, and the airmen's mess is screaming for its grub.'

She stuffed the package under the flap of her respirator and forgot about it until she was outside the airmen's mess, waiting as the corporal and his sidekick checked and unloaded the crates and sacks and boxes. Then, with nothing better to do, she took out the package and opened it. Inside was a keyring, and, dangling from it, a bullet in a shiny net of Duralumin. Wrapped around was a note in Chiefie's scrawl, *Remember you've only eight left, pussycat.*

Six

L ess than eight of his lives were left to PO Dutton, Bunty thought as she listened to his account of last night's raid. Naturally she didn't say so aloud. And in fact, far from depressing him, his near squeaks seemed to have had the opposite effect, inducing a wild exhilaration.

Their Lancaster, B-Baker, had been jumped by a Focke-Wulf in that most crucial time, the run-in to the target, when the aircraft was under the command of the bomb aimer and all the crew were on tenterhooks for him to press the tit. Then, after dropping their load and when turning to leave the target, they'd been coned by searchlights.

'When you lie in that blue light, boy, you know what's coming!' Chris shivered and then unaccountably giggled.

The ack-ack had been fearsome. But he knew better how to deal with it now – they had jinked. Chris said he'd thrown the Lancaster all over the sky like a shuttlecock. Miraculously it had worked. At debriefing, the wing commander had commended them.

'I told you they all think you're a super skipper.'

'And you're a loyal friend, Bunty. I don't know what I'd have done without you.'

Bunty's cheeks flushed with pleasure. As they sat, side by side on the edge of his bed, she thought he was like a child returned from a party.

But later on, like a child, his excitement would topple over. He'd get to thinking about those near squeaks, thinking about the odds of survival and future ops, remembering he still had ten ops to go to complete his tour, and she bet herself there would be tears before bedtime.

At the moment, he was doing what he liked best, just sitting beside her, unwinding, talking about the trip like he wouldn't have talked at debriefing or to anyone else.

Just in case any nosy parker like Sergeant Fisher came in, she was holding a feather duster in her hand, and could immediately go into the domestic routine of a busy little batwoman. Meanwhile, she used the feather duster to tickle his nose or his ears, just to make him laugh even louder.

In the other bed, Mr Bladowski, who had been one of the first to land so hadn't been diverted to Coningsby, was fast asleep, gently snoring. He didn't seem to mind them having a bit of a chat, seemed to regard her these days as part of the furniture.

'So what did you feel when you were in the circuit here and saw there was a Jerry in with you?' she asked in the silence after he had finished describing how one of the 4 Group Lancs had exploded over the target.

'How did I feel? Christ! Shit-scared would be an understatement!' But he laughed as soon as the words were out of his mouth, and she laughed too.

'The bastards! What a dirty trick.'

'Not cricket!' He laughed louder.

'Did they have a go at you?'

'Fired a few bursts. But really they were fastening on the tail of the aircraft that was actually landing.'

'Bastards!' she repeated. 'They only hit the dispersal paint store, I heard. Didn't hit much of the runway.'

'No. They were wide of the mark. Won't hold up ops. Luckily.' Then he thought for a moment, his face clouding, and added, 'Or unluckily.'

Bunty interposed quickly, 'Did they look after you at Coningsby?'

'Bang on! It's a super-duper mess.'

'Good batwoman?' she asked innocently.

'Not a patch on you.' He brought her hand to his lips and gave it a kiss. 'I kid you! It was a batman. Anyway,' he said, his thoughts reverting, 'no ops tonight. We're stood down.'

'Wizzo.'

'I've been saying to myself, Bunty, we should celebrate.'

'We?'

'My pals and me.'

'Oh.'

'*O-oh*,' He imitated her disappointed sigh. 'Don't look like that! You're one of them, Bunty. You're a pal. My best pal.' He squeezed her hand. 'And Blad –' he jerked his head towards his roommate's recumbent form – 'has a birthday. We should celebrate.'

'How?'

'Go and beat up Lincoln. Get a late pass, Bunty. Go in on the liberty bus. We'll have dinner at a hotel. A few drinks. Take in a dance. There's always one on in the church hall. You can ask your chums along. We'll make up a party. It'll be tremendous fun!'

'But I can't, Chris! Officers and airmen aren't allowed to fraternize.'

'Fraternize! That's an awful word!'

'Well, that's what they call it. It's not allowed. They're really hot about officers dating airwomen. I'd be on a charge again.'

'You won't be on a charge, because they won't find out. We won't sit together on the bus. Lincoln's a big place and miles away. Who's to know? Come on! I need to get out! I need fun! And so does Blad.'

She studied his youthful face for a moment, saw the crest of his excitement and relief about to topple. 'All right.' She laughed. 'I'm game. I'd love to!'

After all, she thought, it would be quite an experience, something to write home to her mum about. She had never in her whole life been into a hotel as a customer, though once she had delivered a note from Mr Hardcastle to the Royal back home about a funeral wake that was to be held there. It had looked very posh. She would have to press her uniform and clean her buttons and shoes like crazy to live up to it, but she would give it a go.

Then Chris posed a knotty problem. 'I've had a brainwave! You're such a pretty girl, Bunty. A real pin-up. I'd love to see you in civvies. I like dancing with girls in civvies, holding them.' He spread his hands and closed his eyes dreamily. 'I bet you look smashing. A real Betty Grable. Be a sweetie. Don't wear that horrible uniform. Wear your best party dress for the occasion.'

*　　　*　　　*

85

'I didn't like to say I hadn't got a dress, period! Let alone a party one!' Bunty wailed to Gabriella, as, three hours later, they sluiced their mugs and irons in the greasy vat of water outside the airwomen's mess. 'He was so excited, Gabby. Really, really excited. Just like a little boy.'

'They're all little boys,' Gabby replied cynically. 'And only a boy would ask you to go out in civvies. It's not allowed. If you were caught you'd be for the high jump.'

'He didn't mean any harm. You know what aircrew are like!'

'As I said, like little boys. Did you point out it would be you they punished, not him?'

'No, I couldn't do that.'

'So what are you going to do?'

'I'll try to get a dress. He was really set on it. But if I can't get one, I'll turn up as I am. In uniform. He'll be disappointed. But I can't do anything else. Anyway, are you off duty? And will you come with us? He wants to make it a party.'

'Who's us?'

'PO Bladowski, of course, and some of Chris's crew. They're really nice.'

'Yes. I know.'

'So you'll come?'

'Perhaps.'

'No, don't say perhaps. Say you'll come. Please?'

'All right. I'll come.'

'Carole says she will. She's got a dress. Her mother made it for her eighteenth birthday. She's brought it with her, but she doesn't want to wear it because she doesn't want to be on another charge. She said I could have the loan of it.'

'Will it fit?'

Bunty looked momentarily crestfallen. Then she rallied. 'She says it's loose-fitting.'

'It'd have to be. Very loose-fitting. Anyway, I haven't got a dress. And I wouldn't wear it even if I had. You're a clot if you do. There'll be hell to pay if anyone stops you.'

'I know. But he was really, really keen.'

They had begun to walk back to the billet. Gabby glanced sideways at Bunty and sighed. 'Well, on your head be it! I've got some quite pretty earrings, if that's any good. I've also got a can of imitation silk stockings. You know, leg paint.'

'Oh, thanks ever so. That'd be lovely. And Carole's got some indoor shoes, so I don't have to wear these clodhoppers. We can have a fashion show when we get back.' Bunty skipped along cheerfully. 'Carole's off at five. She's not going to bother with late tea, because the boys are going to buy us dinner. At a hotel. And we're catching the liberty bus at seven.'

Carole was already in the billet. 'Chiefie let me off early. Everything's quiet.' She had made her bed down, unpacked the dress, pressed it and spread it carefully over the hairy blankets. It was of a rich blue silky material with thin shoulder straps, a full skirt and a not too tight waist. But the bust would present problems. As soon as she came off duty, Edith was pressed into service.

She had equipped herself well from the haberdashery department in Edenbridge. Along with her issue 'housewife' (a canvas holdall of needles, pins and thread), she brought out a box filled with cottons and silks and buttons and ribbons.

Carole had given permission for two seams to be let out, and when that didn't accommodate Bunty's bosom, for a small piece of material to be snipped from the underside of the hem, and inserted as a gusset. Edith sat for an hour busily sewing while Gabby shampooed Bunty's thick blonde hair, and Carole painted her legs with the imitation silk stockings.

There was not much make-up to be had between the four of them. However, by pooling their resources, they managed to accent Bunty's pretty little cupid's mouth, and used a blue ops-room crayon round her wide dolly-blue eyes.

Even with the seams let out and the gusset, the dress was tight over the bust. 'But,' as Bunty remarked, 'no worse for being that!'

'You look a million dollars,' Gabby said. 'Edith's done you proud.'

'I know she has. I do wish you'd come with us, Edith.'

Edith shook her head. 'I don't like that sort of thing.' She pursed her lips. 'Arnold wouldn't like me to go either. Anyway, there's a good flick on at the cinema. Mae West.' She almost added, 'You look a bit like Mae West, Bunty,' but she bit her lips in time. Bunty looked lovely, if a bit plump. 'Why don't you try Gabby's earrings?'

They were long and silver and set with what looked like little diamonds. They were the final touch.

'Are they French?' Bunty asked, looking at her own reflection with awe.

'Naturellement.'

'They're really classy.'

'Now,' Gabby said. 'Let's try your greatcoat. Make sure the dress doesn't hang down under it. That would be a real giveaway.' She walked around Bunty, scrutinizing her carefully. 'Nothing shows. Now put the earrings in your pocket. Pull your issue stockings on over the leg paint. It won't shine through. While you're doing that, Carole and I will clean our buttons and put on our faces. Then we're off.'

They anticipated that the dicey part of the operation would probably be the walk to station headquarters, from where the liberty bus departed. Officers, NCOs and RAF police swarmed in that area. Any number of them might have stopped the trio as they marched crisply side by side, feet clicking in rhythm, arms swinging, towards the waiting bus. Their caps sat straight on their heads, their hair was scooped up off their collars, their respirators were correctly slung, their shoes and buttons shone.

But no one stopped them.

The bus was half full. It seemed to be an unwritten rule that the officers (because there were so few of them) should sit in the front seats and the more numerous other ranks at the back. Mr Dutton and Mr Bladowski were already occupying the front seats. They kept their backs turned and stared out of the window as, to the accompaniment of whistles and stamping from the rude airmen, the girls clambered on board.

Then came the first shock. Chiefie was the driver. He observed Carole's discomfiture with grim satisfaction.

'Here, girls! Comfy seat here!' Some of the rough types at the back shouted, patting their knees.

'One more word from you lot, and you're off the bus!' Chiefie rounded on them. 'Sit over there, girls!' He pointed. 'Where I can keep an eye on you. And –' he stood up and addressed the bus as a whole – 'no bloody nonsense from anyone, understand?'

'Yes, Flight Sergeant,' the airmen chorused back dutifully.

'And when you get to Lincoln, don't get tanked up. No drunk will be allowed on the return journey. Remember that! I'm not having any puking on my bus. Nor any offensive or lewd behaviour.' He seemed to fasten his eyes on the officers at the front. 'No matter what rank. Understand? If the AOC got plastered he'd be off my bus like a dose of salts. I'll be watching you all in the mirror, so behave yourselves. Don't play footsie with the girls. Don't sing bawdy songs. Anyone up to anything will get off and walk. Return bus is ten thirty sharp! Not a minute after. No waiting for anyone.'

Then he hitched himself into the driver's seat and started up the engine.

It was a fifty-minute drive into Lincoln, and the blacked-out bus was hot and smelly and slow. Its upholstery was minimal, its springing long since gone.

'Where are we supposed to be meeting?' Carole asked Bunty in a whisper.

'Outside the Station Hotel. It's the biggest and best, Chris says. Not far from where the bus drops us. We just walk straight along that same road. He says we can't miss it.'

'So where are you off to in such a hurry, pussycat?' Chiefie caught Carole's arm as they began to leave the bus.

'We thought,' Carole hesitated, 'we might have a drink.'

'A drink! But you don't drink, pussycat.'

'I do now.'

'Well, mind it's only one. And you girls all stick together.'

'We will.'

'And where are you off to, sirs?' Chiefie asked almost ingratiatingly as Pilot Officers Dutton and Bladowski attempted to slip past him.

'We dance!' cried PO Bladowski, raising a merry hand, snapping his fingers like castanets, taking sideways steps and stamping his feet.

'Good for you, sirs! Sounds a bright idea. I might just go along and do that too. Where is the dance, sirs?'

But they were too wise to tell him. In a flood of incomprehensible Polish, PO Bladowski managed to convey the dance was a private Polish affair, and looking at his watch, hurried Chris away into the darkness.

Striding ahead of the girls, they led the way past a small park towards the station. Ahead of them, they saw a large Victorian building immediately opposite the station. Several cars were drawn up outside. Shallow steps led up to glass swing doors, which intermittently caught an illegal twinkle of indoor light. Thin cracks of light leaked from rows of tall windows. Faint music from an orchestra playing somewhere in the hotel was half drowned by the hiss and shriek of a train blowing off steam in the station opposite; but it was festive and promising and Bunty felt almost unbearably excited.

The two pilots had been joined by two young sergeants, one tall and hefty, the other diminutive. Chris introduced them as 'Jumbo, our bomb aimer, and Rod, our rear gunner. Gabby you bods know already. You've had dealings with her at flying control. This is my special friend, Bunty. And Carole. You might have been lucky enough to be in one of her transports. She's an MT wallah, one of Flight Sergeant Tordoff's harem. That's why he didn't like her being loose in Lincoln.'

'Yes, Chris, we've all met! Hi!' Jumbo put his fingers to his cap.

'Well, let's get inside!' Chris slipped his hand through Bunty's arm. 'Don't want to waste any more good drinking time.' And, nuzzling his nose into her hair, 'Mmm, Bunty, you smell gorgeous.'

The two of them led the way up the steps. Chris pushed open the glass swing doors and pulled aside the inner blackout curtains.

The entrance hall was lit by an ornate chandelier, the biggest Bunty had ever seen. It was covered in dust and threads of cobwebs and she ached to get out her feather duster. But it was still magnificent. Up the wide staircase were gilded wall sconces similarly draped. A well-worn red carpet covered the floor.

Across it in a jerky crablike gait advanced a bent and elderly man in shabby livery of faded purple and gold. He carried, under his arm, a large thin book, and as he neared the newcomers, he lifted a pair of metal-rimmed spectacles that hung from his braided lapel and clipped them on his already pinched nose. He stared at the arriving party with disbelief.

'Yes, sir?' he asked of Chris in a high querulous tone.

'We would like a table for seven, please.' Chris consulted his watch. 'In half an hour please. Give us time for a drink in the bar first.'

'That will not be possible, sir.'

'Why not? Are you fully booked? Then make it in an hour . . . or—'

'That will not be possible either, sir!' the old man announced with satisfaction.

'Well, when can we have a table?'

'Never, sir!' His glassy, hostile gaze travelled round the group. 'Not for this party, sir! Not in this hotel! This hotel –' he paused for effect – 'is for officers only. It does not serve other ranks.'

'Well, I'll be damned!' Chris exploded.

'What is that?' PO Bladowski scowled. 'What is it that old fool say?'

'That they don't serve other ranks.'

'Jeezus Christ! The bloody English! Fight for democracy they say! Who can ever the English understand?' He suddenly lunged forward, grabbed the commissionaire by his lapels. 'These are our comrades! On our crew. We fly with them. I order you to serve them!'

'Leave him alone!' Chris pulled him back. 'The poor old chap can't help it! He's only carrying out the manager's orders!'

'Then send for the manager! At once! Tell him, Count Bladowski would speak with him forthwith!'

'Shut up, Blad, for crying out loud! We don't want a fuss. The girls'd be the ones that would catch it!'

'There is a public house down the road that caters for other ranks,' the old man said, dusting down his lapels.

'Chris,' Jumbo said. 'I've been thinking. Bunty says she's got her civvy clothes on under her greatcoat. She can leave her coat in the cloakroom, then she's a civvy and they'll serve her. You and she and Blad can stay here. The rest of us'll go down the road to the pub.'

'Certainly not!' Chris said. 'Eh, Bunty?'

'No, of course not!'

'Never on your nelly!' Blad glowered. 'Never on your nelly would I eat at this malodorous place. It stinks. Tell your manager! His establishment stinks! No Polish gentleman could eat here undefiled!'

'Shut up, Blad! Let's make a quiet exit.' Chris marshalled them outside. 'We'll probably eat much better down the road.'

'Do you wonder sometime, you English, just what you fight for?'

'Don't start that again, Blad. We all know why you fight.'

'To kill German! To kill many, many Germans!' He repeated that mantra as they marched off down the road, till they reached a public house, outside the darkened doorway of which hung a sign depicting a nineteenth-century musketeer over the caption, *The Volunteer*. 'The trouble is,' Blad said, determined to have the last word, 'you English lack the lust to kill.'

Jumbo pushed open the door of the pub and managed to shove his way inside, holding Gabby and Carole by the arm. The other four insinuated themselves behind. There didn't seem to be an inch of space. The place was packed with servicemen and women.

Behind the counter at the far end, a middle-aged man and his wife were desperately trying to cope with the customers. The air was thick as a London smog, blue with cigarette smoke. Wreaths of it hung in the air like ectoplasm. Chalked on a blackboard above the counter was the evening menu. Bangers and mash or hot onion and potato pie.

Jumbo, being the biggest, elbowed his way to the bar, while Chris gave the woman the orders – three bangers and four hot pies. They ate them standing in the only free bit of space, which was beside a door on which was painted *To the Garden*. Or at least they tried to eat them. The food was hot and delicious, but they had only taken a few mouthfuls when, above the intervening heads and through the murk, they saw the street door open and Chiefie stand framed in the doorway.

He was looking searchingly around before shoving his way in. Without a word said, they all, in one mind, laid down their plates and cutlery on the near end of the bar, crouched down below the level of the counter, turned the handle of the garden door, and prayed that it would open.

It did. They sidled out

They stood for a moment on an unevenly paved patio, drawing in the cool fresh air and letting their eyes get used to the darkness. 'Did he see us?' Carole asked.

'Don't think so,' Chris answered. 'Anyway, it's none of his business. He couldn't do anything if he had spotted us.'

'That wouldn't stop him,' Jumbo laughed. 'I know the bastard. He'd have had our guts.'

They began to pick their way through the back garden of the pub, stumbling over garden furniture, ducking under a washing line. 'He's probably eating up our bangers and mash right now.'

'Not to worry. We'll get some food at the dance.'

But the dance, at what was known as the Sweatbox – a corrugated iron church hall that provided entertainment for the forces – was just as packed as the pub. The air was full of cigarette smoke. It was stiflingly hot and stank of sweat. The food consisted of some tired-looking sandwiches laid out on a trestle table covered in white paper.

The highlight in the midst of all the heat and discomfort was Bunty. When she shed her greatcoat and peeled off her lisle stockings, she emerged like a blue butterfly from a chrysalis to disclose legs painted an elegant silky beige, with straight seams below the dainty hemline of her shimmering blue dress, and swanned on to the floor in Carole's high-heeled shoes.

'You look absolutely stunning,' Chris whispered in her ear as he guided her through the thick sweating wool-clad couples, nearly all in khaki or navy or air force blue, with just a few rather common dresses worn by local girls. 'You're the belle of the ball. Everyone's looking at you!'

'I hope they're not!'

'Well, they are! And I don't wonder! You've got legs like Ginger Rogers! A figure like Betty Grable.' Chris pressed his cheek ardently to hers.

The band consisted of a white-haired old man who nodded his head to every thump of the piano, a kid of about twelve banging the drums, and a fat lady on the xylophone. They played 'These Foolish Things', and Chris crooned it in her ear. 'A cigarette that bears a lipstick's traces, An airline ticket to romantic places, Oh how the ghost of you clings, These foolish things remind me of you.' Then it was 'Wish me luck as you wave me goodbye . . . Give me a smile I can keep for a while, In my heart while I'm away.'

Chris held her so close she could hear his heart beating. And her own heart was dancing faster than the music. 'I do believe,' Chris whispered, 'that I am falling in love with you.'

That was all she needed to make this dance perfect. It was the stuff of fairy tales. Cinderella. Her favourite one. She had come to the ball in the smelly liberty bus instead of a pumpkin, and it was driven by bad-tempered Chiefie Tordoff instead of a proper coachman, but her dress was as beautiful as any Cinderella ball gown. And luck was with her, the bust gusset held. Even when Chris waltzed her out through the rear door, across the scrunchy, cinder-covered back yard, to a bank covered in rough grass, and there pulled her down beside him, she was still walking on air.

At first her only concern was about getting a grass stain, or worse, a dog turd on Carole's lovely dress, so she straightaway hitched the skirt right up so that she didn't, which might have given Chris the wrong idea. For after that she became worried about what Chris was doing to her. But, as well as that, she was also worried that Chris seemed taken aback by her blackouts, and she knew they weren't the thing to wear under a pretty dress, but she had no other knickers of any kind. The two worries jostled for position in her mind. Then the worry of what he was doing became worse than wearing blackouts. She liked it a lot to begin with. The caressing was lovely and exciting. But then she got frightened. She felt it wasn't right. She felt she was no longer in control of herself. She tried to push him and his great big thing away. But by then he was in a real state, more excited than she had ever seen him before, and he kept murmuring that he needed to love her properly, and she thought, best let him get on and have done with it.

She didn't enjoy it. She thought it was horrible, a very messy business, painful too.

She supposed she had, as her mother would have said, lost her cherry, and she should have been worried about it. And at first she was. She thought it was going to spoil the evening for her, but it didn't, because Chris was so sweet to her afterwards. In fact, that was the best bit. He cuddled her and buried his face in her hair and murmured, 'I love you, darling.' And then he went on to say the magic words, 'And now I feel we're as good as married.'

'Do you really?' She wriggled round, sat up and held his face in her hands. 'Really and truly? Cross your heart?'

For some reason, she kept thinking of the posh-looking middle-aged lady in the photo frame, and wondering what she would say.

'Of course I do. Cross my heart. And when all this is over, we'll have a proper white wedding.'

After that they lay for a blissful half-hour on the bank, looking up at the stars, and the fingering of the searchlights. He pointed out some of the stars to her, because they navigated by the stars. The North Star and the Great Bear and Cassiopeia and Orion. Beautiful-sounding names. She repeated them, loving the feel of the words on her tongue and thinking those beautiful stars were the friends of all airmen. It couldn't have been a more romantic evening. Real fairy tale stuff. If he wanted to marry her and he did, for he had said the magic words, then they were as good as engaged. He might even buy her a ring. It was worth all the messy business that went on beforehand, worth even the stains on Carole's dress, which she had already resolved to slip into the officers' mess weekly bag of cleaning. She wondered if it was too soon to write to her mother to tell her she had met her Prince Charming and that they were to be married – a white wedding.

Of course, like Cinderella, she had to be gone before midnight. The liberty bus would leave an hour and a half before, in fact. Ten thirty sharp, Chiefie Tordoff had said. So she and Chris had no time to dance again before she had to cover up her finery.

The arrangement was that the men and the girls would walk to the bus stop separately, lest Chiefie Tordoff was on the prowl.

Bunty slipped early into the tiny ladies' room at the back of the hall while it was still deserted. Through the thin walls, she could hear the sound of heavily shod dancing feet and the orchestra playing 'There'll be bluebirds over the white cliffs of Dover tomorrow, just you wait and see'. There would, there would, Bunty thought, allowing herself one last look at the dream in the fly-speckled mirror.

But the dream was already fading. Her hair looked like a bird's nest, damp and spiky, her make-up all smeared. As for the dress! She wriggled round to examine it and groaned. So many stains!

She held some of the skirt under the cold tap and dabbed the worst of the stains with her handkerchief. Then she put on her thick lisle stockings and her great clumpy shoes, took off Gabby's earrings and dropped them in her pocket, buttoned her greatcoat right up to her neck, put her cap on straight and slung her respirator.

She had just returned fully to earth as it were when the other two girls rushed in, flinging on their greatcoats and bidding each other hurry. 'How did you get on with Blad?' Bunty asked Gabby in a high bright voice as they left. She thought Gabby was looking at her a bit old-fashionedly, as if she knew what Chris and she had been up to.

'Let's say he lusts for activities other than killing Germans!'

Lust was not a word that Bunty greatly cared for at the moment, so she just murmured pacifically, 'Well, he's a Pole!'

'True. How about you and Jumbo, Carole?' Gabby asked as they negotiated the dark pavement.

'He's OK. I like him.'

'Didn't make any passes.'

'Not that I recognized.'

'Rod didn't get much of a look-in, did he?'

'Not with us. He didn't want a look-in.' Carole laughed. 'He made a beeline for a civvy girl. They spent half the time cooling off outside.'

'Talking of cooling off –' Gabby put her hand through Bunty's arm – 'I noticed you were AWOL a long time.'

'Well, it was that hot! I hope I didn't put sweat stains on your dress, Carole.'

'Don't worry. I doubt I'll ever wear it again.'

A number of service liberty buses left Lincoln at ten thirty, so there was a noisy exodus from the dance hall. They joined the stream hurrying towards the bus stop. The three girls tagged on behind a group of army types.

At some distance behind them they could hear Chris and Blad and the others following discreetly.

The night was still fine and a half moon shone. The air smelled cold and wintry. Moved perhaps by the beauty of the night or the romance of the occasion, Bladowski began to sing. He had a nice voice, dark and throbbing. After a while, by the sound of his feet and the clapping of his hands, he had begun to dance, and Chris and Jumbo and Rod were joining in, laughing wildly and singing.

Carole and Gabby smiled at each other indulgently, and Bunty remarked mistily, 'Lovely to hear them so happy.'

Then suddenly, right in front of them, two figures emerged out of the darkness. A baffled torch was shone in their direction. An arm wearing two chevrons waved.

'Airwomen!' shouted an authoritative female voice. 'Halt!'

Two purposeful WAAF police corporals barred their way as they came to a nervous halt.

The torch dazzled them. They screwed up their eyes. The voice shouted again, 'Have you got late passes?'

'Yes, Corporal.'

'Then let's see them! And your twelve fifties.'

The beam of the torch concentrated on Bunty. It seemed to finger her throat where no collar was visible.

'Come on! Pull your fingers out! We haven't got all night. Unbutton your greatcoats. Get out your passes and twelve fifties.'

There was no other course of action open to them except what they did.

The gate to the little park close to the liberty bus stop was just behind them. With one accord the girls fled.

As they dived into the fragrant darkness of the park, they heard the sound of colliding bodies, a squeak, a scuffle, indignant cries and profuse mendacious apologies in broken English.

Dodging through the narrow, winding shrub-lined walkways of the park, Gabby was the first to reach the bus, followed closely by Carole. Then Bunty, breathless and frightened. Jumbo, Chris and Rod were already clambering aboard. Chiefie started the engine as Bunty dragged herself up the steps.

'Get under the seats, you stupid girls!' Chiefie ordered, as the figures of the two WAAF police corporals appeared in the headlights, hands raised authoritatively to stop the bus.

He switched off, heaved himself out of the driver's seat,

drew himself up to his full height and stood in the doorway, arms folded belligerently.

'What is the trouble, Corporal?'

'Three deserters, Flight Sergeant.'

'Deserters? Where, Corporal?'

'Just down the road. Ran off when challenged.'

Chiefie clicked his tongue. 'Men or women?'

'Women. And we suspect one was in civvies.'

'Good God! Might be a civvy masquerading as a WAAF. Don't let them go again, Corporal. Pity you lost 'em. Meantime, don't delay the bus, I am due to leave at twenty-two thirty and it is now twenty-two thirty-five.'

'You haven't seen them, Flight Sergeant?'

'Certainly not! I would have apprehended them. But if they're deserters, they wouldn't come this way, now, would they? Use your loaf. They'd make for the railway station! That's your best bet.'

They thanked him and marched off. Chiefie resumed his seat, started the engine again and pulled away. He said nothing.

The complete silence in the bus was ominous. No one sang. No one even spoke. The atmosphere in the bus was dictated by the set of his head and shoulders, and his angry eyes watching them in the driver's mirror.

After they were clear of the environs of Lincoln, and the road cleaved its way between empty fields, Carole crawled out and began to get stiffly to her feet. 'Get back where you were,' Chiefie hissed. 'You three will stay under the seat till we reach Holmfirth. By then I'll have decided how I'm going to punish you.'

The punishment was not revealed till the following morning. By some tortuous logic, Chiefie had decided that it should be borne entirely by Carole. She was clearly, to him, the instigator of the crime, and it was a serious one. If he reported the girls to the Queen Bee, as he ought to do, they would be court-martialled, and when you added up all their crimes, probably dismissed the service.

It was out of the kindness of his heart that he doled out his punishment. It was surprisingly mild: that she should be on her most hated vehicle, the bomb trolley, for a minimum of the next two weeks.

Seven

Those were weeks that saw, for Bomber Command as a whole, the height of the Battle of Berlin and, for RAF Holmfirth, pinpoint attacks on vital targets before the long-rumoured opening up of the Second Front.

The bomb trolley was laden with smaller than usual high-precision bombs, but it was still a load which Carole instinctively detested. It was the least favourite vehicle for most of the MT drivers, for reasons as varied as their personalities. But all of them shared one common reason – that it was uncomfortable to be perched high up, bumping over the uneven surface of the perimeter track to the dispersals dragging a load that with only a spark could blow the entire station to kingdom come.

The afternoon of the Peenemunde raid was warm and cloudless. A huge tall sky just beginning to tinge with pink arched benignly above the Lincolnshire countryside. The sun glistened on the stubble fields next to the airfield. The scene beyond the dispersed bombsite was as peaceful as the Constable print that hung above their fireplace at home. Home, she thought wistfully, seemed a long way away, her parents distant, diminished figures in a discarded landscape. She drove carefully towards the black silhouettes of the waiting Lancasters.

O-Orange was first, the wing commander's aircraft. Typically, he was there beside it, to watch her being bombed up.

At first, he was too intent on the load to notice who was the driver. Then, when he saw Carole, his expression at first softened and then underwent an exaggerated change. 'Jeezus! You on the bomb trolley! You of all people! How come?'

'Flight Sergeant Tordoff, sir.'

'The man must need his head examining!'

'He does, sir. I wish you'd tell him.'

'Oh, I will! Why the hell did he give you the job?'

'Because he knew I could do it, sir.'

The wing commander gave a snort of disbelief. They both smiled.

'To be truthful . . .' Carole added.

'Which you are!'

'It's supposed to be some sort of punishment.'

'What for?'

'I'd rather not say.'

'Something pretty frightful, I imagine.'

And then he seemed to lose his brief interest in her. O-Orange's bombing-up was complete. The wing commander peered into the bomb bay to check the disposition of the load.

Before she moved off, Carole called to the visible part of him, 'Good luck, sir!'

But he didn't hear her and he didn't turn.

From the balcony, Gabby saw Carole driving the empty trolley past flying control. She waved, and with manifest relief that the bombing-up was done for today at least, Carole waved back. All in all, she felt Chiefie had allowed the three of them to get off lightly for last week's jaunt into Lincoln.

As Gabby walked back into the control room and pulled the blackout curtain behind her, Beaky looked up and smiled. This was always a difficult time, when the target was known, the preparations underway, the names of the crews chalked up on the blackboard, and they had time for thought.

The target, Peenemunde, was, according to their sparse information, a secret weapon base of some sort being built by the enemy. Situated on the Pas de Calais, it was an area Gabby knew a little from childhood. Her father had taken her there for holidays. There were long flat beaches. Sand dunes. An unlikely place for pinpoint bombing.

Gabby had heard nothing since her visit to Adastral House, which probably meant that she had been found unsuitable for whatever job they had been considering her for. In the week since their outing to Lincoln, the losses had been light. But Gabby had felt restless and somehow uneasy, as if something horrible was going to happen. But maybe that was all part of the general tension everyone seemed to be feeling, aware that something must happen soon. But what? And when? And where?

ETD was to be at 2000 hours. In a short time, Beaky would be joining the wing commander and the Met officer for the crew briefing.

Jan had checked the blackout and was sitting at her console rereading a letter from her husband. Beaky had unscrewed his pen preparatory to scribbling a brief note to his wife, when there came a singularly inappropriate but welcome sound – the jingle of an ice-cream van.

Jim the ever hungry pricked up his ears. 'NAAFI van on the road at the back, sir! Mind if I get a doughnut? I missed lunch!'

'An excellent idea, Jim. You might get us all one.' Beaky dipped into his trouser pocket and brought out a handful of change. 'My treat.' The other occupants of flying control cheered.

Jim's eager steps had hardly died away when Beaky lifted his head, listening intently. Wordlessly he pointed to the ceiling, above which vibrated an aircraft's engines. An aircraft approaching fast. Desynchronized engines. Not one of ours. Coming in purposefully low.

Beaky had just opened his mouth to form the word 'Jerry!' when any word was drowned in the whine and crump of bombs that shook flying control to its concrete foundations.

Too late, a voice on the tannoy gabbled out, 'Enemy aircraft. Take cover! Intruder over the airfield!'

The slits round the blackout of the landside window glowed a fierce spurting scarlet. Another heavy crump, then another. Flying control rocked. Just outside, someone screamed; voices shouted orders, then came the clamour of fire-engine bells. And above all the other sounds, the hideous, inappropriate ice-cream jingle, spun by the bomb into an unstoppable hysteria.

For a second, they gritted their teeth and held their breath, waiting for the massive explosion as the intruder found his target and hit a bombed-up Lancaster. Mercifully, none came. The aircraft's engines faded. A few minutes later, a runner came dashing up the steps with the news that all the aircraft were untouched. A stick of bombs had fallen from outside flying control across to D-Dispersal. The NAAFI van had been hit, the two NAAFI girls badly cut by flying glass, and Jim was being carted off in the ambulance.

Gabby ran down the steps and out on to the apron to find out about Jim. Flames licked up into the sky from one of the old dispersal huts. The air was thick with the sizzling smell of explosive and grit, burning wood and spilled kerosene. Thirty yards from flying control, a great ragged hole had been torn in the road. The SPs had cordoned it off with orange tape. The ground in between was slippery with white foam and oil and squashed doughnuts. The ice-cream jingle was still playing but no one was screaming. The SPs said Jim was already in the ambulance.

No one knew, or no one would say, how badly he was hurt. Everyone was hurrying and purposeful, trying to get the flames doused before they attracted the bombs of other intruders.

Gabby skidded over to the ambulance, banged on the side, and shouted, 'Good luck, Jim!' No one answered. It seemed a fatuous thing to do, she thought, watching the ambulance pull away.

As it did so, the all clear sounded.

According to one of the firemen, the other bombs in the stick had straddled part of the perimeter track and blown holes in the main Lincoln road beyond the airfield. No aircraft and no other vehicles had been hit.

In flying control they made another brew of tea and awaited developments. They were beginning to think they had got away with it pretty lightly when, half an hour later, the telephone rang.

Beaky listened, deliberately impassive, to the voice at the other end.

Jim had died in the ambulance.

A blanket of gloom descended on flying control.

Yet, as none of the damage was judged sufficient for delay, the night's operation went on with take-off still scheduled for 2000 hours. A solemn-faced Wingco came into flying control on his way to O-Orange. He showed no emotion at Jim's fate, enquiring only what steps Beaky had taken to get a replacement.

'I got on to Group right away, sir. They'll do their best.'

'Their best isn't usually good enough. Did they say when?'

'No sir.'

'Well, if you don't hear in a couple of days, let me know.'

'Will do, sir.'

Forty minutes later, in response to the green Very light, all four aircraft roared down the runway one after the other and lifted off into a starlit sky.

As the thunder of their engines died away and the planes headed for Peenemunde, back in the married quarters those airwomen off duty prepared for one of the fortnightly kit inspections.

Kit inspections were never a problem to Bunty. She had been brought up to take care of what clothes she had, and never before in her life had she possessed three of everything – three shirts, three bust bodices, three pairs of blackout knickers, three pairs of stockings.

'If you hand me your stockings I'll give them a quick darn,' she said to Carole. 'I've done mine.' Bunty unrolled her canvas housewife, took out her wooden darning mushroom, and slid it down inside one of Carole's stockings. 'Ma'am may be on the warpath tonight.'

Carole looked across at her questioningly. 'Why especially?'

'Sore head. Hangover. From last night. Threw a surprise birthday party in the mess for her dear friend the Wingco. You should have seen the eats! Lobster! Chicken! Pies! Trifles!'

'So why should that make her sore?'

'According to my sergeant, the Wingco only stayed five minutes.'

She thrust her needle gleefully but skilfully into the lisle fabric. The small hole in the heel was darned and the pairs of stockings neatly rolled by the time the flight officer appeared, half an hour later. She had joined the padre to wave a blessing on the Lancasters from the end of the runway, and had drunk a quick libation in the office adjoining the station chapel.

She was flushed and bright-eyed. Her eyes acquired a steely sparkle as they alighted on Carole, standing to attention beside her bed, upon which her kit was, due to Bunty's help, almost mathematically laid out.

'At ease, Kemp,' she snapped crisply, delicately and disdainfully picking up random items – a vest here, a pair of blackouts there – then unrolling a pair of stockings to make sure each one bore a name tape. Disappointed at finding nothing amiss, she turned her attention upon the girl herself, walking around her, eyeing her from head to foot.

'Your hair touches your collar.' She stretched a fastidious finger to lift a brown lock. 'Report to the camp hairdresser for a cut. And report to Flight Sergeant Grimble that you've had it done.'

Bunty's prolific fluffy hair passed without comment. Gabby and Edith were on duty. The flight officer swept out.

'Take no heed of her,' Bunty said stoutly, beginning to stow the kit away. 'She's only taking it out on you because she fancies the Wingco and he fancies you.'

Not true, of course. But a well-worn phrase subsequently taken up by Chiefie Tordoff.

'I warned you, girl,' Chiefie said three days later when, after two successful sorties, the squadron was stood down, 'not to encourage the Brylcreem boys.'

'I don't.'

'Oh, yes you do. I know. I've heard. Chatting up that bastard even when you're on the bomb trolley.'

'Who? The Wingco?'

'Who else?'

'Well, he was chatting to me.'

'Same thing. Takes two to tango.'

'Not even chatting really. Being quite rude. Told me the bomb trolley, with all that TNT, was the last thing I should be on.'

'That's just his way of flirting.'

'How d'you know?'

'I know because I am a man.'

'Is that why you're so rude to me?'

'Don't be cheeky with me, sprog. No, I am never rude. Nor do I fancy you. But he does. He's put in more six-five-eights in the time you've been here than in the three months before.'

'You've never given me one of his jobs.'

'Not bloody likely! See any wet behind my ears? No, I thought not. But, as you're off the bomb trolley, I've got a cushy number for you today.'

'What?'

'Don't sound so suspicious. A little beauty of a job. Delivering instruments to the satellite at Roveton.'

'What sort of instruments?'

'Nothing you can't handle. Take the Hillman van. Come home empty. Except, you pass Thornborough Farm. So, on the way back, pick up some eggs for our fry-ups, eh?'

The fry-ups over the iron stove in the drivers' rest room were one of the joys of night duty. Eggs bought from local farms, bacon scrounged from the messes, bread fried in the fat, and occasionally mushrooms picked in the fields. 'OK.'

'Well, say thank you nicely.'

'Thank you, Flight.'

'Now, don't let anyone thumb a lift from you. Not even the AOC.' Chiefie handed her two half crowns for the eggs.

'Least of all him.' She smiled.

'You're learning, kiddo. I'll make a woman of you yet.'

Flight Sergeant T. Tordoff was not such a bad type after all, Carole thought. This was the sort of trip that made up for the awful ones. The instruments, which she'd picked up from technical stores, looked like oversized egg timers, but the crates were, as Chiefie had said, easy to handle. It was a fine, crisp day. The sky remained a cold, pellucid blue, decorated rather than disturbed by the white woolly skeins of vapour trails. There were still a few haws and a few hips in the hedgerows. A thrush sang. War and bombing seemed a long way away.

The van ran smoothly. Chiefie's directions were easy to follow, which was just as well, because for the duration there were no signposts on the roads, and there was a good deal of traffic, mainly army tanks and lorries. The satellite lay about fourteen miles in a north-easterly direction from Holmfirth. She passed Thornborough Farm in the midst of a little hamlet, presumably of the same name, just off the main Lincoln to Grimsby road. She made a mental note of it for her return journey.

The sun was low in the sky by the time she made that journey, and it was sunset when she reached Thornborough. The farmer was driving his cattle from a pasture on the other side of the road into the milking parlour in the farmyard, which was full of a fine flock of hens scratching in the muck.

She parked her van on the roadside and picked her way

amongst them to the kitchen door. There was an old-fashioned bell pull that didn't seem to work. Having pulled several times, she knocked. Eventually a woman appeared, drying her hands on a checked apron. On a scrubbed wooden table just inside the kitchen were trays of brown eggs.

'How many?' the woman asked, dispensing with any greeting.

'How many can you spare?'

'A dozen. Two dozen. I've had to put prices up to two shillings a dozen.

'Two dozen would be lovely.' Carole proffered the half crowns.

'You can have a few duck eggs for that as well.'

'Wizard.'

'Are you the driver?' the woman asked over her shoulder as she put the eggs into a box.

'Yes.'

'So how about a drop of petrol then?'

'Oh, no!' Carole was horrified. 'I haven't got any. I mean, I've only got what's in the tank.'

'That's all right, love. Easy to siphon out a drop or two.' She sucked noisily through her lips as if on a straw.

'But I can't. I had to fill up and sign for it before I came out. So I couldn't. I'd get shot.'

''Course you wouldn't.'

'I would. It's against the law. I really can't.'

'Well, I'll let you off this time. You're new. You weren't to know. But if you come again, bring a can of petrol. That's the way of doing business. You scratch my back. You know what they say.' Then, magnanimously: 'Now, I expect you'd like to use the toilet?'

It seemed impolite to refuse. It involved a long walk through the farmhouse and up to the first floor, where she was ushered into an old-fashioned bathroom containing a lavatory with a cracked wooden seat. As she returned downstairs, the woman seemed disposed to be conversational, asking her how she liked being in what she called the *WOFF*, and how she liked driving, and if she knew who was going to collect the eggs next time.

When the woman finally released her, Carole picked her way in the dusk through the yard. There was no one about. Within the dimly lit milking parlour, the cattle breathed heavily and snorted, pails rattled, a man's irritated voice shouted.

Along the road outside, there now hummed a steady stream of traffic. Carole unlocked the van, stowed the eggs carefully, started up the engine and pulled away. She felt hungry. She had missed cookhouse tea but she could get a snack from the NAAFI or the Sally Ann. She was mentally deciding between fried Spam or beans on toast, when, a couple of miles beyond the hamlet and still over eight miles from Holmfirth, the engine coughed and then died.

Horrified, she looked at the fuel gauge. Empty.

Enlightenment did not immediately dawn. A hole in the tank? Petrol leak? There had been a slight smell of petrol, now she came to think about it, when she unlocked the van. A loose connection? She pulled on the handbrake, picked up her torch, got out and lifted the bonnet, trying to call to mind all the emergency information they'd been crammed with at MT school.

No sign of loose connections or anything else. She walked slowly and thoughtfully to the back of the van, suspecting now what she was going to find. She beamed her torch on the locked petrol cap. It had been forced. There were chisel marks on the camouflage paint all around, and the cap was so twisted it was amazing it had stayed on.

Not that it made any difference whether it stayed on or it didn't. The petrol had gone. The van was useless. But, by all the rules as well as *Station Standing Orders*, she must stay with it.

Chiefie would go spare. For several minutes, she walked up and down the grassy verge, trying to make up her mind what to do. But everything she thought of, like looking for a friendly pub with a telephone, even walking back to the farm, involved leaving the van, and as *Station Standing Orders* seemed to envisage that the entire German war effort awaited just such an opportunity, she simply had to stay put.

Her only hope, as she stood watching every pair of baffled headlamps that swept by, was a passing Holmfirth vehicle to give her a tow or enough petrol to make base. But none came. Marines crammed aboard a three-tonner whistled and waved.

Then along came a USAAF truck. It screeched to a halt. Backed to come level with her. Out jumped a hefty-looking sergeant, who uttered the blessed words, 'Wanna lift or a tow, ma'am?'

'Oh, thank you. Thank you. A tow please.'

'How far are you going?'

'Holmfirth.'

'No problem, ma'am. Right on my route. I'll take you all the way!'

She almost threw her arms round him.

Her feeling of immense thankfulness was only slightly diminished by the thought of Chiefie's face when she trundled into the sector, courtesy the USAAF. Chiefie rated the Yanks on the same level as the Brylcreem boys. Jealousy gnawed at his vitals every time he saw one.

Minutes later, as the sergeant fiddled with the towrope and the lights, another vehicle drew up behind the van in an arresting screech of brakes.

A figure jumped out in exaggerated alarm. 'What in God's name is going on, Sergeant?'

A tall figure crossed the spidery beams of light from the headlamps and tapped the sergeant authoritatively on his shoulder.

'Are you making off with our van, Sergeant?' a familiar voice asked. 'And our driver?' A battered cap was pushed to the back of the newcomer's head. He shoved it further, running his hand through his hair as if in alarmed perplexity. The American sergeant got to his feet and grinned good-humouredly. 'No, sir! Nothing like that.' He glanced at Carole sideways, adding with shy gallantry, 'Though I don't say I wouldn't like to, sir.'

'You would regret it, dear boy!' the wing commander muttered. 'My God, you would!' And then, as the sergeant began explaining the situation, he airily took charge.

'Very kind of you, Sergeant. Thanks for coming to the rescue. We're very grateful. But not to worry. Don't go to all that trouble. You can unfasten the rope. She doesn't need a tow. This is one of our vans. Holmfirth's. She's one of our drivers. And, luckily, I always carry a spare can of petrol. I can give her enough to get her home.'

After the Yank had been reluctantly prised from his rescue,

and as they watched the jeep's tail lights disappear into the darkness, the wing commander turned to her. 'You don't change, do you?'

'Why don't I?'

'God alone knows!'

'I mean, why do you think I don't change?'

'I think, my girl, that you are drawn to trouble.'

'As the sparks fly upwards?' She laughed tentatively, suddenly acutely shy.

'Something like that.' He lifted the can and began to pour petrol.

'I've noticed that whenever I see you, you're in trouble.' He paused. In the glow of her torch she saw him frown. 'No, that's not fair. Not true either. But whenever I see you . . .' He looked sideways at her, his expression suddenly earnest and profound. 'I know I'm in trouble. Or going to be.'

She inhaled the sickly sweet smell of the petrol as it mingled with the night smells of the countryside and the scent of crushed grass under their feet. It was a potent, strangely haunting and portentous mixture.

'Why? Why are you in trouble?' she asked breathlessly as he brought out a pocket knife, snapped it open and tried to straighten the damaged cap.

'You're not stupid,' he answered brusquely. 'You can guess why.'

'I can't.'

'Of course you can.'

'I don't dare.'

He wiped his hands on a handkerchief, staring down at her, eyeing her keenly.

'In case it's true? Or in case it isn't?'

'In case it isn't,' she said.

'Is it true?' Chiefie demanded in righteous indignation the following day. 'Is that what really happened?'

He had been off on a run to collect oil filters from the maintenance unit when they arrived back, so the third degree had had to wait until Carole reported for duty the next day.

'I don't tell lies,' she answered boldly.

'Sez who?'

'Sez me.'

'Maybe you don't.' He stroked his chin thoughtfully. 'At least, not often. Not as often as most people. Point is, have you told me the whole truth?'

'What is this? Some sort of kangaroo court? D'you want me to take the Bible in my right hand? The whole truth and nothing but?'

'Not a bad idea. And don't be so cheeky, sprog. You're getting cheekier by the day. No, it's not a court, it's a friendly inquiry.'

'You could have fooled me.'

'Most men could fool you.' He scowled darkly. 'For a start, fancy letting some bastard siphon off your petrol.'

'I wouldn't if I hadn't stopped to get your eggs. You told me to.'

'So I did. But not at that price! Nearly a full tank!'

'The farmer's wife asked me for petrol. She seemed to expect it. D'you usually give her some?'

'I have been known to.'

'Well, there you are! You encourage it. That's black-marketeering!'

'Don't you preach at me, pussycat! You've no right to climb up into the pulpit! What happened after the Wingco had put petrol in your tank? Did he try to put anything else in?'

'What do you mean?' She flushed angrily.

'Did he try to take advantage of you?'

'You sound like the *News of the World*, and that's a filthy suggestion!'

'Well, did he?'

'Of course not! I'm insulted! It's foul of you to suggest it!'

'Did he sit in the van with you?'

'Just while I switched on and checked the gauge.'

'Put his arm round you, did he?'

'No!'

'Try to kiss you?'

'If he had, I'd have kissed him back.'

'Oh, would you now, Miss Cleverpants!'

She nodded, hugging the memory of that moment to her. The first time anyone had ever kissed her like that.

'And then I suppose he escorted you home like a proper gentleman?'

'He drove behind me till we got to the airfield, yes. To make sure I was all right.'

'Very touching.' Chiefie got out a filthy handkerchief and pretended to dab his eyes. 'Then what?'

'Then I got to the section and signed in. You know the rest.'

'Oh no I don't! What did he do then?'

She shrugged. 'Drove off to the mess, I think.'

'Didn't he give you a lift to the Waafery?'

'No, of course not.'

'Liar!'

'I'm not!'

'Yes you are. I've proved it. He did give you a lift. I know you went in his bloody car. I could put you on a charge!'

Carole held her breath and said nothing.

'God alone knows what happened in the car.'

'Nothing.'

'So what did you do while you were doing nothing?'

'We talked.'

'What about?'

'This and that.'

'He told you all about himself and how he'd never met anyone like you before.'

It was true. He had told her little revealing things about himself. Shown his vulnerability. How, before an operation, he always turned his alarm clock upside down, put it the right way up when he safely returned. All the same, she shook her head.

'Any snogging?'

'Of course not!'

'Of course not!' He mimicked her tone. Then he lowered his voice to an accusing growl. 'Then how come you lent him your handkerchief? And how come it's covered in lipstick?' He retuned his voice from growl to high falsetto. 'Oh, sir! Silly me! I've put lipstick on your face. Let me wipe it clean.'

'You don't know it's mine.'

'Well, with that womanizer you have a point. But this exhibit has got C in the corner, and it smells of you.' He opened a desk drawer, brought out the handkerchief and waved

111

it in front of her. 'I found this when he brought his car in this morning. The clot walked right into my trap. Your five hundred check's due on your Humber, sir, I said, all smarmy and efficient. So, like a lamb, in he brings it. I made a point of doing the check myself.'

'Went over it like a Scotland Yard detective, I suppose?'

'That's right, pet. I never miss a trick.'

'I hope you thanked him for his help yesterday.'

'Oh, I did, darling. And I refilled his can, when I'd have liked to refill his backside with my boot. And I gave him three eggs.'

'Thank you.'

'Then I told him if he fooled around with one of my drivers, I'd have his guts for garters.'

'You didn't!'

'No.' He sighed heavily. 'I didn't. Rank is rank. Officers are officers. Aircrew are angels. Brylcreem boys can do no wrong. But, in a better world, I would have.'

A week later, at domestic evening, Bunty was thinking wistfully in terms of a better world and how different things might be. In a better world, she would be already married. She would be pleased that her period was late. She would be whispering coyly in Chris's ear about a happy event. Of course, she still had hope that it wasn't a happy event and that a late period didn't mean anything at all. But something told her that it did.

'What's up?' Carole asked bluntly, as the two of them knelt side by side on the linoleum of number five married quarter, polishing vigorously. Gabby was on duty, so Bunty and Carole were alone.

Despite that fact, Bunty looked nervously over her shoulder before croaking, 'What d'you mean?'

'You know what I mean.' Carole rubbed a lump of wax into the uncooperative linoleum. 'You look miserable. It's not like you. Have you and Chris fallen out or something?'

'No, 'course not. We never will. I'd never quarrel with Chris no matter what. And he wouldn't with me.' She wiped the back of her hand over her sweaty forehead. 'You see, we're engaged.' She looked challengingly sideways, as if daring Carole to contradict her.

'I know. You told me. We're really pleased for you. We all like Chris.'

Bunty looked slightly mollified.

'So, it's not Chris,' Carole prompted.

'No. At least, not exactly.'

'How unexactly?'

'Could be just a bit.'

'Is it because he's on a forty-eight-hour pass?'

'No. He's gone home for it. I'm glad.'

'Something he's said? Or –' she paused a long time – 'done?'

Bunty didn't at first answer. She screwed up her face and blinked her eyes. Then she mumbled in a choky voice, 'Something we've both done.'

Carole sprang to her feet, snapping the lid on the tin of polish.

'You didn't . . . ? You haven't?'

In answer, Bunty pulled herself off her knees by grabbing the end of Carole's bed, and then threw herself on it, grinding her clenched fists into her eyes and sobbing. 'Yes I have! I didn't mean to! But I have! I did!'

'When?'

'At the dance. In your dress. It was awful of me. Really wicked. I'm sorry. I really am. And . . . now . . . now . . .'

'Now?'

'Now I haven't got my monthly. And that means . . . doesn't it? And if it does, the WAAF'll throw me out. And my mum and Mr Hardcastle won't have me and . . .'

Carole sat slowly down beside Bunty and took one of her greasy hands. The MO's lectures on their initial training came vividly and terribly to mind. She made quick calculations. Three and a bit weeks since the dance in Lincoln. It must have been at Bunty's most vulnerable time.

What was the MO's word for it? Ovulation. That's what it was. On the other hand, Carole tried to assemble her thoughts. When she spoke, she picked her words slowly, carefully, as she strove to navigate through the minefield of her own ignorance. 'I suppose it could mean that, but I think you'd have to be very unlucky. For it to be that, I mean.'

'But I am unlucky,' Bunty wailed. 'My mum always said so. If anything was going to happen, it'd always happen to me! Mr Hardcastle said I always got the slug in the lettuce.'

'That's silly. Of course you're not unlucky. You're very lucky. You're lovely-looking and people like you. And you're engaged to Chris.'

'Sort of. I haven't got a ring yet.'

'Well, even sort of.'

'And how long will I have him for? 'Specially if I tell him I've got a bun in my oven.'

She put both her hands dramatically on her stomach.

'But you haven't got one for certain. You might just be late. Lots of girls are when they join up at first. It's the different life.'

'How d'you know?'

'Judy in MT told me.'

'The one the squadron calls Juicy Judy?'

'Some of them do. She's all right.'

'She gets around, doesn't she?'

'I suppose.'

'Did she tell you anything else?'

'Like what?'

'Like what to do if it is?'

'Not really. Though she did say once when she was late, she had a double gin and a hot bath.'

'Fat chance of a hot bath.' Bunty began to cry quietly and despairingly. 'I can get the gin but it makes me feel awful.'

'Well, I think if you were pregnant you'd have other signs.' Carole screwed up her eyes trying to remember. 'As soon as the billets have been inspected, I'll look out my notes from Bridgnorth.'

'It's Corporal Cummings doing the billets tonight. She won't take long. She's better than Flight Sergeant Grimble.'

'Anyone's better than her.'

They laughed weakly.

More cheerfully, Bunty suggested, 'And when she goes, we can pop over to the Sally Ann and get some chips. I really fancy chips these days.'

Now that's a bad sign, Carole thought, but kept her own counsel.

Eight

Over in flying control, Beaky was also keeping his own counsel. This time in the teeth of the wing commander's interference.

'I told you, Beaky, to get in touch with me if Group didn't come up with Jim's replacement.'

'I think you did mention something of the sort, sir.'

'You think! You bloody well know! And I didn't just mention, I told you to let me know.'

Beaky gritted his teeth and said nothing. The wing commander was as usual using the three-day stand-down to improve the collective efficiency and to get up everybody's nose. Gabby, sitting at the R/T set, shot him a sympathetic smile, and pretended to be busy sorting NOTAMS.

'Luckily for you, Beaky, it so happens that I can help.'

'How, sir?'

'I have a supernumerary W/Op air gunner.'

Beaky pricked up his ears. He rested his elbows on the desk and put the tips of his fingers together, listening politely. 'Tell me more, sir.'

'A laddie called Bob Halliday, Flight Sergeant. Was with the squadron before we moved down here.'

'So, I wouldn't have met him?'

'No, He's been out of action for a year. A good type. I've had him on my crew. One of our best W/Op AGs. A real gen merchant. His Lanc took a hit over Düsseldorf. He got badly burned in the face and hands; McIndoe's lot at East Grinstead have patched him up. But I'm not letting him go back on flying yet. At the moment he's doing sweet FA in the orderly room.'

'So you want him usefully employed.'

'Got it in one, Beaky.'

'Does he want to go back?'

'On ops? Raring to go. Keeps batting my ear to say he's not a filing clerk.'

Beaky shook his head. 'You boys never learn.'

'Anyway, he's all yours if you'd like him.'

'I'd like him very much.'

'Good show. But I should warn you –' he swept an apologetic glance round control to include Gabby and Lyn – 'he's not a pretty sight.'

One of the wing commander's little understatements, Beaky later reflected when Bob Halliday reported for duty next day.

F/Sgt Halliday was not a pretty sight. He was a tall, broad-shouldered young man, and he wore on his battledress top the ribbon of the DFM. His scrubby brown hair bristled up like a brush from an almost unreal, somehow manufactured face, which was half lean and pallid, half the shiny pink of recently grafted skin. He had no eyebrows and no lashes, but his brown eyes were bright and compelling; and though they were direct and perfectly friendly, they held a mocking gleam as if challenging anyone to flinch.

Or to flinch from his handshake. According to the citation, he had tried to smother the fire on the Lancaster, suffering multiple third degree burns. His flying gloves had stuck to his fingers. But his grip was firm, his deep voice clear and resonant.

Beaky had no doubt that Bob would be an excellent operator, an asset to the team. But it was Bob Halliday's effect on another member of the team that surprised him.

From the moment Bob and Gabby exchanged glances, something happened. Beaky could hardly believe his eyes. The attraction between them was obvious. Beaky wrote later that night to his wife:

It reminded me of when you and I met, dear. We knew at once, didn't we? And, as with us, I can understand what he sees in her, but not her in him. Gabby, the aloof, the fastidious, seems equally enchanted. If it were not a disparaging analogy, because the young man in question is a splendid, intelligent chap, I would be minded of Titania and Bottom and casting around for Puck and his magic juice.

116

Magic juice was exactly what Bunty was casting around for. She had taken a strong dose of Epsom salts. By dint of boiling pans of water, she had managed to get enough for a scalding-hot bath. It had made her buttocks sore but done nothing else. She was now awaiting a bunch of parsley which one of the officers' mess cooks had promised to liberate for her. Parsley, according to gossip in the NAAFI, was the cure for both irregularities and pregnancies.

The photograph of Chris's mother remained unimpressed. Her expression was still kindly, but slightly severe these days. Reverently polishing that photograph, Bunty reflected that Chris would be with his mother now, or, as he was due back that afternoon, just taking leave of her. What were they talking about? Had he mentioned Bunty to her? Told her that he and she were engaged, or as good as? That he was in love for the first time? That, when the war ended, they would have a white wedding. And hearing all this, was his mother pleased?

Three hours later, rather daringly, she asked him that question. She happened to be in the mess office, signing for some more cleaning fluid, when Chris put his head round the door.

'Oh, there you are!' He smiled warmly. 'I've been looking for you! How about rustling up some tea? I know I'm too late for mess tea, but see what you can do, eh? And –' he patted his weekend bag, his smile broadening – 'I've got something special for you.'

She flushed scarlet with pleasure. Sergeant Fisher noticed. He pursed his lips and raised his funny little eyebrows several times warningly. But she didn't care. Although she couldn't be absolutely sure, she could guess at what Chris had brought her – The Ring. She hoped it would fit, but that wouldn't matter, because rings could be altered.

She hummed as she walked through to the mess kitchen to scrounge something nice for Chris. 'What've you got to be so cheerful about?' Corporal Butterworth, the WAAF duty cook, asked her dourly.

'Nothing really. Mind if I make some tea for one of my blokes?'

'Suit yourself. There's some sandwiches left if you like. And that yellow slab cake.'

'Thanks ever so. Any jam?'

'You can scrape some out from that tin behind you. Don't fill him up too much though. There's an op on later. We'll be frying their bacon and eggs in another few hours.'

And even that information didn't depress Bunty. As she set out a nice appetizing tray, she kept thinking about The Ring. Would it be a real diamond? A sapphire? Chris had once said that she should wear sapphires because of her blue eyes. A ruby? A good wife was above rubies. She remembered Mr Hardcastle liked to quote that when he was persuading widowers to stump up for some really expensive coffin. But whatever it was, it didn't matter. If it was just a plain old curtain ring she wouldn't much care.

'Just tell me what it is,' she said, setting Chris's tray on the chest of drawers in his room, and then holding up her face for him to kiss her.

'Tell me you've missed me, first of all.'

'Oh, I have!' She sighed. 'Did you miss me?'

'I'll say I did!'

'I thought about you all the time.'

'Me too.'

'Did you . . . ?' She turned, in respectful acknowledgement, to the photograph, then moistened her lips, proceeded cautiously. 'Did you tell your mother about me?'

'Of course I did.'

'Oh, Chris!' Bunty was quite overcome. 'Was she pleased?'

'Very.'

'Honestly?'

'Yes! Ra–ther! And very grateful!'

He was fiddling with the catch of his weekend bag. 'So grateful that –' he snapped the bag open, and, smiling as triumphantly as a conjurer bringing a rabbit out of a hat, produced a parcel, much too big for a ring. 'She sent you this.' Proudly he held out the brown paper parcel to her.

'For me?' Bunty quavered. 'She sent it for me?'

'Yes, my love! For you. Take it. Sweet of her, wasn't it? There, there.' He put his arm comfortingly round Bunty's shoulders. 'You're quite overcome, aren't you!'

Tears had certainly sprung to Bunty's eyes. A parcel from

his mother? Not from Chris himself. She took the square parcel uncertainly. 'What is it?'

'Open it and see!'

She tore at the paper. A faint hope still remained. Perhaps there was a ring inside. His mother's. A family heirloom. That was why she had sent it. The ring was originally hers, but so pleased was she that she had taken it off her finger to give to her son for his intended. And with something else. Some personal gift perhaps. That might be it. Sure enough, under the brown paper were two separate parcels, each wrapped in pink tissue. The larger and more solid one contained a box far too big for a ring. She tore aside the pink paper. A be-ribboned box of chocolates. Very nice, difficult to get, expensive chocolates. The sight of them made her retch.

'Mother gave up her sweet coupons especially to get you those.'

'That's so kind of her,' Bunty breathed chokingly.

'You'll like the other present too.' Chris was chewing a sandwich and watching her indulgently as she ripped aside more pink paper. Out dropped a pair of fine silk stockings. Flesh-coloured, delicate and, like the chocolates, expensive.

'More coupons!' Bunty forced a grisly smile to her face. 'She's given up more coupons. Clothing ones this time. Your mother is ever so kind.'

'I told her about your coming to the dance with that awful leg paint on. That was why she sent you those.'

'Did you tell her what happened?'

'Happened?'

'At the dance?'

Chris was pouring himself a cup of tea. The hand holding the teapot paused in mid-air. 'Some of it, yes.' He frowned. 'What especially did you mean?'

'About you and me . . . and . . . well . . . afterwards?'

'Afterwards?'

'Outside . . . doing it . . .' She hadn't meant to put it so baldly, but it just came out like that.

He looked absolutely appalled, almost disgusted. 'Of course not, Bunty. That wouldn't be right at all. Not to one's mother. Now would it?'

She was about to agree that it wouldn't when PO Bladowski

119

came in, saw the tea tray and begged her to get the same for him. Then, suddenly serious, the two pilots commiserated about it being Frederikshaven again.

Another attack by ten Lancasters on the aero engine works at Frederikshaven took place a week later. Take-off was scheduled for 2300 hours. By ten o'clock some of the crews were crowded around the table in flying control, drinking coffee and chatting to their erstwhile colleague, F/Sgt Bob Halliday.

Beaky still heartily approved of his new R/T operator. He was efficient and conscientious, and knew how to handle the crews. He was a good link between the airmen and the flying control staff. Beaky had at first toyed with the idea of putting Gabby and Bob on different shifts because of their obvious attraction to one another. But so decorously did they behave, and yet so clear was their mutual affection, that he hadn't the heart to separate them. *Especially*, as he wrote to his wife, *under the circumstances*.

As for Bob Halliday's scarred face and hands, no one noticed them any more.

At the McIndoe unit in the Queen Victoria Hospital, they had given him art lessons to encourage the use of his burned hands. He made sketches of all the staff, but mostly of Gabby at her R/T set. In quiet moments, she was helping him to improve his schoolboy French, and he was showing her how to dismantle and rebuild a wireless set.

The raid that night was again being led by the wing commander in O-Orange.

'This time next month,' Bob told the wing commander, 'I'll be coming with you.'

'Yes, you do that, Bob. Taffy here's just keeping the seat warm for you. Three more trips and he's on rest.'

'Cheer up, Gabby!' The Wingco patted her arm as he left flying control. 'The war may be over by then.'

'He can't wait to get back, sir.'

'Well, there's one born every minute.' The wing commander checked his watch with the clock on the wall. 'Time we were off. Be seeing you!'

Out in the darkness, the aircraft had been bombed up and, tonight, loaded with a new device, packages of what was known as Window, metal strips to confuse the enemy's radar; the bowsers had filled up the tanks with 100-octane fuel and left. From the balcony of flying control, Bob and Gabby stood silently watching the scene below.

This time next month. She touched his hand. This time next month maybe she herself would be away. She hadn't told him about that yet. Even if she were allowed to, she wouldn't know how.

Bob had a simple touching certainty that their destinies were joined. Somehow they would get through all this and settle down together. Perhaps it was the war. Or perhaps it was the sort of people that they were. They felt their affair had a calm inevitability about it. They worked together. They listened to the aircraft departing and they listened for their return, chatting desultorily, telling each other about their childhoods, while Mr Birdsall wrote to his wife in a silence broken only by the shifting of the hot coke in the stove and the scutter of field mice around the pipes.

On their off-duty periods, they rode bicycles loaned to them from stores, exploring the flat countryside, watched a calm day fade at last light and saw the rosy winter afterglow. They ate bread and cheese lunches at pubs, went to the pictures at the Odeon in Lincoln, held hands in the back row with all the other courting couples; kissed, but nothing more.

The airwomen, Gabby had discovered, were divided into those who did and those who didn't. The latter outnumbered the former; for two reasons. They were woefully ignorant and they didn't know exactly how it was done. On the other hand, they had some idea of the consequences and certainly feared them.

The aircrews were similarly divided into those who wanted to live their brief life to the full, go to bed with as many girls as possible, and those more cautious and considerate who didn't want to leave behind a little bastard for their girlfriends to cope with.

If the girl in question were a WAAF, then she was really on her own. There was no help to be had for girls like Bunty. The stations couldn't wait to get rid of them. Airwomen discharged for pregnancy were listed amongst a station's casualties.

As Gabby and Bob came in from the balcony, the crews were testing their equipment and armaments at dispersals around the blacked-out airfields. The air vibrated to the harsh throb of revving engines.

Just before twenty-three hundred, the wing commander, in O-Orange, was requesting permission to taxi. One after another, the rest of the aircraft followed suit, taxiing round to the runway's head.

The walls of flying control shook, the metal windows vibrated like chattering teeth as O-Orange accelerated to take-off power. A tiny blink of light from the control hut by the runway gave take-off permission. O-Orange roared down the runway, the exhausts glowing like red-hot coals. Then the black shape lifted.

'O-Orange airborne twenty-three ten.'

One by one, Bob chalked the departure times on the blackboard. Then flying control settled down to listen to their frequencies and wait. There was nothing to warn them that tonight would be worse than any other.

Just after midnight, Bob made a thick potent mixture of Camp coffee and Nestlé's milk while the girls monitored the R/T and W/T messages. Gabby had only taken a couple of mouthfuls when abruptly a voice crackled through on the D (distress) frequency.

'T-Tommy returning to base.'

A glance at the board. T-Tommy, Chris Dutton.

'Position, sir?' Gabby asked.

'South-east of Dungeness. Ailerons damaged by cannon. Pouring hydraulic fluid.'

Beaky, listening intently, exchanged a glance with Bob. A belly landing.

Beaky came over and took the microphone. 'Bombs?'

'All but one jettisoned.'

'And that one?'

'Four-hundred-pounder. Seems to be stuck.'

'Dear God!' Beaky sighed to himself, and while Gabby vectored T-Tommy back to base, picked up the direct line to the station commander.

Five minutes later, the group captain was breathing noisily down their necks as the fire engines and ambulances tore down to the runway's end. All inessential personnel were being evacuated. The runway was being soaked in foam.

The flight commander of A Flight was summoned. He reassured the group captain that Chris Dutton was a first-class pilot and steady as a rock.

Chris's voice when it came over the R/T again was half drowned in static but steady enough. Risking the attention of an enemy hit-and-run raider, airfield lights were switched on.

In the tension of the moment, the group captain roughly pushed aside Beaky, took charge himself and barked directly to Chris Dutton. 'Can you get your wheels down?'

'I don't know, sir.'

'Indicator light?'

'Not coming on, sir.'

'Then do a low sweep over the field. We'll all be out there looking.' He covered the mike with his hand. 'Hell's bells, a belly landing and a bomb up his backside! Jesus!'

Then he strode to the door that gave on to the balcony. With his hand on the blackout blanket, he said, 'Stay where you are, Beaky.' He addressed Gabby, Lyn and Bob, 'You three youngsters, out here with me. Keep your eyes skinned. Don't dare blink.'

'Thank God for the moon!' the GC breathed, as the Lancaster bore down through the torn cloud to become spotlit in a sudden beam of moonlight. T-Tommy swept so low over the tower that they could feel the fiery heat of its engines; its vicious slipstream blew them all back against the wall. The moonlight, the diffused glow from the airfield, was just enough for them to distinguish the wheels lowered.

'The CO burst back into the tower and snapped into the microphone, 'T-Tommy. OK! Undercarriage lowered!'

'But is it locked down?' Bob murmured.

The GC held up his hand with his fingers crossed, and spoke again into the mike.

'T-Tommy, pancake. Softly as you can, for Chrissake. Don't want to bust your cookie. Grease her down, boy!'

The GC kept the microphone gripped in his hand while they all stood by the big window and watched T-Tommy as he gained enough height to line with the runway. He began his descent.

123

As he swung from side to side, the watchers assessed his chances. And theirs. There was a helluva lot of explosive hanging just above their heads. In thirty seconds, they would be standing there letting out a sigh of relief, or blown to kingdom come.

Bob squeezed Gabby's hand.

'This is when we're all glad we've led such blameless lives,' the station commander joked valiantly.

And into the microphone, 'Easy does it, Chris. Level out a bit. Easy. You're doing fine.'

There was a moment's almost unbearable suspense as the huge machine hovered. Then the wheels connected with the runway. Another moment's suspense. The undercarriage held firm. The Lancaster slewed a fraction, then settled.

'Bloody marvellous landing, Chris! Cat pissing on glass!' The GC let out his breath in a great explosion of relief, as the Lancaster decelerated down the runway and then on to the perimeter track. 'Dispersal right away. The armourers'll deal with your bloody bomb.'

Immediately the group captain was out of the door and running down the steps of flying control.

'Well, well, well!' Beaky blew out his cheeks and sighed with immense relief. 'That sort of moment is very good for the soul. It reminds me of all the things I have left undone, and it fills me with the desire to do them forthwith.'

He glanced over his spectacles at Bob and Gabby. They had each returned to their separate tables. Gabby was entering a pile of NOTAMS in the log book. Bob was busy writing on the back of a message flimsy. Three words, *Je t'aime*.

'Why are you grinning, Sergeant Halliday?' Beaky asked him.

'Because, sir, I was thinking exactly the same as you. I remembered something very important I hadn't done.' He got up and took the message he had written over to Gabby.

'I'm glad to hear it, Bob.'

Beaky pulled his writing paper pad towards him and, inspired by those moments of self-enlightenment, began to write a letter to his wife, much more affectionate than usual. Two hours later, the first of the returning bombers that had got through to the target was back in the circuit.

*   *   *

124

The tension of Chris Dutton's return soon subsided. The news from dispersal was good. The bomb had been safely dealt with and carted away. None of the crew had been injured. They were all back in their billets by the time the first aircraft landed.

'Dare we hope for a full house?' Beaky asked with cautious optimism as the homecoming Lancasters followed each other in rapid succession, and one by one the blackboard boxes were filled with chalked-in times of return. It was first light, time for optimism and thoughts of bacon and egg breakfast.

Now the aircraft roaring over Holmfirth were high fliers going on to airfields in Yorkshire and the north.

'O-Orange isn't back,' Bob said tersely, jerking his head at the empty box on the blackboard.

'Give him time, laddie!'

'He should have been the first back.'

Bob walked over and stood between Gabby and Lyn as they sat at their sets, listening intently to the gabble of dots and dashes clamouring through the ether.

'He'll be along,' Beaky had just remarked, when PO Bladowski's crew came clattering in. And with them a cold cloud of foreboding. Some of the euphoria after a success-fully completed operation was missing. Jumbo had seen O-Orange being attacked by Wild Boar fighters shortly after they crossed the coast. He was jinxing around the sky, trying to shake them off. Then they themselves were coned and lost sight of O-Orange in the melee over the target.

A second crew came in and reported an unidentified Lancaster going down in flames.

'Any idea whose?'

'Not a clue.'

'See any parachutes?'

'No.'

'He's probably landed somewhere else,' Gabby suggested. And, turning to Beaky, 'Shall I send out a Darky?'

'Yes, do that.'

But they were already sure that he hadn't diverted. Above them, the sky seemed to empty. The sets were filled with cracklings and gabblings and random broken-off voices. The

Darky line remained silent. The night's raid was over. If anyone were returning, they would have come back by now.

Time ticked by. They kept glancing at the clock.

'He'd be out of fuel now,' Bob remarked in a deadpan voice, going out yet again on to the balcony as Gabby put down the telephone on the last call.

Five minutes later, the station commander breezed in, his face flushed, his eyes bloodshot.

'As if we hadn't had enough for one night!' he exclaimed indignantly. He made straight for the coffee table, and lifted the huge jar of crew rum. He poured them each a generous tot. 'Here, get this down!'

'Shall we report the Wingco missing, sir?' Beaky asked.

''Fraid so. It's a bloody bad blow to the squadron. And to the group. Just when we need to be hitting them for six.'

When Bob reappeared from the balcony, he handed him a tot of rum and remarked cheerfully, 'One must look on the bright side. You should be glad I didn't let you twist my arm to get back on ops.'

For a moment, Gabby thought Bob was going to throw the rum in the CO's beefy face, but he simply grimaced, downed it, and grimaced again.

Less than an hour later, as a fiery red sun rose, the day shift came on.

'Mind if we go round to dispersal?' Bob asked Gabby, as they put on their caps and slung their respirators.

'Of course not. I'd like the walk. I don't want to sleep.' I don't want to be the one to tell Carole, she might have added.

Together they walked round to the perimeter track. Peewits rose from the rough grassland. The wind now had gone round to the east, and it brought in a faint tang of the salt marshes. Along the road beyond the perimeter, a farm tractor was hauling a load of beets. It all seemed totally at peace.

But at O-Orange's dispersal a strange vigil was taking place. The ground crew night shift had refused to go off duty and were sitting on upturned toolboxes waiting for their Lancaster to return.

Nine

'And a bloody long wait they had, sweetheart,' Chiefie told Carole the following afternoon. 'I'm surprised you weren't there with them. Stargazing. You and the Wingco being that thick!'

'We weren't thick. Anyway –' she caught her breath – 'what would be the point?'

'Quite! I'm glad you've got a bit of sense! Just you carry on regardless! More fish in the sea than ever came out!'

Carole clenched her teeth and said nothing.

'I've given you a nice job today, pet. Just to be kind: officers' mess rations. After all, as we were saying in our mess, if the Wingco had got away with it, he'd have appeared by now. If he'd lobbed down anywhere, we'd have heard. Remember, we've losses all the time. Just because he's got red hair and three rings round his sleeve, doesn't mean he's any different.'

'I didn't say it did.'

'Besides, the bastard might be a prisoner of war. Might just turn up. He's a bad penny if ever I saw one.'

'Stop going on about it! Just shut up!'

'Oh, dear me, pet! That's a bloody rude thing to say to your boss! Insubordination! I could put you on a charge for that!'

'Try to!'

'I might just at that!'

'You'd look even more of a fool!'

'Would I now, Miss Saucypants! What's got into you, canny lass? It's not my fault your fancy man's got himself shot down!'

'He wasn't my fancy man.'

'Well, what was he?'

'It's none of your business.'

'C'mon.'

'Why can't you leave it alone?'

'I want to know, I've a right to know. I'm not handing over the Ford keys till you tell me.'

Carole sighed. 'He was someone I liked.'

'Oh, now we admit it, do we? Someone you fancied?'

'Oh, for God's sake! That's enough. I've told you.' Carole reached over suddenly, snatched the keys from his hand and slammed out.

She had just checked the oil on the Ford transit and filled her up at the yard pump, when Chiefie sauntered out of the office doorway and stood beside her.

'Well, your fancy man won't be hanging round here no more, no more! Flying Officer Wright's just had a call from his buddy in Intelligence. They've monitored the German radio, Lord Haw-Haw. Five of the crew baled out, possibly six. Five are POWs. Wingco went down with his ship.' He drew in a deep breath. 'Good chap really. I felt the same as you. He was someone I liked.'

'I hate you, Chiefie,' Carole snapped, got into her truck and drove off at speed.

Bunty was in the officers' mess kitchen scrounging another late tea tray for PO Dutton when Carole arrived with the rations.

Bunty's moods were in a state of constant flux. For a precious few hours she had been ecstatic because Chris was the man of the moment. Everyone said he had done a fine job. There was talk of a gong. A DFC. He was on top of the world. And, Bunty thought, no one could accuse a pilot with the DFC of having the dreaded LMF. But this morning after he had heard that the Wingco was missing, Chris had sunk into a really bad state. So bad that even PO Bladowski had remarked about it, and you had to be very bad to get through to him. Last night she had lain awake in her billet, trying to sort through how to tell Chris that she was pregnant. She was sure of it now. She had been sick again, her nipples were feeling tight and stretched like they said they would in Carole's lecture notes, and the parsley hadn't worked.

Over and over again, she had gone through different ways of telling him. The laughing way; the good news way; the saying I'm sorry way, even the frightened way. Because she was frightened all right.

But this morning when she had seen him, she knew she never could tell him. She couldn't add any more to what he had already borne. No one but she knew what he was like inside. What a nervous little boy he was. How stretched to his limits. He put on such an act with the rest of the squadron. No one knew how that terrible landing ordeal had brought him nearly to breaking point, or how the news of the Wingco's death had just about completed it.

The Wingco, though he was only young, was what the RAF called a good leader. He pulled them all together, especially young ones like Chris. Another Wingco would be posted in quickly, and life and operations would go on. But she knew the Humpty Dumpty eggshell that was Chris had been pushed off the wall, and she doubted he would ever get himself together again.

Then, standing in the kitchen, Bunty recalled to herself other people who would be miserable today.

'Sorry about the Wingco,' she whispered to Carole, pouring her a mug from Chris's pot. She almost added, *It was a good thing you two didn't get too thick*, but decided best not. 'Have one of those scones as well,' she added in a rush of sympathy, taking one off Chris's tray. 'Cheer yourself up.'

'How about you?' Carole smiled determinedly. 'Do you still need cheering up?'

'I do that.'

'Nothing's happened?'

'No.' Then Bunty noticed that Corporal Butterworth, who was known as a sneak, was listening rather too curiously. She picked up her tray. 'Well, mustn't keep his lordship waiting.'

A moment after she had disappeared, Sergeant Fisher put his head round the kitchen door. 'I've checked the rations, Carole. Everything's OK. But I wonder if you'd like to step into my office, I'd like a word.'

His office was cluttered. Already they had begun to clear the personal effects of the missing crew for transmission to stores. 'Sorry about all this, dear.' Sergeant Fisher waved a hand towards a chair. 'Do sit down. All this grieves me, it

129

really does. I'm not made of stone. But life must go on. Their replacements'll be in before you've time to say Jack Robinson. I hear the new Wingco's already on his way. And I've got to put the chaps in somewhere. I need their rooms clear.'

'That's all right.' Carole averted her eyes from the most distant pile, where the Wingco's cap and his best blue uniform were clearly visible.

'But,' Sergeant Fish said portentously, 'the Wingco asked me to do something.' He jumped up and unlocked the cupboard behind his desk.

Out of it, he brought a small alarm clock with a smiling yellow sun on its face.

'He asked me to give you this if he didn't come back. He said he told you he always used to turn it upside down when he went on a trip and then right way up when he got back.'

'Yes.'

'They all have their little superstitions.' Sergeant Fisher smiled with sad indulgence. 'S/L Palmer always has to go backwards through the swing doors. Beresford used to have to pee on the tail, Mendip won't go off without his girl's scarf tied in three knots. Bladowski has to kiss me on both cheeks, silly man. But there you are!' He thrust the clock into her hands. 'This is for you. Don't cry. He said to keep it upside down till he gets back.'

He turned to open the door for her. 'And sometime, dear, when you're feeling more your sparkling self, I'd like a word about Bunty. Corporal Butterworth seems to have the idea . . . But never mind, she's probably wrong. Anyway, there's no urgency. Time will tell.'

Time did tell. The wing commander did not return. He was officially posted missing, believed killed. The new wing commander, Ken Clark, arrived and was killed on his third operation. Bunty's period did not materialize, but other symptoms did. Every day that went by, she became more desperate.

A cold Lincolnshire winter had set in. On the first domestic evening of December, Bunty begged Edith to get out her Ouija board and see if Arnold could advise her what to do.

For once Carole and Gabby were off duty on domestic

evening, and so they had a quorum. Carole was willing to join in, but Gabby had to have her arm twisted. She made her usual protest about it being superstitious nonsense at best, a cheat at worst. But these days, since the advent of Bob Halliday, she had been so much more approachable and co-operative.

'I'll clean your shoes,' Bunty offered as an inducement, 'if you'll join in. And your greatcoat buttons.'

'So long as you know it's nonsense, and so long as it doesn't take more than half an hour. I'm meeting Bob in the Sally Ann afterwards.'

An hour later, when F/Sgt Grimble had been and noisily gone, and their kit had been safely stowed away, Edith unwrapped her Ouija board. As usual, what she called the seance took place in the tiny kitchen at the back of the married quarter.

That afternoon, Edith had liberated a small paper bag full of what the coal merchant described as best nutty slack from the coal dump. Bunty had similarly liberated a hunk of margarine, which they had learned could be used instead of firelighters, and collected sufficient twigs from the narrow garden at the back of the officers' mess to start a blaze in the kitchen stove.

With the blackout in place, the kitchen looked quite inviting in the scarlet homely glow of the old iron stove and the emergency candle flickering on the draining board.

'Now, now,' Edith said, unwrapping a glass and setting it in the middle of the board. 'No need to look like that, Gabby. It's just an ordinary tooth glass, officers and sergeants for the use of, which I liberated from stores. Now all we do is sit around and put our fingers on it.'

They had to find something to sit on. The married quarter was only equipped with the luxury of two folding chairs. Edith, as the maestro, laid claim to one, and Gabby, since she had to go quickly to meet Bob, was allowed the other.

Bunty and Carole had to go to the bother of unmaking their beds and arranging the three biscuits in a pile.

'Now, if you two are hoping for a message –' Edith looked invitingly at Bunty and Carole – 'you need something belonging to the dear one. Or which the dear one has touched, just to put in your lap.'

'What if the dear one isn't dead?'

'Passed over, you should say,' Edith corrected.

'Well, what if he hasn't passed over? What if I just want advice about him? And what I should do?'

'You still hold on to something he's touched, and then we wait and see.'

Avoiding Gabby's cynical gaze, Carole furtively brought out the Wingco's little alarm clock, while Bunty fiercely clutched the flesh-coloured silk stockings.

'Are we ready now? All of you put your fingertips on the glass. Don't press! Don't push! We don't want any cheating.' She closed her eyes. The nutty slack in the stove shifted. The candlelight wavered and smoked in the draught. Edith seemed to the others to grow waxy pale in the flickering light.

After a moment, she asked in a stagey, sepulchral voice, 'Are you there, Arnold?'

Nothing happened.

It was like some terrible bastardization of the R/T, Gabby thought, relaying messages on the Darky line to overdue men, desperately asking them to answer. She stirred uncomfortably. If it hadn't been that she was so sorry for Bunty, so sorry that Bunty felt she had to descend to this, she would have got up and marched out.

'Are you there, Arnold? Knock once for yes.'

From somewhere, from Edith's raised foot, Gabby suspected, came a loud knock.

Gabby exclaimed derisively. Edith hissed her to keep quiet.

'Arnold dear, do you have a message?'

Another loud thump.

'Is it a message for me?'

Two thumps, so hefty that the table shook. 'God in Heaven!' Gabby exclaimed. 'That was certainly someone's foot!'

'You're saying no, Arnold. The message is not for me. Is it a message for one of my friends?'

Apparently it was. Another loud thump.

'Can you give us the friend's initial, dear?'

Now the glass really moved.

'You're pushing!' Gabby accused. 'I felt it!' She flushed with fury as the glass sped round to the letter G.

'G!' Edith exclaimed. 'For Gabby, dear?'

A single thump for yes.

'What do you want to tell her?'

The glass was whipping around the board before Gabby could get to her feet. P-O-S-T-E-D, it spelled out.

'Oh, don't get up now, Gabby!' Edith shrilled. 'You'll break the fluence. You'll upset Arnold! And Bunty and Carole won't be able to find out what he is going to tell them.'

But although Gabby remained seated, scowling at the Ouija board, Arnold must already have been upset. He was giving no more messages. Bunty wept with frustration.

Edith let out a long sigh and said these seances always took it out of her; would Bunty be a dear and fetch her a wad from the NAAFI? Shamefacedly, Carole stowed the Wingco's clock away in her locker. By mistake she put it the right way up. She wasn't sure if that was a good sign or a bad. Probably a bad.

Altogether it had been a stupid evening. She wished she hadn't taken part in it. Worse still, the following week, Arnold's prediction came true – Gabby was posted.

The news of Gabby's posting was telephoned through to flying control from the station signals at 2030 hours on the third of December.

The last of the night's heavily laden Lancasters, D-Dog, had just become airborne for their raid on Düsseldorf, the roar of its climbing engines was still echoing above them. Jan was chalking D-Dog's precise take-off time in the last box on the blackboard. She paused, hand upraised, as Mr Birdsall called over to Gabby that a special Air Ministry posting had been signalled through for her.

Gabby was sitting at the R/T. Bob Halliday was kneeling close beside her at the leads for the R/T set, trying to improve the reception, which had become racked by interference. For a moment, they all seemed to freeze.

And so began, Mr Birdsall wrote to his wife half an hour later in the lull between take-off and return,

a memorable evening. Bob Halliday was really knocked off his perch. He will miss Gabby terribly. I shall miss her myself. I

133

can hear you saying that I've found in her the daughter we didn't have. Perhaps that is so. I would be proud if she was my daughter, and tonight, I felt almost in loco parentis. You know, I worry about what is going to happen to her. I have a shrewd idea what this mystery posting is about; Gabby's fluent French, the imminence of the Second Front make me uneasy. Initially she is posted to Stoney Cross in the New Forest, leaving Holmfirth in five days' time. Just long enough, as I pointed out, wistfully, for her to get all the signatures to clear the station.

Immediately I said that, Bob looked up at Gabby and said loudly, in front of us all, 'Just long enough to get a special licence. We can get married before you go.'

And that was it. The strangest proposal I have ever heard, and in the strangest place. But then we live in strange times. The happier events of life become unreal, while death and destruction become our reality.

As Beaky knew, but could not mention to his wife, the death and destruction of war were now daily becoming more intense, the scales of victory or defeat ever more finely balanced. Allied bombers were facing much stiffer resistance. The enemy's production of night fighters had not been halted. They were putting up more night fighters than ever before. The Kammhuber tactics had increased the kills from anti-aircraft fire. Despite new aids such as Oboe and Window, there were dark predictions that taking the bombing into the heart of Germany would result in the Battle of Britain in reverse – the incoming bombers would be shot out of the sky by the defending fighters and gunners, fighting like the Battle of Britain pilots for their homeland.

'At a time like this . . .' Gabby made a token protest.

'At a time like this,' Bob repeated, 'it's all the more important to have whatever time we can together.' Still kneeling, he reached up and took her hand. 'Anyway, that's what I want. Always supposing you'll have me.'

'Of course I'll have you.'

From her seat in front of the W/T set, Jan clapped loudly. Beaky abandoned all pretence of not listening and, as he wrote to his wife,

I beamed on them in a fatherly manner. As they embraced, Bob sought permission from me to be off early shift tomorrow in order to thumb a lift into Lincoln to buy a special licence, which I gave gladly with my blessing.

Almost immediately another blessing came their way. The much maligned padre added his blessing when he entered flying control like a sodden spectre as the staff of flying control stood drinking the health of the happy pair in aircrew rum.

Dutifully, but reluctantly, he had stood by the end of the runway lifting his hand in blessing as, one by one, the black, heavily laden Lancasters staggered off into that damp December night. Trails of cloud touched the tops of the hangars and the dense air made take-off dicey; and, as always, the padre's heart was uneasy. How to reconcile those brave young men with what they had to do, how to reconcile Christ's teaching with the bombing of cities?

The padre had been assured by the station commander that his presence by the runway helped morale, a sort of physical manifestation of God being with our boys in a task which some of the more sensitive found disturbing. The padre had been joined that night by a disparate group of WAAFs of all ranks waving handkerchiefs; one of them, the blonde batwoman called Bunty, was dabbing her eyes and sniffing noisily as the last glow of the last Lancaster died into darkness. The padre had wondered if he should go to her assistance, offer her comfort, a suitable text perhaps. But he had never been good with weeping women.

Now, in the warmth and light of flying control, he seemed to step into a different world. All seemed cheerful. Joyful even. The staggering bombers clawing their way up into an inhospitable sky were here translated to chalked letters and figures on a blackboard, all safely airborne, all under control.

He took off his sodden overcoat, warmed his hands at the glowing iron stove, accepted the generous measure of rum that Jan poured into a tin mug and handed him.

Gulping it gratefully, he described the news of the forthcoming wedding as 'manna from heaven'.

'I get weary of funerals,' he sighed. 'And even more weary of writing to bereaved relatives, grieving parents, young wives.' He almost followed Bunty's example and sniffled into the dregs of his rum. Then he had a most wonderful idea.

'Might I offer you,' he asked Gabby and Bob, 'a blessing in our RAF chapel after the civil ceremony?'

The happy pair looked very doubtful. Aghast even.

'But we're not churchgoers,' Gabby protested. And, with her usual honesty, 'I always manage to get out of church parade, because I was brought up a Catholic. And, as you know, the station warrant officer always orders, "Fall out the Catholics and Jews."'

'Ah, yes. I don't like that much. Not very Christian. But it is *King's Regulations*.'

'I like it.' Gabby smiled at Bob. 'I fall out! I'm no longer a Catholic. But I still fall out.'

'And I'm nothing.' Bob spread his hands ruefully. 'Absolutely nothing.'

Nevertheless, despite their reluctance, Gabby and Bob were persuaded that it would be a good excuse for a party. The padre brought out his diary from the breast pocket of his uniform.

'You'll have to get permission to marry from the station commander, but that's just a formality.' He riffled through the pages.

'Shall we say Saturday?'

Thus, Beaky added in a postscript to his wife,

it was all fixed up here in flying control as we waited for the bombers' return. A midsummer night's dream continued here. Not a romantic place, I can hear you say. But surrounded as it is by sudden death, horribly mutilated men, exploding bombs and inescapable fear, it is an oasis. And, as an extra lucky bonus, that night the bombers all returned.

'I'm real sorry you're leaving. But you are so lucky!' Bunty sighed enviously, as she watched Gabby begin to sort through her kit in the upstairs room of the married quarter. 'To get married. To have a blessing on the station. That's real romance.

Can we all come? Can I ask Chris? I think it might give him the idea!'

'Has he still not got it?' Gabby asked.

'No such luck.'

'D'you mean you still haven't told him?'

'About my bun? No, I can't. I really can't. I'll never dare. It'd upset him. He was all shaken up after the last do. I had to stay and talk to him for hours.' She sighed and shook her head. 'Anyway, I don't really know for certain yet, do I?' She patted her stomach.

'How late are you?'

'I've missed another month.' Her eyes filled with tears. Then, ever hopeful, 'But one of the cooks in the mess told me something. Her mother used to help girls that got into trouble . . . she told me what she did.'

'What was that?'

'Just something she says might work.'

'Which is?'

'I'm not telling anyone till afterwards. Till I see whether it does or not.' Then, in a more practical tone of voice, 'Would you happen to have any spare Elastoplast?'

'I might have.' Gabby looked surprised at the apparent change of subject. 'I think I've got some here in my locker.'

She reached to the back of the shelf in her metal locker. She felt momentarily overwhelmed by the events of the last forty-eight hours, as if life had gone too quickly ahead of her. To be posted for special duties, and to be about to get married. Each a big step in her life. Everything had happened so suddenly, even for wartime, that she could hardly believe it was for real.

'Oh, thanks ever so. You'll be the first to know if it works.'

But it didn't. The cure was a simple one. According to the cook, all you had to do if you suspected you were pregnant was to put some Elastoplast tightly over your navel. The unborn baby breathed through his mother's navel. That's what your navel was there for. Everyone knew that. So stop up your navel. No air, no baby. It just shrivelled away.

To make certain, the Elastoplast should be in position for

at least twenty-four hours, when, with luck, Bunty's period would magically appear. But Bunty was, as her mother so often said, dead unlucky.

'No luck?' Gabby asked Bunty commiseratingly on the Thursday before her wedding. Gabby was about to race around the station obtaining a clearance signature from every section, as laid down in *Station Standing Orders*.

Edith had forgiven Gabby's cynicism at the Ouija session and had lent her a bike from stores to get round the station quickly. After all, Edith could afford to be generous. Arnold had been vindicated. Gabby had indeed been posted as he had foretold. So, with the generosity of the righteous, Edith had also liberated from stores a brand new shirt for Gabby to wear at her wedding. Carole had given her a new Van Heusen collar to go with it, a much prized item for which one had to give up a clothing coupon. Carole had also queued up at the NAAFI to buy a tin of Nivea cream for Gabby's prenuptial beauty treatment.

That Thursday afternoon, Gabby had something more important than beauty on her mind. Bob still didn't know the implications of her posting.

There was no operation scheduled for that night. The station was quiet, as Bob and Gabby showed their 1250s at the guardroom and strolled out through the main gate, turning east towards the flat scrub that edged the sea marshes. They sat on the remains of a crumbled stone wall, watching the sun setting over the estuary, gilding the shallow wavelets, listening to the melancholy call of the oystercatchers and the cry of the waders.

Bob slipped his arm round her shoulders, took off her cap and kissed her lips. 'What is it? Tell me? I've always known you held back. That there was something you couldn't tell me. Was it someone else? Someone before me?'

He heard her out without interruption, those dark compelling eyes fixed intently on her face.

'At least,' she said shakily, alarmed at his stricken silence, 'it wasn't someone else.'

'I wish it had been,' he began vehemently, and then stopped himself. 'No. That's not true.'

'Do you still want to marry me?'

'More than ever.'

He didn't try to dissuade her. He accepted that she must do what she felt she must, that it was all part of being the person he loved, that it was no different from his going back on operations. They clasped each other, half in agony, half in something like bliss, as they listened to the small sounds of the countryside around them, murmuring over and over again, 'If only this could last for ever.'

The sun disappeared. The shallow estuary waters were bathed in the soft pinky-grey last light. They began to devise a code so that they could communicate with one another when all her letters from now on would be censored, and discussed how, if she were dropped in France, she could get some word through to him that she was still alive.

At the Lincoln Registrar's Office of Births, Marriages and Deaths, Carole sat on a form in the corridor beside Beaky. The corridor was crowded with young servicemen and women. It smelled of damp uniforms, mostly khaki, and the lilies which one of the brides to be was clutching.

'I have seldom seen a sadder but prouder bridegroom,' Mr Birdsall whispered to Carole, as Bob Halliday hurried by them. 'I understand Bob had difficulty in booking a slot,' he went on, 'so many men and women getting married before they go overseas.' Then, peering over the heads of the waiting couples, 'Ah, Gabby is beckoning us! Our turn now!'

Gabby looked radiant. The girls in married quarter five had shampooed her hair and done her make-up. Her hair hung shiny and loose on her collar. Lipstick had been acquired from the cookhouse, where the cooks were running a lively little business making lipstick from lard and cochineal – at threepence a lipstick, it was a snip. Bunty had given some of her precious eyeshadow. Buttons and cap badge and shoes had been shone by Carole, Gabby's uniform pressed by the meticulous Edith. Throughout the brisk ceremony, Gabby held Bob's hand tightly. Beaky thought she looked suddenly very young and vulnerable.

An almost Christmassy atmosphere prevailed at the station chapel blessing. Earlier on, Bunty, Carole and Edith had scrambled through the perimeter fence and cut branches of holly and holm oak and whatever shrub or tree still remained green. These they had arranged in pots in front of the altar, intertwined with streamers of silver window strips. The padre had togged himself out in his surplice and stole and stood with his hands outspread to welcome them.

Men from the squadron and a number of airwomen filled the rows of chairs. A little fluster of surprise went round the group assembled in front of the wooden altar when Flying Officer Caldbeck arrived with F/Sgt Grimble in attendance.

With great restraint, the flight sergeant bit her lip and refrained from calling the company to attention. Like the Queen Bee, to whom she stuck like an obsequious shadow, she entered with her head suitably bent, her sharp, always angry eyes travelling over the bride as if she ached to tell her to get her hair off her collar. Instead, like her Queen Bee, she shook the hands of the happy couple and wished them well.

'Why are you crying?' Hermione Caldbeck turned suddenly to ask Bunty crisply. 'On such a happy occasion!'

'The words are so lovely, ma'am,' Bunty sniffed, fearful that ma'am might guess something else was wrong.

Although Bunty had asked Chris to come to the blessing, he hadn't appeared. He had excused himself on the grounds that weddings weren't his line, which didn't cheer her, and that anyway he was developing a nasty cold.

Which was a worse worry. She had an awful feeling that he was going to try to get off ops. And that would eventually mean LMF. But even if it didn't mean that, he might get himself so nervous that he would make a mistake and get killed. That was why she wept.

Even the champagne that Beaky had bought to celebrate the happy occasion didn't help. They drank it in the lobby of the station chapel because they couldn't all join up together anywhere else, because of being a mixture of commissioned and non-commissioned ranks.

Bunty was glad to get back to the officers' mess. But within minutes, Sergeant Fisher had called her into his office. He couldn't wait to tell her that, half an hour ago, Mr Dutton had been admitted to sick quarters.

Then he began asking her disturbing questions. How had Mr Dutton been lately? Did she think he had been off colour ever since the bomb incident?

'It's only a cold he's got, isn't it?' she asked airily. 'That's what he told me.'

'Mmm, well maybe.' Sergeant Fisher eyed her sideways. 'And how about you, Bunty? Are you all right? You haven't caught anything off him, have you?'

And that was a funny question. She bridled. 'What could I catch?' she asked.

'Germs, dear, what else?'

Bunty didn't sleep a wink that night. She got up early and made them all a cup of tea. She helped Gabby check she'd got her railway warrant and rations and all her forms, and they debated whether or not it was worthwhile collecting her rations for the journey. They decided it wasn't. Then she and Carole walked along with Gabby to MT, where Carole had promised there was a truck going to the railway station.

They helped Gabby climb into the three-ton Ford with her kitbag. The truck was already three-quarters full of airmen and airwomen. But Bob Halliday had been one of the first aboard, keeping a place for Gabby.

Out came a hand, grasped Gabby's and pulled her up. The new Mr and Mrs Halliday cuddled together for the last brief ride to the station.

Carole blinked her eyes. The truck, crowded with men and women, suddenly reminded her of a film she'd seen at the camp cinema, *The Scarlet Pimpernel*. The noisy truck became a tumbrel. She had an overpowering feeling that the happy couple was rattling along, not to the railway station but to their deaths.

Ten

In the event it was Chris who died. He had his two nights in sick quarters. Bunty was allowed to visit him on the excuse that she needed to take in some books and his mail. Among the mail was a letter from his mother, and Bunty sat quietly but eagerly by his bed as he read it. She hoped that it would mention her and that he would hand her the letter. But it obviously didn't.

'Is your mum well?' she asked.

'Yes. Bang on.'

'And your dad?'

'He's always fit.'

He folded the letter and put it back in the envelope. But he took her hand, pulled her over to him, and gave her a brief kiss on her lips. Then he asked her to come again and bring some buns and such like from the mess, as sick quarters food was foul.

But the next day when she called at sick quarters, the MO was with Chris, so she just had to leave the buns and sandwiches, and anyway, the MO was clearly passing him fit for duty, because by Wednesday Chris was back on operations again.

The operation was to Rostock on the Baltic, a tough target for the Lancasters, but because of the presence of the Heinkel factory in the Marienehe suburb, one much favoured by command.

The Lancasters were bombed up with a high proportion of incendiaries. Most people knew by now that Rostock was a mediaeval city full of wooden buildings. So, fires would be started and then the Lancasters would drop their high explosives into the fires.

The bomb trolleys had left the aircraft and returned to the dump when Carole drove Chris and his crew to their aircraft, B-Baker. Chris looked pale, his eyes red-rimmed. He sat at the back of the Commer with his crew, and all through the short journey he was laughing and cracking jokes with them.

Cracking them very determinedly, a bit discordantly, Carole thought, wondering if the crew noticed. Maybe not. They all laughed heartily, greeted B-Baker as an old friend, their favourite aircraft, they said; Chris slapped her camouflaged sides as if she were a horse. Chalky White, the bomb aimer, peed against her nose wheel for luck.

Carole hung around until after take-off. She wanted to be able to tell Bunty that she had seen him off. The sky was clear and there was a bombers' moon. Already the grass between the peri track and the runway was crisp with frost.

Six hours later, as she waited at dispersal for the bombers' return, the temperature had dropped. The grass was white in the baffled headlights. The moon was intermittently hidden by trails of cloud. It was numbingly cold.

She wet her finger and held her hand out of the side window to try to guess the direction of the wind. From the north-east. Helpful to the bombers, and the visibility was good for landing.

Shortly before three, she felt the sky begin to vibrate with the first sound of the bombers' return, the sound swelling to a throaty continuous roar, the sky filling with black bat shapes homing in from the coast. She watched some of them sweeping over her to the airfields of the north. She could smell the acrid heat of their glowing exhausts, feel their slipstreams rock the truck.

Then the Holmfirth aircraft were detaching themselves from the stream, descending into the circuit. On came the runway lights. She tried to count the black shapes circling like moths. She thought she counted eleven.

Then a quick flick of light from the controllers' caravan, a green light, and the first Lancaster was landing. The other ten followed in quick succession.

As far as she could see, B-Baker was not among them. She waited and waited. But the crew of B-Baker did not return. Her truck remained empty.

Before she returned to the MT section, she drove round to flying control in the hope that they had had a Darky from B-Baker, or that the Lancaster had diverted to another station.

Bob Halliday shook his head. He made her a cup of bitter

brown tea laced with Nestlé's milk. Beaky said they would be ringing round shortly to other stations in the group, that B-Baker was not yet officially missing, but they all guessed that it was just a matter of time. As they waited, they talked about Gabby. She had telephoned to say she was comfortably settled. Living out, and in the lap of luxury. Bob was hoping to meet her for a forty-eight in London, and their honeymoon.

Then, when Beaky officially confirmed B-Baker as missing, Carole could no longer postpone returning to MT, and to the married quarter, to tell Bunty.

'So, that silly girl's boyfriend got the chop,' F/Sgt Tordoff said as Carole signed in at the section thirty-six hours later.

'We don't know that for certain. He may be a POW.'

'In that blaze? Doubtful. Besides, Bladowski's crew saw him go down.'

'Who told you that?'

'Jumbo. We were sharing a noggin in the mess. He saw it with his own eyes. B-Baker took a direct hit. Exploded before he hit the ground.'

Carole shivered but said nothing.

'How did she take it?'

'Bunty? Numbly.'

Chiefie clicked his tongue in the nearest he got to sympathy. 'You'll just have to tell her about all those other fish in the sea. You girls have got to learn to get yourself a nice reliable ground type like me.'

'I'd rather be a nun.'

'Thank you, Miss Cleverclogs, and here's me giving you the officers' mess ration run, so you can have a chat with her.'

From the group of drivers by the stove, someone started to sing the popular Arthur Askey ditty, 'Big Hearted Arthur they call me, Big Hearted Arthur that's me!'

'That's it, laugh, you ungrateful bastards! You won't get a better big-hearted boss than me!' He tossed Carole the keys of the ration lorry.

'Thank you, Flight Sergeant.'

'Actually, Sergeant Fisher asked specially for you. Reckons you're an honest type. Some of these bastards –' he stabbed an accusing finger at the group by the stove – 'aren't above liberating officers' goodies. Like that big tin of biscuits they're guzzling now. Where the hell did that come from?'

Leaving the clamour of denials, Carole made her exit, drove round to the issue end of the airmen's mess, checked the rations being loaded and then drove the short distance to the rear entrance to the officers' mess.

The sun was setting in a cool rose and violet sky. She could see her breath in the frosty air. In another few days it would be Christmas. She had not drawn Christmas leave, and in a way she was glad. She was being slowly hammered and welded to fit into this strange unnatural community, and beginning to feel more at home in it than in the outside world.

It was warm in the officers' mess kitchen, and fragrant with the smell of tonight's steak and kidney pie. Corporal Butterworth checked the rations, initialled the flimsy and handed it back for Carole to have countersigned by Sergeant Fisher.

There was no sign of Bunty, who was often to be seen in the kitchen, scrounging an extra tray of tea and sandwiches for one of her boys. No sign of her in the corridor that led to the rooms, or in the laundry room.

'Come and sit down, my dear,' Sergeant Fisher invited affably when she knocked on his door. 'I'd like a word with you.' He lifted his pen. 'Corporal's checked everything, has she?'

'Thoroughly.' Carole smiled.

'Good-o.' He signed his name with a flourish. 'Some of your colleagues are a bit light-fingered. Jam, butter, biscuits, sausages . . .' He tut-tutted. 'But that's not what I wanted a word about. It's about Bunty. I want your advice. From a feminine point of view.'

Carole spread her hands helplessly. 'What can I say? She's grieving about Mr Dutton.'

'We all are, dear. We're all grieving for them all. And I did warn her. I warn you all about aircrew. They rarely make it to the altar.'

'Bob Halliday did.'

'But he's temporarily grounded. When he goes back on ops, it'll be curtains.'

'I hope not!' Carole exclaimed. 'Anyway, what d'you want me to say to Bunty?'

'Well, for one thing, tell her to cheer up. To look on the bright side. She can be such a jolly girl. The boys really like her. But now she's a wet weekend. She's bad for morale. And I've got the new Wingco arriving this evening. Sorry, dear. I know there was a little bit of something going on between you. But that's life. The king is dead, long live the king. I don't want any miserable faces. Life must go on. The war must go on.'

Life went on. The war went on. The new wing commander arrived, a bold, blond press-on youngster of twenty-three. Bunty's manifest misery began to try Sergeant Fisher beyond endurance. Once again, on the pretext of her honesty, he asked for Carole to do the ration run to the officers' mess.

'I now know,' he told Carole sternly, 'that there is something wrong with Bunty. Grief is not enough. This morning, I had her into my office; I was being very nice to her. Then suddenly her eyes rolled up into her head. I could only see the whites.' He shuddered. 'It was awful. And then she keeled over.'

'Fainted?'

'Yes. Didn't she tell you?'

'No.'

'And before that, Corporal Butterworth heard her puking in the officers' lavatory. She must have been taken short while she was changing the beds and just dived in there. And Corporal Butterworth is of the opinion that Bunty is pregnant.'

'Oh.'

'Is that all you've got to say?'

'Well, I can't think of anything else. Have you asked Bunty?'

'I'm going to.' Sergeant Fisher shoved out his jaw. 'I've made up my mind. I shall ask her outright and have no nonsense.'

She denied it of course. 'I had to, Carole. I had to tell a porky,' she said, as another domestic evening, the last before Christmas, arrived. Edith had done her cleaning and nipped round to the Sally Ann to buy three comforting doughnuts, their speciality. 'Just think what would have happened. Sarge would have sent me to Ma'am. Ma'am would have thrown clause eleven at me, and I'd have been out on my ear. No money, no nothing, and nowhere to go.'

146

'Can't you go to your mother?'

'She wouldn't have me.'

'How d'you know?'

'Because I know my mum. I've lived with her long enough. Even if she wasn't having it off with Mr Hardcastle, she wouldn't.'

'Have you any aunts or uncles?'

'No.' Bunty shook her head.

'Well, at least write and ask your mother. Just try. If she says no, she says no. You'd be no worse off.'

'I wouldn't know what to say to her. How to begin.'

'I'll help you write the letter. If you told your mother what a marvellous person Chris is, and how brave, maybe she'd understand.'

'I'll have to try something. Corporal Butterworth talked to me this afternoon when I was in the kitchen pressing Mr Bladowski's uniform. I didn't admit I was pregnant but I knew she knew. She went on about sometimes it could be got rid of with a knitting needle.'

'My God, Bunty! You can't try that!'

'Why can't I?'

'Because you can't. You'd give yourself blood poisoning or something awful. And it probably wouldn't work.'

'Being me, it probably wouldn't,' Bunty agreed dolefully. 'But what can I do?'

'Stick it out for a while. But sooner or later you'll have to go to the MO.'

'I won't. I can't! I'm going to stay here till the last moment, in case Chris comes back. I want to be here.'

'But when you begin to show?'

'Everybody puts on weight. It's the food and the marching. And Edith says she'll wangle me bigger skirts and things from stores.'

'Edith knows, does she?'

'She's guessed. She said we could ask Arnold what to do. She wanted to have a seance tonight, but I didn't feel in the mood.'

'Then let's get that letter written tonight, and see what your mother says.'

147

Bunty's mother didn't say anything. The reply, when it came, was immediate, but it was from Mr Hardcastle, and it was written on his special undertaker's printed paper, with his name and address in black Gothic lettering.

The letter wasted no time in polite niceties. It came quickly to the point. It said that Bunty's mother regarded her as dead. So dead that, in all kindness, he had generously offered to put up a small tombstone for her. Her mother, regarding her daughter as dead, could therefore have no more correspondence with her.

However, he himself would give her a kindly word of advice. In his frequent and harmonious contacts with all the churches in Stoke, he had learned that the Church of England Moral Welfare Department ran homes for fallen women. He suggested that Bunty, as a fallen woman, now qualified for their help and should contact a home near Lincoln, but not, please, near them.

It was a cold and gloomy Christmas, despite the efforts of the senior officers. A foraging party had gone out and acquired a fine tall Christmas tree by digging it up from the plantation round the reservoir. It was erected on the parade ground and decorated with silver baubles and streamers of Window. Dances were laid on in the various messes on Christmas Eve, and the usual feast on Christmas Day. Barrels of beer, masses of turkey and ham and sausages, vats of mashed potatoes and turnip and lashings of gravy, all served to the airmen and airwomen by the officers. Even the Queen Bee twittering around, laughing with her fellow officers as she dropped plates of food in front of the other ranks. When the pudding was being served, the station commander stood on a chair and told them how marvellously they had all worked that year and how, very shortly, the Hun would be on the run.

But the new Wingco had gone missing, another was on the way, and it seemed to many people as if the Second Front was never going to open up.

In the New Year the trucks carrying the crews out to their aircraft were full of fresh-faced boys straight from Initial Training Wing. So many of the old ones had gone, either posted to another squadron or missing. The one item hailed as good news was that Bob Halliday had passed his medical to go back on ops.

'You'd think he'd have learned his lesson, wouldn't you? With a face like that.' Chiefie remarked scornfully to Carole as they sat drinking tea by the stove in the rest room at the MT section. It was a crisp January morning and the coke in the stove glowed frostily. 'But he hasn't. He laid on a thrash in the mess to celebrate last night.'

'He couldn't bear to hang around while his friends were on ops,' Carole said.

'Even so, he should've been thankful. Mind, the squadron was thankful to have him back. He didn't have to twist this new Wingco's arm no more, no more. They're bloody short of trained crews. The sergeants' mess is full of kids now. It's like an infant school. The ink isn't bloody dry on their numbers. Some of them are no older than you, sprog.'

'You can't say worse than that.' Carole smiled.

'You can't, pet.' He yawned and stretched his arms above his head. 'But it was a good thrash. I had a noggin or three. I might just put my feet up for an hour. It's bound to be quiet. The squadron's stood down. Rainstorms over Europe. Nothing moving.'

In the expectation that there would be few demands for transport, Chiefie had generously allowed two of his married drivers to have sleeping-out passes. Fenella, the other duty driver, had finished the ration run and been sent by Chiefie to see if she could scrounge another bag of firewood from stores. The section seemed unnaturally deserted.

Then, just as Chiefie was about to swing himself on to the bunk, the telephone rang. He scooped up the receiver, frowning. His frown deepened. His whole body stiffened as he listened to the voice at the other end.

Carole had stood up and was bending over the stove, adding more boiling water to the stewy brew inside the metal teapot. He stared across the room at her speculatively.

'OK! Roger,' she heard him say. 'Yep! I got a driver available! Will do!' He hooked back the receiver on to its cradle. He took a deep breath, rubbed his hands together and gave her a secretive inward-turning smile that made her instantly

149

suspicious. 'Got a job for you, pet! Right up your street! Cushy number! Lovely day for a drive!'

'I've had some of your cushy numbers.' She looked at him warily.

'Well, this is cushy. Promise! Cross my heart!'

She had heard of his promises too, but she just asked, 'Where to?'

'RAF Driffield.'

She raised her brows. 'Quite a way.'

'So what? If you're good, you can take the Humber.'

'There's a catch in it.'

'No, there isn't. Pick up a visiting VIP.'

'Uh-uh! That's it! The AOC!' She groaned, and automatically looked in the broken mirror beside the stove to see if her hair was short enough.

'No. Not exactly the AOC. But smarten yourself up. Don't let the section down.'

'Do I ever?'

'Appearance-wise, no.'

'Where do I report?'

'Their officers' mess. He'll be ready to leave.'

'What's he coming here for?'

Chiefie shrugged. 'God knows! Ours not to question why. Just bring him here.'

'Anything else? No eggs to be picked up?'

'No. Just get there and back. Don't give any lifts. Don't ask any of your pals if they'd like a little run out with you.' He unhooked the Humber keys from the board and tossed them to her. 'Apparently this VIP has a short fuse.'

'I'm used to bosses with short fuses,' she flung at him over her shoulder as she pulled the door closed behind her.

Outside, she stepped daintily over the puddles of oil in the section forecourt, walking up to the parked Humber.

With masterly insensitivity, Chiefie had given her, not the station Humber, but the wing commander's car. That was the trouble with Chiefie, he could be kind, but he could also be cruel, whether deliberately or not, she never knew.

She inserted the key in the lock. Today Chiefie was being cruel. For, within this carefully valeted car was the history of

150

her fragile, tenuous affair with the Wingco. The dent above the nearside wheel that had brought about their first meeting was so skilfully repaired that it was invisible. But she knew it was there. The seat was adjusted to his long legs, because his replacements had not lasted and had never driven the car. The carpet round the pedals was scuffed with his shoes. She could see the ghost of herself sitting in the passenger seat at their last meeting, hugging herself with excitement and trepidation, naive, ignorant, unsure how to respond to him, awed a little by the chasm between them, but most of all by the new sort of man he showed himself to be: gentle, diffident, disarming. She was more at ease with the shouting, angry, demanding wing commander.

'If anyone suspects there's anything between us, it'll make life difficult for you,' he had said, sliding his arm round her shoulders. 'And difficult for me maybe, too. I'd always sworn I wouldn't be serious about any girl while I was on ops.'

Then he had gone on, just as Chiefie had scornfully suggested, to say, 'But this is different. You're different, I can't stop thinking about you.'

'Is that bad?'

'For me, very bad. You haunt me.'

'So, what do you want to do?'

'To kiss you.'

And, having kissed her, very excitingly she thought at the time, he had drawn away, sighing heavily. 'And that makes it worse. Infinitely worse. You're just a kid, aren't you? You should be back at school. You don't even know how to kiss properly.'

She had felt deeply offended. 'I'm sorry.'

'Oh, God! Don't be sorry! I love you for it. It just makes me more of a bastard. I'm five years older than you, Carole.' He had made the gap sound unbridgeable. 'But really I'm ten times as old. A hundred times. I'm old in here!' He thumped his chest. 'And you're a kid. A schoolkid. You're still in gymslip and black stockings.'

Those, apart from goodbye, were the last words he had spoken to her.

But if she was a kid, she was growing older all the time.

In the weeks since he had been shot down, she had aged as many years. She blinked her eyes, stabbed the key into the ignition. If he hadn't died, he probably wouldn't have wanted anything to do with her anyway. Men were fickle, men liked sophistication, Bunty said. Girls who knew all the answers. Who'd been around.

She adjusted the seat fiercely, as if banishing him; then she adjusted the mirror. Fleetingly, faintly, she seemed to see his face behind the glass, his brows puckered, his mouth rueful, his red hair rumpled.

She turned the key savagely, slammed the engine into gear, released the brake and roared out of the forecourt, along the deserted main camp road.

She stopped, engine still running, at the guardroom gate and showed her 658 to the SP, returning his smile frugally. Often, when the squadron was stood down, there would be a knot of off-duty airmen and airwomen, hoping to thumb a lift; but luckily, today there were none. She accelerated out between the bare wind-bitten hedgerows, her face set, wishing she were driving any other vehicle than this one.

For if she had haunted the Wingco, he certainly still haunted her. She felt as if he were sitting in the seat beside her. His face was superimposed over the sunlit wintry landscape. She opened the window and the smell of the sea and the mudflats blew in. A sad, uncomforting smell.

On these occasional trips when she was totally alone, she tried to think, to sort herself out. As the miles spun away under her wheels, she tried to adjust herself to the unnatural life and unnatural death all around her, to the quick flowering relationships and the swifter cutting down of them. She tried to come to terms with the youngsters she ferried to the aircraft, some of them boys of her own age, straight from school, for whom she waited but who did not return, and to come to terms with the awful work they were ordered to do.

She tried to think about her friends. She tried to guess what Gabby was doing at this moment; what Bunty was going to do about her pregnancy; whether Edith would ever give up talking to her dead Arnold and form a real relationship; what all of them would be doing this time next year. But today she

152

couldn't focus on the problems of her friends. The Wingco's face remained superimposed.

Above her arched an almost cloudless sky A flight of Spitfires in tight formation roared over towards the sea, a Lysander, like a daddy-long-legs, hovered above a field of old cabbage stumps. But she hardly saw them. She hardly saw the heavy army lorries trundling in the opposite direction, the tanks. An army on the move. The war gearing up to something.

The turning to Driffield would have caught her unawares if she hadn't spotted those distinctive huge peacetime hangers, the tall water tower, the Lysander now coming in to land, its spindly shape on the east–west runway.

She slackened her speed, stopped at the red and white pole across the road and showed her identity card and 658 to the SP. A corporal emerged from the guardroom behind him and told her to report to the officers' mess, which was straight up the road, and then immediately left beside the flagpole.

Driffield was a peacetime RAF station built to last, with sturdy brick buildings set in grassy spaces planted with trees. A sweeping drive led up to the large neo-Georgian officers' mess. Three wide stone steps, protected with sandbags, led to the entrance, a glass swing door.

As she was about to stop the car in front of the steps, the glass door spun, refracting the sunlight, and in it, again, she saw the Wingco's ghostly face. She saw the red hair shoving up under the battered cap, the grin on his thin face.

At first she thought she was hallucinating. She was so overwhelmed, so excited, so frightened that her foot was paralysed on the accelerator. Her hands gripping the wheel jerked uncontrollably. The front wheel caught the pile of sandbags beside the steps. She could hear the bumper protest as it took another dent. The revving engine coughed harshly and then died.

'You don't change!' The Wingco shook his head in mock reproach, as Carole stepped sheepishly out of the car. Then, regardless of the watchers in the mess, he threw his arms round her, twirling her off her feet, swinging her dizzily round and round. 'Thank God for that!'

153

Eleven

'Thank God!' Flight Officer Caldwell exclaimed four hours later. She had appointed herself the spokeswoman for the welcome party foregathered inside Holmfirth officers' mess. Word of the Wingco's escape through occupied France and his return had travelled like wildfire round the station. All that was known was that he had survived the crash, been hidden by the French Resistance and then somehow made his way home.

'Thank God indeed,' the padre echoed.

'Couldn't have come at a better time.' The station commander clapped the Wingco on his shoulder. 'Your successor didn't stay the course. This'll pep up the squadron. And things, my boy, are hotting up.'

'We've all missed you.' The Queen Bee slipped her hand through his arm and gazed up at him beguilingly. 'There's going to be a thrash in the mess this evening. It's all laid on.'

She was reluctant to let the Wingco be spirited away by Olive Spinks, the Intelligence officer. Luckily Olive was quite old, late thirties, an ex-librarian and reassuringly plain. To her, the Wingco again told the story of his escape.

A bowdlerized version of the Wingco's escape gradually found its way into station lore.

Attacked by Me-109s, the Lancaster was severely damaged by cannon fire, its rudder shot away. The Wingco had managed to hold it until his crew had baled out. Then he had crash-landed the aircraft in a field just over the border in France. He had been hidden by Resistance workers until he was fit to make the journey, then passed down the network to the coast. A French fishing boat had taken him halfway across the North Sea, where he was transferred to a coble putting in at Grimsby. The worst part had been convincing the Grimsby police that

154

he wasn't a Nazi infiltrator, and they had escorted him to the nearest RAF station.

'A feat of endurance reminiscent of Air Commodore Bennett's escape after bombing the *Tirpitz*,' Beaky remarked to Gabby's replacement, a black-haired ex-actress called Poppy, with the vivid blue eyes and darting movements of a kingfisher. *And who, I fear*, Beaky later wrote to his wife,

> may be equally brilliant at catching fish. More aircrew than ever hang around. But not Bob Halliday. He is now a very much married man, although, alas, he still awaits his honeymoon. Gabby is only allowed to write a certain number of letters. But occasionally mysterious signals come over the W/T in their special code. Not according to *King's Regulations*, of course. But I turn a blind eye, or rather a deaf ear.

A consistently deaf ear was being turned by the new W/T operator, Poppy, towards Edith's invitations to explore the future via the Ouija board. She had been allocated Gabby's old bed in married quarter 5, but had immediately asked the admin corporal if she could change her billet and sleep in one of the Nissen huts, because Bunty's weeping kept her awake.

'You've got to do something about that silly cow!' she told Carole. 'When she isn't weeping, she's puking.'

'She's upset. But she's been a bit more cheerful since the Wingco came back. She reckons her boyfriend might come back too. Give her time.'

'And what good will that do? She's pregnant, isn't she?'

'You haven't said that to anyone else, have you?'

'Not so far, But why shouldn't I? She's got to do something. I need my rest. I can't start falling asleep on duty.'

'None of us can.'

'Well, you talk to her then. You know her better than I do. Tell her to go and get her discharge. You'd think she'd be glad to get it. I'm warning you here and now. If you don't do something, I will.'

Whether she did or not, whether it was simply F/Sgt Grimble's never-failing nose for misdoings, two days later Bunty was told to report to station sick quarters.

155

F/Sgt Grimble was waiting for her. Bunty was ordered to submit to an examination by the grey-haired medical officer, Doc Malone, who looked as reluctant as Bunty to take part in the proceedings.

An hour later, Bunty was marched in front of Flight Officer Caldbeck, wearing her cap and without escort, because she wasn't on a charge.

'Although, if I had my way,' the Queen Bee told her sternly, 'you would be on a charge. You have behaved shamefully. You have broken *Station Standing Orders*. You have betrayed your trust. You joined up to serve your country, not to engage in sexual adventure.'

Having delivered herself of her peroration, Hermione Caldbeck allowed herself to discuss practicalities.

'You know you will be discharged forthwith under clause eleven?'

'Yes.' Bunty snuffled.

'Yes, what?'

'Yes, ma'am.'

'That you will be entitled to pay until the end of this week and a railway warrant to your home.'

'I can't go home!'

'Why not?'

'My mother doesn't want me.'

'That's hardly surprising. But it's no use crying. There are homes for fallen women. Run by the churches. You must contact one of them. However, perhaps when you get home, your mother will look after you.'

'She won't.'

'The baby's father then? Do you know who he is?'

'Of course I do.'

'You're sure?'

'Yes, I am.'

'Or have you been with several men?'

'Of course not.'

'No of course about it. I know something of what you girls get up to. So, have you told him?'

'He's not here any more.'

Two minutes later, she was in the orderly room collecting

156

her railway warrant, though she knew she wouldn't use it, her £1 6s pay, and a form to clear the station. Her first port of call was the clothing store, where Edith took her clearance chit to the sergeant for signature, and then whispered that if she went out to the back she'd find a bicycle she could borrow to get herself round the other sections.

'And we'll have a seance with the board this evening. It's the only way you're going to find out what's going to happen to you. Arnold will help you decide what to do. Carole's off, I know, because she's duty driver tomorrow.'

'That only makes three of us. Poppy's on duty and anyway she wouldn't join in if she wasn't.'

'Well, three it will have to be.'

'You won't ask anyone from the other billets, will you? I don't want everyone to know.'

Edith pursed her lips and said she wouldn't, and forbore to add that everyone else either knew or guessed.

'I guessed weeks ago,' Sergeant Fisher sighed when he signed her chit. 'But I was too well mannered to say.'

Bunty gave him a snuffled thank you.

'I'm sorry it's come to this, dear. But I did warn you.' He sighed. 'It's Mr Dutton, isn't it?'

'Yes, Sarge.'

'And you didn't get a chance to tell him?'

'No, and I'm glad I didn't. I would've felt it was my fault that he got the chop. For worrying him.'

'Well, you both should have thought of that before. Both, my dear. It takes two. But I'll tell you something, Bunty. If I were going to get the chop, I'd be glad to think I was leaving behind a little Sergeant Fisher. PO Dutton was a fine man. He'll have a fine son or daughter.'

Bunty wiped her nose and nodded. In these months as an airwoman, she had learned a lot. She realized it was unlikely that Sergeant Fisher would ever go through those actions with a girl which would result in a little Sergeant Fisher. Nevertheless, his remark planted a tiny seed of comfort in the barren landscape of her misery.

The tiny seed was gently nourished that evening as the three of them, Carole, Edith and Bunty, gathered round the kitchen

157

table in their married quarter. Carole had persuaded Chiefie to part with three of his latest batch of farm eggs. She had also scrounged round all the messes – the officers', the sergeants' and the airmen's – for sliced bread, a lump of bacon fat, Spam and a block of bright yellow slab cake, to make a tolerable farewell feast.

And, despite the fact that they hadn't a quorum for the Ouija board, Arnold obligingly appeared almost at once to the three of them.

There was no Gabby to protest that his knocking sounded like a heavy shoe, and if none of them quite believed, they all wanted to believe, and longed for a message to be spelled out.

'Is that you, Arnold?' Edith asked, then, twisting her mouth into a whispered aside. 'Sometimes you get mischievous spirits.'

Arnold loudly confirmed that it was indeed he.

'Bunty, who's sitting here, is very anxious, dear. Have you a message for her?'

Arnold had.

'You know she's got a little problem, Arnold. What should she do about it, dear?'

Suddenly the glass went crazy, spinning round the board, hardly stopping at each letter long enough for them to spell out the message.

'Go,' Edith interpreted loudly, 'to . . .' Then the glass described a series of little squiggles, as if Arnold's spirit didn't quite have the strength to reach the letters.

Then, getting his vigour back, in rapid succession: M-O-T-H-E-R.

'No!' Bunty shrieked. 'I am not going to my mother!'

She half rose from her seat.

But she was forestalled by two loud knocks and Edith shrilling, 'That's Arnold. He's still with us and he's saying no!'

She waved Bunty into silence, drew a deep breath and explained as calmly as she could, 'Two knocks means no! We've got Arnold's message wrong. That's what he's saying. Isn't it, Arnold?'

Arnold banged once with a resounding 'Yes!'

'Sorry, love!' She smiled apologetically at the ceiling. 'We're getting a bit het up. Don't be cross with us, we'll try again. Are you ready to give it to us, dear?'

One rather sulky knock and they pressed their fingers once more on the glass.

This time it spun with weight and purpose. *Go to*, was the same. Then, instead of the little squiggles came quite distinctly, *His*.

'Go to *his* mother!' Edith squealed with delight, then sat back smiling and sighing and spreading her hands in triumphant exhaustion.

'Thank you, Arnold. Thank you!' she said to the ceiling, then carefully withdrew the Ouija board and wrapped it in its piece of cretonne.

'Now, what did I tell you?' she addressed the others. 'You're a couple of doubting Thomases. It's an effort for him. But Arnold always helps.'

'It has helped, hasn't it, Bunty?' she asked a few minutes later, tucking into the egg and Spam sandwiches. 'Don't you think you might do as Arnold says, dear? Go to his mother?'

'I'd never have the cheek.'

'Why not?'

'Just wouldn't.'

'They might like to know.'

Bunty blew out her lips derisively.

'You wouldn't know till you told them,' Carole said.

Bunty shook her head. 'Anyway, they're posh.'

'So what?' Carole asked.

'And he's their only son.'

'They might be glad something's left of him.'

'Funny you should say that, Carole. That's what Sergeant Fisher said.'

'Well, there you are! I can help you write the letter if you like.'

Then they both remembered the dismal results of the letter to Bunty's mother, and Mr Hardcastle's reply, and the matter was dropped while they rounded the evening off with Camp coffee and Nestlé's milk. Carole had already decided she would talk to the Wingco about Bunty now that the secret was known;

now the worst had happened and the WAAF had thrown her out.

She didn't know him well enough to guess how he would react. He might reckon that she was ruining one of their brief snatched and secret times together with an insuperable problem.

She had only met him twice since his reappearance, both occasions carefully planned. On the first, she had gone alone into Lincoln on the Liberty bus; this time, thank God, it was not driven by Chiefie. Then she had waited for him in the porch of the cathedral, the only place she knew except the sweatbox and the unwelcoming station hotel, where they refused to serve other ranks. He had arrived in the Humber and driven her to a little pub he knew by the river. They had sat in a dark corner of the bar, drinking wine and eating fresh-caught trout.

'Tell me about you before we met. What did you do? Where did you work?'

'For my uncle. Driving a newspaper van.'

'And before that, you were at school. Of course you were! Did you have a boyfriend?'

'No. I didn't know many boys. It was an all-girls' school. I met a boy I quite liked at the church beetle drive.'

'A beetle drive! God, the depravity!'

'He took me to the pictures.'

'Back row?'

'No. He was at school too. We sat in the cheapest seats at the front. Threepence each.'

'What did you see?'

'*The Invisible Man.*'

'Very appropriate.' They both laughed immoderately.

'What about you?' she asked, stopping her laughter. 'I bet you had lots of girls. Still have.'

'No, I haven't! I had. But not now. No one else, I swear. Nor will have.'

Big, wonderful, promising words! Did she believe them? She wasn't sure.

Prosaically, she asked, 'What did you do before you joined up?'

'I never went to a beetle drive. That I swear.'

'You did other things.'

'A few.'

'Such as?'

'Well, I didn't want to help my father on the farm, so I went to university. Mechanical Engineering. Took a private pilot's licence. Joined up.'

'What will you do afterwards? After the war?'

'If there's an afterwards, which I doubt! God knows! I can't waste time thinking about that!' He laughed away the moment's solemnity by saying that meanwhile he intended to finish her education. She must regard him as her teacher. He was now going to teach her how to kiss.

The lesson continued at their second meeting five days later. It followed the same pattern – the liberty bus, the walk to the cathedral. This time she had to wait for half an hour before he came. As she sat on the stone bench in the south porch, the air raid warning howled. She watched searchlights fingering the sky. They clearly found nothing. The sirens were followed almost immediately by the all clear and the noise of the Humber engine fiercely accelerating.

'Sorry about this!' The Wingco burst out of the darkness. 'Your bloody Queen Bee kept me talking.' He took off his hat and fanned his face with it. 'She tried to cadge a lift into Lincoln. I had the devil's own job to shake her off.'

'Shake her off.' The three words seemed to echo round the high roof of the porch, momentous and malevolent. Cautiously, Carole suggested, 'She's got a crush on you.'

'She's a crush on most men.'

'Especially pilots.'

'The girl has good taste.' He sat down beside her on the bench and took her hand. 'The point is, if you get in her way she can really hurt you. If she suspected about us, she could put you on a charge and get you posted. We'll have to be careful.'

Being careful involved finding another pub further away than last time, miles north in a nameless little hamlet. There were two soldiers propping up one end of the bar, and a naval lieutenant at the other end with a fluffy-haired girl in a tight scarlet suit whom the soldiers were eyeing enviously.

The interior was shabby, the bar scantily stocked, with a large notice warning *No Whisky*. But there was a log fire and food was on offer, and it was too far for anyone from Holmfirth.

Sitting by the fire, eating their Spam and beans and chips, she tried to tell him about Bunty. He listened, but he made no comment other than to say, 'Let me think about it,' which was probably his way of saying he wasn't interested, and that his mind was on other things.

Then, as soon as the meal was finished, and they were in the car again, he pulled her into his arms, telling her, 'Here beginneth the second lesson.'

Carole was remembering the strange exciting feelings engendered by that second lesson when Edith prodded her back to the present with her sharp little elbow.

'Point is, even if we get the letter written, what is Bunty going to do as of now?'

Bunty drained her mug and banged it heavily on the table. 'I'm not going home.' She set her cherubic lips stubbornly.

'Well, you can't stay on here. Once you've cleared the camp, you'll have to go. Ma'am'll have you escorted off the station if you try to stay.'

'Could you get a room in the village?' Carole suggested. 'Some of the men live out. Two of our drivers do.'

'But how do I get a room?'

'You just ask, silly,' Edith said. 'But anyway, I've an idea. So you might not have to ask. I know someone that takes in lodgers.'

'Do you really?' Bunty immediately brightened. 'Who?'

'Fred Burford's wife. He's the coal contractor. He owes the stores a favour. Well, you know what coal men are! He comes in with his truck over the weighbridge, goes out without unloading and comes in again. I've seen him do it. Sometimes several times. And he knows I've seen him.'

'Oh, Edith, could you ask them if they'll have me?'

'If either of you've got two pennies on you, I'll pop along to the phone box and ask them now.'

Edith had just departed on her errand of mercy when another insuperable problem overwhelmed Bunty.

'But what am I going to do for money? Mrs Burford'll want paying. I've only got that one pound six shillings pay on me.'

*   *   *

That problem was solved the following day. Bunty went into the officers' mess to say goodbye to Mr Bladowski and her other officers, and of course to Sergeant Fisher.

All of them kissed her, including Sergeant Fisher, and told her to be sure and write to let them know how she got on. 'We'll have a squadron reunion when it's all over,' the aircrew promised. 'And you'll be our special guest.'

Sergeant Fisher's help was more immediate, though it wasn't really his idea at all. He said, opening a drawer in his desk and taking out an envelope, 'This is from the lads. They wanted to say thank you. So they had a whip round in the mess to give you a farewell present. They couldn't think of anything to buy in the time, and I said you wouldn't want liquor and you don't smoke. So would you mind having this?'

He passed the envelope over to her. 'Take it away and open it quietly some place. Remember it's no more than you deserve.'

But it was. Much, much more. Inside were six big white elegant five pound notes with their lovely copperplate writing. Thirty pounds, almost as much as she would earn in a year. It was enough to pay her digs for weeks and weeks, and, in that time, Chris might reappear or, when she managed to write the letter, his parents might reply to her.

The Burfords' cottage was in the centre of Holmfirth village, only two miles from the airfield, and according to Edith they were both pleased to welcome her. Bunty's volatile spirits soared.

She left her kitbag and cardboard case at the MT section because Carole had said she would get the first available transport to drop off her luggage at the Burfords'. Carole wasn't around. So Bunty set off to walk, confident that life wasn't going to be so bad after all. Throughout good days and bad, there was one thought that kept her going. Chris had said that they were as good as married. I'm not a fallen woman, she told herself, walking between the winter-brown dykes, no matter what Mr Hardcastle and Ma'am say, I can hold my head up. I really am married.

Twelve

'I've always sworn that I wouldn't get married. Not while the war's on.'

The Wingco squeezed Carole's hand and his face took on an expression of deadly seriousness. 'Can you understand that?'

Two days after Bunty took up residence at the Burfords', the Wingco and Carole were sitting side by side in the fateful Humber outside group headquarters. Like everyone else on the station, like everyone in the whole service, the Wingco had learned to Work the System. Knowing Carole was duty driver, he had put in a 658 for the squadron car to take a senior officer to a conference at group headquarters. The officer being himself, the conference being to pop his head round the door of the chief operations officer and bind away about replacements and the iniquities of Bomber Command.

If Chiefie had been suspicious, he gave no sign. And, as the Wingco remarked to Carole, you had to do that sort of thing if you were a senior officer and you had fallen in love with an airwoman.

'And have you?'

'You know I have. But I still wouldn't get married.'

'I didn't suggest you did marry me,' Carole said coolly, maintaining her dignity against a rush of anger. 'I'm not sure I would marry you if you asked me.' Her cheeks flushed furiously. 'I hate you when you talk like that. Hate you!'

'But you know bloody well why!' He grabbed both her arms. 'I swear I'd ask you to marry me tomorrow if the war was over.'

It was all so like what Chris had reportedly said to Bunty. 'I don't think you want the war to be over! I think you men love it!'

'My God! Do you? Do you really? Then you're a bloody fool!'

'I'm sorry. I shouldn't have said that!'

'No, you bloody well shouldn't' He folded his arms across his chest, frowning through the windscreen. Then his mood melted. He took her hand again. 'I understand though. I sounded a pompous bastard. Me not prepared to marry you. That I should be so lucky! But I find all this so frustrating, don't you?'

She nodded.

'Snatching these little bits of time together, always looking over our shoulders, afraid someone will see us.'

'So why not get married?'

'You should be able to guess.'

'Because you don't want to enough.'

'You know that's not true!' He drew a deep breath. 'Quite simple, really. Because I don't want to make you a widow.'

'But at least . . .'

'No, don't argue. I won't make you a widow. I won't marry you! But I won't ask you to go to bed with me either. I've seen what happens.'

'You mean, like Bunty and Chris?'

'I've seen so many others. But yes, that's what I mean.'

'She'd have been happier now if he had married her.'

'Possibly.'

'Certainly.' Carole clenched her fists with frustration and banged them on the wheel. 'They would have had some time together. She'd have been his next of kin, the first to know if he came back. Or didn't. The RAF would have looked after her instead of chucking her out like rubbish . . .'

'Don't get worked up!' In another change of mood, he took her hand, holding it in both of his. 'Don't cry.' He kissed her fingers one by one like a parent kissing a child. And then, as if all her distress was for Bunty, and their own situation completely forgotten, he went on soothingly, 'I'll do what I can to help Bunty. Tell her not to write to Mrs Dutton yet. I'm writing to her anyway. Several bods went missing while I was away. The adjutant wrote to the relatives of course, but I want to do that now myself. I know them all so well. They're like family. I can tell their relatives things no one else knows. Sometimes that helps. I can tell Mrs Dutton about Bunty. See how she reacts. That's better than Bunty writing herself. Leave it with me.'

He looked suddenly so kind, so adult, so thoughtful and reliable that she felt guilty because her gratitude was shot through with resentment that they had stopped talking about themselves, their future, and he had escaped into that other self, that of the squadron commander doing his best for his men.

Then, after resentment came suspicion. That suspicion was deepened when, waving aside her thanks, he suggested that at the next squadron stand-down, she applied for a sleeping-out pass and that they booked into some hotel a long way away, perhaps Cambridge, where no one knew them; separate rooms of course, not asking her to sleep with him. Just to be together.

Yet neither resentment nor suspicion prevented her doing exactly that.

In the event, she had to wait for the second squadron stand-down at the end of February before Chiefie would sign her sleeping-out pass. He did so reluctantly, grumbling that the section was overworked, and no one had ever seen him applying for a sleeping-out pass.

'Well, I haven't had one since I came here.'

'Maybe you haven't wanted one before!' He looked at her accusingly. 'You were a nice girl when you came here. Butter wouldn't melt in your little mouth. But nice girls don't stay nice for long. They go off like milk. And now you're doing like the rest of 'em. Falling for the Brylcreem brigade.'

'No, I'm not.'

'Well for one of them. So watch it. You'll get let down in the end.'

'Apart from that, do I get my SOP?'

'You're getting bolshie as well as going off. I like it not, sprog! You'll only get it if you promise not to use it for what I think you're going to use it for.'

'That's too complicated to follow.'

'Well, if you want it spelled out, no getting into bed.'

'You're being crude.'

'I'm being truthful. And if he's truthful, that's what he has in mind.'

'You're wrong!'

'I wish I were.' He signed the form with a flourish and a heavy sigh. 'Now watch out when you take this for your Queen Bee's signature. She'll know about you and him. And she has a dirty big sting in her tail.'

The Wingco said the same, after they had made their separate ways to Holmfirth station. 'Hermione's sidekick is on the platform,' he whispered in passing at the ticket office.

So, for the first part of the journey, Carole and the Wingco sat in separate compartments. He travelled in the first-class carriage with the Queen Bee's sidekick, an elderly admin officer who was an air commodore's widow. Just as well, because the third-class compartments were crowded with Holmfirth personnel and they would have been spotted together by someone.

But when they changed trains at March for the shorter leg of the stopping train to Cambridge, there was no one else on the platform in RAF blue, so they both clambered into a third-class compartment, picked their way over the stalwart legs of land girls, all fast asleep.

Squeezed happily side by side, they held hands as they jerked and rattled through the rich loamy brown landscape. A pale sun struggled through the overcast sky and gleamed on the slices of turned earth. Peewits rose at the passing of the train They were escaping Holmfirth together. It was all going to be special, she told herself. What her grandmother, who was Welsh, used to call one for the box.

At Cambridge, the station platforms were thick with RAF and USAAF uniforms from 8 Group stations, and so they were unnoticeable and anonymous amongst them.

Cambridge looked so beautiful. The sun was low in the sky, sinking behind dark stratus clouds; it gilded the pavements as they walked to the big comfortable hotel. It glowed benignly on the Georgian façades of the buildings and turned their ancient windows to a fiery copper.

Once through the glass doors, the Wingco seemed to change,

to shed the job, the unbearable responsibility, to become a young man in his twenties, ardent and unsure. In the shadowy lounge, fussed over by an elderly waitress, they drank tea and ate crumpets.

'I've given you real butter,' the waitress whispered.

Carole smiled. There was a popular song that winter called 'He Wears a Pair of Silver Wings'. They were all suckers for wings.

Before dinner, they walked across Parkers Piece to the river, sat on a wooden seat and watched the new moon rise over Emmanuel. When he kissed her rapturously, for the first time she felt it was not enough. When they strolled back to the hotel, her feelings were not of delight but an aching dissatisfaction.

But the luxury of even a wartime hotel was soothing. To have hot water that flowed freely into a bath that actually had a plug, the feel of warm dry towels, the privacy of one's own room. Then the sumptuous meal of off-the-ration food: smoked salmon, roast duck, followed by a pudding made of bright-pink artificial cream. The table was lit by three-branch candelabra. The same elderly waitress whispered that sir's was all breast. She had asked the chef specially.

The dissatisfaction gave way to cosy domesticity as they drank coffee and brandy in a corner of the lounge. Best not to go into the bar, they had decided, lest by some mischance they met someone they knew.

He kissed her goodnight at the top of the mahogany staircase, then held her hand as they sauntered to the door of her room; another kiss, tender but undemanding, the kiss of a settled relationship.

'See you . . .' he said softly and paused, holding his breath, waiting for her to invite him inside and let him break his promise.

But she didn't. Though she ached to, she couldn't.

'Yes.' She nodded. 'See you in the morning.'

Their rooms were on the same floor, one each side of the staircase. She listened to his disappointed footsteps, their echo diminishing along the creaky polished boards. For a while she half expected him to come tapping on the door. Every time she heard the boards creak she held her breath, wanting and not wanting, not sure what she would do if he did come, and wondering what exactly one did anyway. The Bridgnorth notes and anecdotes of the MT drivers were an inadequate guide for what Bunty said was a mucky, messy business really. Carole fell asleep thinking that maybe her affair wasn't all that different from Bunty's. She slept soundly and woke to the brightness of a cold winter morning, simultaneously relieved and disappointed.

'There's a market on in the square,' the Wingco told her, holding a chair out for her at breakfast. He looked fresh and smart and relaxed. 'We might prowl around. There's not much on the breakfast menu. Ersatz sausages and fried carrot instead of tomato. Or an egg.'

The elderly waitress brought him two plump poached eggs, the toast again buttered with the real stuff. 'We see you boys go over every night,' she murmured admiringly. 'It's nice to do something for one of you.'

Just around the corner from the hotel, the market blossomed in the square under tattered red and white and yellow awnings. Stalls piled with local vegetables, mostly potatoes, turnips, kale, red and green cabbages, boxes of cress; others selling home-made bread and fatless cakes were sandwiched between stalls where sad second-hand clothes flapped on metal rails and small furtive antiques vendors displayed old trinkets, battered silver and cracked china.

The Wingco made straight for one where a white-bearded old man sat smoking a clay pipe behind trays of old jewellery. He must have explored the place before, because he and the old man exchanged winks.

The Wingco went through the motions of examining a line of rings, picking up one here and there and then putting it down again, saying nothing.

Then he paused over a small Victorian ring of turquoises and amethysts surrounded by seed pearls, easily the most beautiful piece of jewellery on the stall.

'Try it on.' The Wingco lifted her hand and slid the ring over her third finger. It fitted perfectly, as snugly as Cinderella's slipper. Today, after all, promised to be one for the box.

'Like it?'

'I love it.'

'And I love you.' He closed her hand over the ring. 'Remember. I love you always, no matter what.'

The old man removed his clay pipe, placed it down carefully and offered to put the ring in a box, but she needed to wear it at least for a while. Once back at RAF Holmfirth, she wouldn't be allowed to wear it, at least not on her finger. So the Wingco bought a silver chain for her to wear it round her neck till the war was over. Then . . .

At that moment, standing in the cool sunlit square surrounded by the colour and good-tempered clamour of an English market, she felt she belonged to him. As Bunty had said, as good as married. But it was too like Bunty. Probably all over the country there were girls who felt they were as good as married to men who went away and never came back, either because they couldn't or because they didn't want to.

But that shadowy thought quickly passed. They wandered blissfully around the market, holding hands, the ring digging into her finger from the pressure of his. Then, lured by the smell of baking potatoes, they bought two from a woman presiding over a glowing charcoal stove. They ate them as they wandered round. The air smelled of fresh fruit and flowers and vegetables, the sun glowing on their faces, replete with food and warmth and well-being.

Suddenly, Carole spied a familiar figure, pausing, skulking almost in the shelter of the old clothes stall. A figure no longer in uniform, dressed in a country tweed skirt and jacket, but instantly recognizable.

'Gabby!' Carole waved and shouted.

Gabby heard her and froze. Her eyes met Carole's. They filled, not with pleased recognition, but with dismay and pain. Then she turned, pushed past a stout woman fingering the old clothes and ran.

Gabby kept on running for the length of one row of stalls. Then she slackened her pace, swearing under her breath in French.

These days she spoke French, wrote French, thought French,

170

dreamed French. Bit by bit, on her training, she had sloughed off the English side of herself, erased most of her English. All that remained of her English connection was her marriage to Bob Halliday.

She was now nearing the end of her SOE training. She had sailed through the language component, the self-defence and weapons, the cross-countries. Before she left Holmfirth, Bob and she had worked out a code for getting messages to each other, so she knew that Bob was back on operations.

She would have given anything to talk to Carole and to find out more. But today was her final passing-out assignment. This was to avoid her minder, Henri, and reach the railway station without being intercepted by him.

The day had begun with a session on the firing range. Then evasion exercises. She had been driven in an old Ford from the SOE safe house near Huntingdon, along the Cambridge road, where she was dropped at the turning to Longstanton. She had been given a small parcel, which she was to drop in the second wastepaper basket on the down platform at the railway station, avoiding any sightings en route, and taking no more than one and a half hours.

She had had to walk part of the way, chary of accepting lifts, lest it were one of Them, the observers. She had come three miles in the cab of a beet lorry, and another couple of miles on a tractor.

An hour and fifteen minutes had already been expended when she saw Carole and, not altogether surprisingly, the Wingco. The sight of them filled her with a mixture of longing and despair.

The last third of a mile from the marketplace to the station was likely to be the most difficult. Emmanuel Street was thick with shoppers, ideal for her cover, but also ideal for her observers'. She kept a sharp eye on reflections in the shop windows, and twice brought out her mirror and scanned the faces behind her.

The wide shallow station approach was, in contrast, a bleak no-man's land, over which cars and trucks moved at speed, but where pedestrians were easily identifiable. Worse still, she thought she could glimpse a distant figure like that of Henri, lurking by a telephone box at the station entrance.

A bus crawled by, making for the station. She almost boarded it, but decided it was too risky. Then, grinding its gears behind the bus, she saw a council swill lorry. She lifted her thumb, gazed up imploringly at the driver.

'I'm only going to the station, ducks,' the red-faced, reassuringly genuine-looking driver said reprovingly. 'It's only a hundred yards. Hardly worth you getting in. Can't you walk that bit?'

'My feet hurt.'

'OK, then, love.' He reached a hairy arm over and opened the passenger door. 'It's a bloody awful smell. And that seat isn't that clean. But if your feet hurt . . .'

She scrambled up. The smell was much worse inside, but the journey was mercifully short. Luckily, on account of his stinking load, the driver pulled into the coal yard at the side of the main station.

'Would you mind,' Gabby suggested to the driver, 'if I slid and got out of your door? There's a man over there I don't want to meet.'

'Oh, I get you! Pestering you, is he?'

'Yes. Has been all morning.'

'The bastard! Well, I'll give him such a clout if he comes over!' He raised his big grease-stained fist.

'He won't. He won't see me if I get out your side.'

She slid down and, screened by the truck, opened the side gate, raced over the footbridge as if dashing for a train, and dropped her package in the second waste bin with five minutes in hand.

Later that afternoon, she wrote her last letter to Bob on English soil before starting on the final leg of her journey.

Thirteen

Bob picked up her letter from his pigeonhole in the sergeants' mess before walking into the dining room for his pre-operational meal of bacon and eggs. He slipped her letter into the breast pocket of his battledress top to read when the briefing was over. As usual before an operation, the dining room was loud and lively with convivial chatter. A little forced perhaps, but conveying the right impression of KKL — Kouldn't Kare Less.

The target was briefly speculated upon; a few were making bets on it, ranging from Aachen, a short straightforward flight, to Regensburg in Bavaria, or worse still, Milan, a bloody long and dangerous haul; others were happily flirting with the girls serving the meal, persuading them to spoon an extra egg or two on their plates. Jumbo was on his third egg as Bob slid into the chair beside him. For this operation, Bob was joining Jumbo on Bladowski's crew, because Bladowski's wireless operator/air gunner had been rushed to hospital with a suspected appendicitis.

'How did Blad take it?' Bob asked Jumbo.

'Glad to have you aboard.'

Bladowski was well known for his obsession with killing Germans. According to the grapevine, his whole family had been slaughtered by them. Everyone on his crew had to be on the top line, 100 per cent. Bob looked down at his damaged hands.

'Are you sure?'

'Absolutely.' Jumbo buttered a large roll and plastered it with marmalade. Then, just in case the target was somewhere like Regensburg or, worse, Milan, he and Bob and most of the crews helped themselves to a handful of wakey-wakey

173

pills from the big bowls left invitingly on the serving tables, before, comfortably gorged, they left the mess for the briefing room.

The briefing room was a large wooden hut filled with benches. At the far end of the hut was a raised platform, and behind it a huge map of Europe densely packed with little black swastikas along the entire coast from Norway to Portugal. To one side was a blackboard on which was pinned another map, but this was concealed behind a red curtain, which, at the climax to the briefing, would be drawn aside to disclose the target. From the ceiling, beside a card printed in big black letters, YOUR ENEMY, hung models of German aircraft – mostly Messerschmitt 109s, twin-engined Messerschmitt 110 fighters and Junkers 88s. Jumbo ducked his head under them as he and Bob slid along the third bench.

Playfully, Bob reached up and flicked a Ju 88 into a spin. The string must have been weak, or he had flicked it harder than he had intended. The model fell to the ground, to the cheers of the rest of the crews. It seemed to be a good omen.

'That'll teach him to crack nuts in church.' Bob laughed, making the most of it.

Then he bent to pick up the model. Whoever had made it had left a sharp edge to the tail. It caught the side of Bob's thumb, drew blood. The skin of his hands was thin. They bled easily. Bob scrubbed his thumb irritably with his handkerchief. The model had turned into a bad omen.

He was still frowning when the first technical officers trooped on to the dais. A moment later the Wingco joined them and announced, 'Gentlemen, the station commander.'

Everyone jumped to their feet and stood to attention.

It was a moment that the group captain savoured. He marched in briskly, stamped up on to the platform, tossed his gold-acorned hat on to the table, smoothed his hair and smiled at the assembled crews.

'OK, gentlemen,' he called down to them breezily. 'Sit yourselves down. Light up!'

Outwardly, they relaxed, lounged back in their seats, lit their cigarettes and looked up at the red curtain as if they were in a cinema, the big film about to begin, and they were about to be pleasantly entertained. Inwardly, they waited, breaths held, for the moment when that curtain would be drawn back and their target disclosed.

When the moment came, the group captain pulled the cord, there was a quickly suppressed exclamation. Berlin. The big one. There it stood in its criss-crossing of red and white tapes, yellow turning markers, the ugly red and orange splodges of ack-ack positions. The exclamations were quickly stifled as the group captain's booming voice congratulated them on being chosen to bomb the Hun's heartland, and piously wished to God that he could come with them.

For Bob, it was certainly being thrown in at the deep end. But it meant the war was moving to its climax. There would be the big battle for the air over Germany. But soon it would be over. Gabby and he would be together. He patted his breast where Gabby's letter waited to be read, and began to take his usual meticulous notes. He had forgotten about the Ju model, forgotten to worry about his burned hands.

Half an hour later, the letter was still unread. Having pulled on his flying boots, collected his flying clobber and parachutes and rations, Bob went out early to the aircraft. They were still being bombed up. He stood in front of the Lancaster and watched the long articulated bomb train make a wide sweep and then stop neatly alongside their aircraft, J-Jig. From the cab of the tractor, a hand waved to him. Bob smiled wryly. Carole must have got into Tom Tordoff's bad books again.

Carole mouthed, 'Have you heard from Gabby?'

Bob nodded and put up his thumb.

Then the armourers were seizing the bomb load and carefully latching the target indicators, the high-capacity bombs, general-purpose bombs and incendiaries into their calculated slots. The bomb trolley moved off to the next aircraft.

Bob walked round the back of the dispersal huts and sat himself down on the grassy mound that covered one of the air-raid shelters, savouring his momentary isolation. A near full moon had risen behind the woodland to the south-east of the airfield, whitening the grass, its light almost strong enough to read by. He took out Gabby's letter, opened it and spread it on his knee. Then he brought out his torch and shielded its

175

narrow beam with his cap. Before he began to read, he had guessed it was her last before going on operations, but the confirmation still hit him hard.

He sat for several minutes, watching the moon clear the treetops, his hands clasped round his knees, choked with the fear that, caught as they were in these crushing forces, in these cataclysmic events, he was never going to see her again.

Determinedly, he dismissed that fear. He folded the letter, pressed it to his lips and slipped it back in his pocket. Then he jumped to his feet and went back to J-Jig to join the others.

His fears for Gabby and for what might lie ahead for both of them became only one fear. Fear of failure. Fear of letting his skipper and crewmates down.

When he had clambered on board J-Jig, stowed his parachute and was about to push the sealed escape kit down beside his radio console, he held the kit for a moment in his hand. It contained a silk map of Germany, dried fruit, counterfeit German money and a compass. He thought of the much more lethal escape kit that Gabby would shortly be given.

It was as if the powers that be had decreed that a secret agent's last glimpse of England should be a picture-book epitome of an English country house. The moon, the necessary moon for an SOE drop, was rising over the South Downs. It gleamed on stone-mullioned windows, whitened the grass of the lawns, made solid triangles of the yew trees, which flanked the entrance and sculpted the tall Elizabethan chimneys of a typical squire's residence.

The blackout was perfect. Not a chink of light showed from inside. Everything was peaceful. The lane to the manor had been a wandering branch of the main southbound road, and that had given way to a neglected private drive, now little better than a farm track.

A honeysuckle branch, denuded of leaves, trailed over the stone porch. An espalier rose webbed the wall either side. The door was of heavy, studded oak, a tiny spyhole just visible at eye level.

Henri, Gabby's minder, jerked the iron bell pull three times and then twice more. He turned to smile down at her reassuringly. They had never been allowed to get to know each other. All knowledge was dangerous. She was just another Joe he was delivering.

The door was opened quietly by a young woman who drew them quickly inside, behind the blackout curtain. She was hand-picked, Gabby thought, to blend perfectly with her surroundings – light-brown wavy hair framing a smiling untroubled face, a young face, apart from the shrewd bespectacled eyes. She wore a well-cut skirt, blue twinset and a string of pearls. Nothing could be more normal, more innocent, more fitting. She spread her arms wide in welcome. 'Henri! How good to see you again. And Gabby!' She leaned forward and kissed Gabby's cheek. 'Welcome, Gabby. I'm Lisa. You must be tired.'

'Not really. But very glad to be here.'

'Well, come along in.' She led them across the stone-flagged hall, their footsteps echoing hollowly. A rich smell of cooking wafted in from the kitchen. It mingled with the scent of dried lavender and pot-pourri in large bowls on the oak chest. From the garden came the voices of children, still playing in the moonlit garden. A man's voice, presumably Lisa's husband, announced, 'Dinner will be in half an hour.'

It was like stepping into a play. A play of comfortable middle-class normality far away from the war, in which the family were the repertory actors, she the visiting star for the night. The repertory actors would perform again, night after night. A guest like her would be welcomed. Dinner would be served. A comfortable night or maybe more, depending on the weather and the moon, after which the guest would depart. A new guest would arrive, and the same lines would be spoken.

'I'll show you to your room, Gabby, and you can freshen up.' Lisa opened the door to a small room in the eaves. Beneath the low, raftered ceiling was a comfortable-looking bed with big pillows and a patchwork quilt, a washstand with a flowered china ewer, an elderly armchair and a large full-length mirror. Like the moon, the mirror was of paramount importance.

'The bathroom's next door. The water's hot. Have a bath if you wish. We usually congregate in the bar downstairs for

177

a noggin before dinner. We've some bods who arrived back last night from France. They'll be pleased to see you.'

At the door, she paused. 'After dinner, you should be able to get a little sleep. I'll wake you. Ralph, my husband, will drive you to the airfield.'

'Do you know when?'

'O-one-hundred hours. Just time to eat, sleep an hour or so, and check yourself over.'

Checking herself over meant saying goodbye to her present self, examining her body, her clothes, everything she carried, for any association with Britain and her past life.

Before she went along to explore the bathroom, she opened her bag and took out Bob's letters, read them over again, then tore them in pieces, preserving until last the tiny fragment of the last letter, in which he had written in his neat hand, *Remember, I love you.* That she put on her tongue and swallowed.

Sentimental, but that was what she had been taught to do with paper that mattered. She tried to laugh at herself but failed. Then she crept quietly down the corridor to the bathroom.

In the enormous old-fashioned iron bath that stood on four claw feet in the centre of the room, she used her English soap for the last time. She lay in the warm water, scrutinizing her own body suspiciously, as if it were a partner she couldn't trust. How, they had all been asked, would their bodies stand up to Gestapo torture? Her carefully manicured nails, for instance, being torn out by the roots? Her head held underwater till she was almost drowned? Constant bright light? Constant beatings? The electric wand applied to her genitals? Rape? How would she stand up? As always, the answer was that she didn't know.

She stepped over the side and towelled herself dry. Back in the bedroom, she again examined every garment before she put it on. Nothing to identify their origin, or the material. No labels, not even the trace of one having been there.

Before going downstairs to join the others, she looked at herself in the long mirror. Her appearance was not improved. At training school, her hair had been cut to a style halfway between a bob and a shingle. Very French. Her eyebrows had been plucked to fine lines. She had lost weight. Her face looked more gaunt. Greta Garbo without the glamour. She was not allowed to use English lipstick any more because the shades were different from the French, so, apart from her dark eyes, her face was colourless.

Yet, despite her appearance, the Frenchmen greeted her warmly and gallantly. Ralph, Lisa's husband, tall and tweedy and pipe-smoking, the quintessential squire and perfect partner for Lisa, introduced himself as their conducting officer as well as host.

At dinner, a special feast of roast Sussex chicken and garden vegetables, Gabby sat between two Frenchmen, returning Joes, whom Ralph had picked up from Tangmere in the early hours. They plied her with the wine they had brought in, and suddenly one of them rushed upstairs, came down and presented her with three stems of lily of the valley, picked before dawn in Provence.

By an unwritten code, no one discussed their work. The talk was of anecdotes before the war, their explorations of the Sussex countryside on a previous stay, the kindness of their hostess.

At ten o'clock, at the same time as PO Bladowski opened the throttles on J-Jig and Bob Halliday checked the calibration of his guns, Lisa suggested Gabby should snatch an hour or so's rest.

'But before you sleep –' Lisa handed Gabby a scrap of paper, on which was scrawled a poem – 'memorize this.'

> The life that I have
> Is all that I have,
> And the life that I have is yours.
> The love that I have
> Of the life that I have
> Is yours, and yours, and yours.
> A sleep I shall have,
> A rest I shall have,
> Yet death will be but a pause,
> For the peace of my years
> In the long green grass
> Will be yours, and yours, and yours.

179

The words chimed eerily with Gabby's own feelings, but she knew they were no sentimental outpourings, but carefully crafted to embody her own executive agent's code system. She lay on her bed awake, repeating the lines aloud until Lisa called her.

'This is it,' Gabby said, more to herself than Lisa. She swung her legs over the side of the bed, and opened the black-out curtains. The sky was cold and clear. A full moon rode free of any cloud above the treetops. For a moment, she shivered, her teeth chattered uncontrollably. Then she dressed and descended to the sitting room for the final search. Her pockets were turned out again, lest a stray bus ticket or a coin or a handkerchief had been left in them.

She was allowed to keep the lilies of the valley, because they were French. She slipped them through the buttonhole of her black jacket. Then Ralph handed her a false French identity card and ration card. From now on, she was Marie Leclerc, a shop assistant. He also gave her a wallet of French money, a fountain pen which squirted tear gas, and a wooden cosh that could be concealed in the sleeve of her jacket.

He put a small Smith and Wesson into her hand, murmuring, 'I know you can use it.' A smiling reference to her high performance at target practice. She clenched her fingers over it. The feel was comforting and empowering. As the weapons instructor had drummed into them, 'If there is no way out, at least take one of them with you.'

Gabby also accepted the French cigarettes, although she rarely smoked, some French matches, a miniature compass, magnifying glass, binoculars, French maps painted on gossamer-fine silk, a toothbrush and some gritty-looking French soap.

Lisa watched her pack away the soap with a sympathetic smile. It was she who gave Gabby the final piece of equipment.

In the kindly tone of a considerate hostess, she inquired if Gabby would like some cyanide, and, when Gabby nodded, added, 'Just slip off your jacket.'

Then out came her workbasket. A needle was threaded. It was so disconcertingly ordinary and homely it carried Gabby back to her schooldays, her mother hastily mending a torn school skirt, or, not so long ago, Edith stitching the gusset into Bunty's dress. Only now, into each of the cuffs of Gabby's jacket was being stitched the tiny phial of cyanide for when the Nazi torture became utterly unbearable and even the bravest might betray their comrades.

Twenty minutes later, as J-Jig shuddered and bounced in the hot smoking cloud of ack-ack over the target, Gabby was sitting in the front seat of Ralph's old Lagonda being driven over the last curve of the moonlit downs. The Lagonda's shadow flicked beside them, as they dropped down to the flood plain of the Arun. Ahead was the thin silver horizon of the Channel, all that separated them from Occupied Europe.

From behind Gabby, Henri leaned over eagerly, his hand resting on her shoulder. She found it reassuring. He had completed a spell with SOE in the sector toward which they were heading. He knew its terrors, its swift arrests, its heavy casualties, its torture, and yet he couldn't wait to get back. Her own excitement, her emotion at her return to France, was tempered by self-doubt, by the awful question she kept asking herself, how would she measure up?

Ahead now lay the main road to Chichester and the west. A few Army lorries were grinding along, but at this hour, the traffic was light. To the right, the square tower of Boxgrove Priory loomed solid and somehow indestructible against the paler sky; a few minutes later, the airfield materialized, the wire fence holding in tall angular hangars, the box of flying control, the water tower, the lines of huts.

Ralph didn't approach the main entrance. He continued on past the gate and the guardroom, and headed down a village street, past a pub, a village store, a telephone box, and slid the car to a halt outside a long high hedge.

Their arrival must have been observed. Tall gates of slatted wood, barely visible in the hedge, swung silently open. Ralph turned the car in. The tyres crunched over a short gravel drive and stopped at the back door of a red-brick, ivy-hung cottage. Ralph switched off the engine, and waved to Gabby and Henri to get out.

The door was opened by a burly RAF sergeant whom Ralph

addressed as Bill. He led them into a warm, oak-beamed kitchen and waved them to two chairs by the blazing fire. To reach them, they had to squeeze past a metal table, laden with files, which acted as an unobtrusive barrier. The kitchen was a disconcerting mixture of Sussex countryside comfort and secret war. It seemed to act as a guardroom. There were R/T sets against the walls; an airman sat in front of a W/T set, his back to them. There were several telephones, one the special top-secret red scrambler telephone. A couple of packed parachutes lay on the farmhouse table in the centre of the room.

Bill put a mug of coffee in their hands, invited them to sign the lines book which lay beside the parachutes. There were no introductions, no conversation. As soon as they had drained their mugs, Ralph indicated they should be on their way.

As they left, the young airman at the wireless set began tapping out a short message to be sent out on the World Broadcast of the BBC.

Gabby paused to listen to the sequence of dots and dashes. '*Madame a acheté deux chapeaux.*'

Their reception committee in France would be listening in to that BBC broadcast, receiving the message that two Joes were now on their way.

Leaving the cottage, Ralph turned right, and drove a little further along the road. The village almost immediately petered out, but the airfield fence was still visible on their left. In it, they saw a narrow back entrance that gave on to the perimeter track. Nothing was visible beyond the perimeter track but large flat fields of newly turned loamy earth. Ralph turned in the narrow entrance and drove about fifty yards.

Out of the moonlight, alone on a grassy dispersal like some giant man-made daddy long legs, solidified the gawky shape of a Lysander. Its fuselage was painted matt black, which gave it a more sinister air, and a large torpedo-shaped extra fuel tank was slung under its wing.

'Here we are!' Ralph called cheerfully. 'Your carriage, ma'am!' He leaned over to open the door for her. 'Everyone in the village thinks the Lizzie is for air-sea rescue. We try to keep them thinking that!'

As Gabby stepped out of the car, she could smell the sea

and the dew-soaked spongy turf. The smells mingled with the scent of the lily of the valley in her buttonhole. There was near silence except for the hum of vehicles on the main road, the screech of metal on metal from the repair hangar, and the tinkle of drain water into the dyke between the fields and the perimeter.

Then there came the clatter of feet on metal. Down the ladder on the port side of the Lysander swung a figure already goggled and helmeted, wiping his hands on a greasy rag. Their Lysander pilot.

'Two more Joes for you!' Ralph told the pilot without introducing them.

They all shook hands. Ralph confirmed to the pilot that the call letter for the landing was G. Then he turned to Gabby, wished her Godspeed, and bent down to kiss her cheek.

She pulled the lilies from her buttonhole, held them to her lips, then handed them to Ralph, asking if he would send them to Sergeant Bob Halliday at Holmfirth. Unsurprised, clearly used to such last-minute requests, Ralph nodded and put up his thumb. Then he clapped Henri on the shoulder and watched Gabby and Henri clamber into the aircraft.

Their meagre luggage was stowed under the pilot's wooden hinged seat. They were shown how to clip the observer-type parachutes on to their harness. Then the roof was slid shut. The pilot primed and started the engine, tested the controls, the brake pressure, then opened her up to cruising altitude and requested take-off clearance. The moment had come.

Out of the window, Gabby watched Ralph walk on to the grass clear of the slipstream. He stood, holding himself very erect, as if making his body form a salute as the pilot turned the Lysander on to the long flarepath. He was still there as the pilot eased the throttle fully open and took off.

They flew low. Almost at once they were over the seaside town of Bognor, with its long spindly pier. Then town and pier vanished, the last of England fell away and there was nothing below their wheels but the deceptively smooth waves of the Channel.

Crouching in the cockpit, the three of them kept their eyes skinned for enemy aircraft.

A few minutes out, the pilot requested a scan from Blackgang radar station, named after the most bloodthirsty gang of smugglers in Sussex history.

Beyond their starboard wing tip, two fast black shadows crossed a shaft of moonlight, Messerschmitts heading north, thankfully away from them. Below, a heavily laden merchant ship was creeping up from the Western Approaches.

The outside temperature had dropped. Along the leading edges of the wings, sparkling in the moonlight, a rime of ice crystals had formed, adding to the aircraft's weight, decreasing its manoeuvrability. The pilot glanced out, frowning. For a craven moment, Gabby longed for the pilot to abort, and take them back to England.

Then, ahead, a darker line of grey. Searchlights to port, a few orange splodges of ack-ack fire. The pilot descended lower still, to little more than cliff-top height, to avoid the Kammhuber radar. The Lysander's wheels seemed to brush the hedges.

They were over France. Henri grasped Gabby's shoulder as if to share her excitement. But she felt nothing except a cold apprehension. Her teeth chattered. She rubbed her hands, pretending it was just the cold.

'Watch out now for high-tension cables,' the pilot told them. 'Some are marked, but some aren't.'

He spread out his carefully prepared strips of map, and studied them. The other two screwed their heads round, trying to map read over his shoulder, and at the same time watch the grey ground whizzing below them, searching desperately for landmarks.

'The Loire,' Gabby called out, as she spied a silver curve of river. But the sight of it failed to lift her spirits.

According to the pilot's briefing, twenty-eight miles inland from the coast, they should see a small hamlet round a church with a tall, thin spire. Beyond the church, there should be a large cattle farm with outbuildings that formed a courtyard. To the east of it, a line of poplars, and then, shielded between farm and poplars, a spinney with a large rectangular field beyond. The drop field.

There was the hamlet, surely? The church, the farm, the poplars.

The pilot went round to take a better look. They all stared down, their eyes watering with the effort, their hearts hammering.

Satisfied, the pilot fired off the recognition letter of the day, G.

Immediately below the Lysander's starboard wing tip, a white light bloomed briefly. The pilot flashed in return.

Below them now, three white lights formed themselves into the inverted L designating the field, and the waiting reception committee.

'OK. All set? Down we go!'

There was no time for a circuit. No time for more checks. The pilot pushed the throttle forward. They all gritted their teeth, and prayed that it wasn't a trap. All the same, they tensed their muscles, prepared themselves for the rattle of machine guns, strained their ears for German voices.

But there was nothing as the Lysander's wheels bumped over the uneven grass, except the backfiring of her engine. The Lysander had barely come to a halt before steps sounded on the ladder, and the door was dragged open.

A broad-shouldered man in a black hooded cape helped Gabby and then Henri to scramble out. Bright eyes in a red farmer's face inspected her. Suddenly strong arms embraced her. The man smelled reassuringly of the night air and the farmyard.

Two shadowy figures emerged from the spinney, ran silently past them and climbed aboard the Lysander in their places. Somewhere an owl hooted. A cold wind rustled the dry twigs in the spinney. Far away a car accelerated along an invisible road.

Henri addressed the red-faced man as Armand. He led them to the far edge of the field, where a van was parked in the shelter of the spinney. A bespectacled dark-haired young man in his early twenties stood beside the van, stamping his feet with the cold, impatient to be off.

By the time they were settled in the van, and the young man introduced as Guillaume, the Lysander had taken off again. They caught a last glimpse of it hedge-hopping towards the coast, as they began their half-hour journey to their safe house.

*   *   *

185

The safe house was a small isolated pig farm halfway up a shallow hill. They travelled by narrow country lanes, turned along the main highway only for three miles or so, left it to cross an iron bridge over a railway line. The moonlight gleamed on its tracks; there was a signal box downline from the bridge, the red glow of a signal, random pinpricks of unguarded light. They passed few vehicles – a couple of old lorries, a bicycle, what looked like a German staff car with two motorcycle outriders.

From the meagre conversation in the van, Gabby gathered that Henri was to leave the next day by train to join another group, that Armand was her group leader, Guillaume his lieutenant; and, ominously, that their previous radio operator had been arrested, fortunately miles away and, unlike the radio operator of a neighbouring cell, not while on duty.

Two or three miles beyond the railway track, they turned up a pot-holed access road, which climbed the shallow hill to their safe house. It stood, a ragged scatter of low buildings with no other habitation in sight.

The kitchen was large but not furnished for comfort. It smelled of a mixture of pig food and apples and herbs hanging from the rafters. Armand's wife, Hélène, a silent, tight-lipped lady with her hair sternly scraped up into a bun, was busy by the black iron stove. Without speaking, she doled out a bowl of thick soup to each of them, and handed round a basket of black bread. Guillaume lifted a jug in the centre of the table and filled their glasses with red wine, dark and delicious. At the same time he inspected Gabby like an elderly schoolmaster over the top of his spectacles.

When Hélène showed Gabby to her room, she still didn't speak. Gabby tried addressing her in French, but as if forever schooled into silence, she simply shook her head.

Still in silence, she showed Gabby up the two flights of steep and narrow stairs to her room in the attic.

Gabby drew back the curtains and looked out at the hillside, and tried, as she had been taught, to figure out her means of escape should the Gestapo come. From her small window, high in the eaves, to the ground was a precipitous drop. There was some cover as far as the outbuildings. But beyond that, all the way down the hillside, just a few wind-bitten shrubs.

The sky was paling into first light. She could see across the valley to the railway track. She heard the distant sound of an approaching train. There must be a tunnel just further up the line, for the train suddenly burst out in a huge rattle of wheels and a great gust of steam. It was pulling a dozen or so slatted cattle trucks.

The signal close to the bridge was at red. The train screeched to a graunching halt, let out a huge hissing cloud of steam. And as the steam drifted away, Gabby saw a chilling sight. Behind the slatted sides of the trucks, heads moved; not the heads of cattle, but human heads. Human fingers grasped the slats, human faces peered, thin human arms thrust out imploringly, while, above the hissing of the steam, the cold morning air was pierced with the keening sound of human despair.

Gabby stared transfixed. She knew the Nazis had embarked on a terrible programme of so-called racial purification. The Einsatzgruppen in Poland and then in France and Holland had begun a bloodbath, slaughtering men, women and children, transporting Jews, Poles, Gypsies, dissident French and Dutch to death camps deep in Germany. What Goebbels called 'the house-cleaning of Jews, the intelligentsia and the clergy'. Gabby had read some of the secret information. But seeing it . . .

She covered her mouth with her hand to stop herself shrieking out!

The red signal changed to green. The death train whistled, blew steam, the pistons clanked and turned. The imploring arms were swept away behind a white hissing cloud, but still Gabby stared helplessly. When she finally clambered into the big feather-pillowed bed, and fell into an exhausted sleep, the rat-a-tat-tat of the train, the arms, the dreadful keening sound haunted her dreams.

But she awoke a few hours later to sunlight through the crack in the curtains, her resolve strengthened. She repeated to herself the lines of her transmission code, no longer afraid, knowing she was not helpless.

Across the Channel, a more clouded dawn had broken over RAF Holmfirth.

Bladowski and his crew were drinking rum in operations and being debriefed by Olive Spinks. Above their heads the same models floated, turning harmlessly in one of the many cold draughts.

Bob looked up at them wryly. The Junkers 88 was rethreaded and back in place. He wondered if it was still smeared with his blood. He glanced down at his thumb. It seemed a long time since last night.

Bladowski was in a triumphant, expansive mood. He waved his tin mug towards the model and for the second time told the Intelligence officer that not only had they dropped their bombs on the target, but also that Bob had bagged a Junkers Ju 88R, as their photos would show.

Olive turned her sharp eyes to Bob.

'I reckon I got him,' Bob, always strictly accurate, said soberly. 'I saw him dive. One engine was on fire. He was trailing smoke. I didn't actually see him go in.'

He looked down at his hands again. When the Junkers 88 fastened on the Lancaster's tail, they had just begun their bomb run. Jumbo was lying in the bomb bay, the bomb tit in his hand. Bob had been manning the gun in the rear turret. The great ugly black shape of the Junkers, spitting fire, seemed about to burst through the perspex of the turret.

He hadn't been afraid. Just frightened of failing. Frightened his eye had lost its judgement, that his withered fingers would be clumsy. Since his crash and the fire, and those months of skin grafting, he had always mistrusted his hands.

This was his first kill since rejoining the squadron. Yet he didn't feel good about it. Just glad he hadn't let down the rest of the crew.

'You got him all right,' Bladowski said. 'Otherwise we wouldn't be here. Jumbo takes so long pressing the tit!'

Then, still in a high good mood, he put his arm round a shoulder of each of them, and, walking them towards the door, executed a little dance and sang 'Jeszcze Polska nie zginela', 'Poland still lives'.

But at least he didn't say, last night we killed Germans.

As they were leaving, the Wingco and his crew came in for

debriefing. He pressed Bob's shoulder, and murmured, 'Well done!'

Emerging into the intermittent sunlight, Bob decided not to go back to the mess with the others on the waiting transport. Instead he walked up the steps to flying control.

Beaky was just taking over the morning shift. He waved him to a chair beside the stove. Jan poured him a mug of coffee. Then Beaky handed him a message flimsy.

'Came in about ten minutes ago,' Beaky said, smiling.

The message was from Gabby. It consisted of only three letters and two numbers. But it told him she had arrived safely without incident and was already transmitting. He glanced across at Beaky.

'Good news?' Beaky asked him.

'I'm not sure.'

But, in the relief after his fight with the Junkers, he allowed himself to hope that things might yet work out.

And, as an added bonus to a day that had at least begun hopefully, a signal came in that the squadron was stood down for thirty-six hours.

'Thirty-six hours stand-down!' Chiefie Tordoff exclaimed as Carole reported for duty at noon. 'Those Brylcreems get spoiled rotten!'

'You don't mean that!'

'Mebbe I do and mebbe I don't.' Chiefie scowled at the papers he was shuffling on his desk and then turned to stare at her again. 'You look in need of a stand-down, canny lass.'

'It's always tiring on the bomb trolley.'

'Is it now!'

'Yes.'

'We all have to do it, you know. Duty is duty.' He frowned at her again. 'At least if they're stood down we won't have many 658s this evening, will we, pet?'

'Thank goodness!'

'Tired?'

She nodded.

'Still worrying about the Brylcreems?'

'No.' The Wingco had returned safely. That was enough

189

for today. But she still had Bunty and her problem. 'Just tired.'

Chiefie eyed her critically. 'Then go back to your billet, girl! Go to bed! And don't come back till this time tomorrow! You make me feel tired just looking at you!'

Thankfully, she went back to number five married quarter and did exactly as Chiefie had told her. She must have slept for a solid fifteen hours. She was vaguely aware that Edith had, at some point, brought her in a mug of tea and a jam butty, for a cold mug and a soggy sandwich were by her bed when she woke.

The billet was empty. She dressed and stacked her bedclothes into the liquorice-all-sort shape which the RAF demanded; she walked to the Sally Ann, drank a cup of coffee and bought two jam doughnuts in a bag, the most the girl behind the counter would let her buy, to take to Bunty.

The morning was breezy but fine; small clouds hurrying before a cool east wind, but there was a reassuring scent of spring in the air and, on the most spindly of hedges, little blobs of green. Keeping a sharp lookout for Flight Sergeant Grimble and any admin corporals, who would certainly stop her and demand to know why, if she was not on duty, she had not been on morning parade, Carole set off towards the guardroom. Because of the stand-down, the station was quieter than usual; there was very little road traffic and not an aircraft in the circuit. She kept looking over her shoulder in the hope that she might see the Wingco's Humber sweeping by. But the only vehicle that passed her was a Queen Mary grinding in with a section of Lancaster fuselage.

At the guardroom, she booked out and headed for Holmfirth village and the Burfords' cottage.

Fourteen

Bunty was sitting on a stool at the back of the cottage peeling potatoes for Mrs Burford, who had gone to the other side of Holmfirth to see her sister. Bunty was wearing a voluminous smock. She looked heavily pregnant now and disconsolate. But she cheered a little at the sight of the doughnuts, and ate them wolfishly.

As Carole sat herself down on the step beside her, Bunty told her that the honeymoon period with the Burfords was over. Mr Burford had shown himself to be an MTF-er, the initials standing for Must Touch Flesh, and he found Bunty's generous figure irresistible. Although he was an ugly little chap, he was used to getting his own way with the house-wives, because he was the coal man and fuel was scarce and Lincolnshire was cold. 'He's always telling us what a woman'll do for a bag of coal. And he reckons I'm fair game. No better than I ought to be. Because of . . .' She stroked the now well-developed bump.

Carole murmured indignantly and sympathetically.

'I sometimes promise myself – if he puts his dirty hands on me just once more, I'll kill him!'

To add to that problem, Mrs Burford had noticed her husband creeping up on Bunty, patting her bottom, peering down her blouse, trying to touch her up, and from the stray remarks Mrs Burford kept making, she wanted Bunty gone.

'Where would you go?'

'I dunno.'

'You haven't heard from your mum, I suppose?'

'No. Nor will I.'

Carole wanted to ask Bunty if she had heard from Chris's parents, but she couldn't be certain the Wingco had written

191

to them. He'd probably forgotten all about Bunty and his promise, and who could blame him?

'There's the home, the Church of England home, the one near Lincoln, the one Ma'am mentioned.'

'I know there is. I've thought a lot about it. But I don't want to go there.'

'I know you don't. But just for a while. You'd be near. There'd be no Mr Burford to bother you, Edith and I could come and see you. We can always get lifts into Lincoln. And Chris could still find you there when he gets back.'

'If he gets back.'

Carole said nothing. Until now Bunty had always been so full of hope. It was never if but when.

'Because I don't reckon now,' Bunty said loudly and clearly and with bitter conviction, 'that he will come back. Ever!'

In a way, though the words fell out of her mouth like bricks, she felt better for saying them. Her hope had finally died. It was a relief to say so loud and clear.

Mr Hardcastle, the undertaker, had a favourite text for the bereaved family of any long-suffering corpse who had endured periods of hope followed by disappointment and death. 'Hope deferred maketh the heart sick.'

Bunty could say amen to that. Hope had been deferred too long. Her heart was truly sick. She had passed through the time of wanting to get rid of the baby. Now she wanted to be brave and bring up Chris's baby, but she didn't know how. On that last day when she had signed out at the officers' mess, she had gone into the dining room and looked down at those two innocent-looking bowls of pills, one bowl of wakey-wakeys and the other of sleepy-sleepy pills, and she had been sorely tempted to take a handful of the sleepies, and swallow the lot.

But she wouldn't, of course. She wouldn't let down a hero like Chris. She would look after his son, for she was sure it would be a son. But how to support the two of them? How to find a place to live? How to get a job with your only reference stating that you'd been kicked out of the WAAF?

'At least,' Carole was suggesting, 'we could thumb a lift into Lincoln and have a look at it.'

'Oh, I dunno. D'you mean now?'

'Why not? It'd be somewhere to go. After we'd looked at the home, we could get a cuppa somewhere or look at the shops. I don't have to go on duty till five. It's better than waiting here for Mr Burford to pop back home and catch you on your own.'

'Anything's better than that!' Bunty agreed, and for the first time smiled wanly.

'Well, come on then!'

One of the great advantages of the Burford cottage was that it was right on the main road. And one of the advantages of the squadron being stood down was that a number of Holmfirth's personnel were taking a day off in Lincoln. Several of the boys owned their own bangers, decrepit cars which they had bought for a few pounds and done up themselves.

But, as it happened, the first vehicle along the road was the Queen Mary which had passed Carole on her way to the cottage. Now empty, its fuselage section safely delivered, it was on its return journey to the Derby maintenance unit.

The driver pulled up promptly and shouted to them to hop into the back. It was uncomfortable but at least it got them there. The driver dropped them on the main road round Lincoln about a quarter of a mile from the cathedral.

The Church of England moral welfare home was a further mile's walk away. It was a big Victorian stone house set behind a high privet hedge. A large painted board at the double iron gates proclaimed its purpose, *For Fallen Women*. Both girls averted their eyes from the sign, peering up at the dark stone façade nervously, and then cautiously pushing open the wrought-iron gates. They crunched up a short gravel drive to a flight of three stone steps leading up to a brown front door. There was a long wrought-iron bell pull beside it, with a notice that said, *Pull and wait. Do not enter without permission.*

'Don't let's,' Bunty said. 'I don't want to go in. It looks awful. I'd rather go back to the Burfords.'

'At least try.' Carole stretched out her hand and pulled the bell. The sound echoed emptily. Then the echoing peals died away, to be replaced by approaching footsteps, heavily shod feet on a flagged floor. The footsteps stopped. A key turned.

The door was cautiously swung back by a girl with a white cap on scraped-back hair and a moist red nose. She wore a long starched white pinafore, which almost reached to her bare ankles and her clogs.

'Yes?' she asked sharply and unwelcomingly, wiping her nose with the back of her hand.

'May we see Matron?' Carole asked.

'I dunno. Have you got an appointment?'

'No. But we really would like to see her.'

The girl's wary glance took in Bunty's figure and she appeared to relent. 'I'll go and ask her. Stay there. I'll be back.'

With that she shut the door firmly. They stared at the brown door, listening to her footsteps fading into some echoing recesses of the house, and then, minutes later, to them returning.

Once again the door was opened narrowly. 'Matron says she'll spare you five minutes. You can come in. Wipe your feet.'

She opened the door just wide enough for them to step inside. Then she locked the door again. The hall was only dimly lit by a single stained-glass window depicting a ghostly pale Christ on a black cross before a storm-clouded sky.

The girl waited till they had wiped their feet on the rectangle of doormat, the only piece of covering on the flagstones of the hall.

'Matron says she'll see you in the dining room,' the girl said, clumping ahead of them into a large room with a lofty corniced ceiling, furnished with a long, well-scrubbed wooden table and chairs, ten each side. As with the hall, this room was dominated by the crucifixion, this time a huge dark painting above the marble fireplace, showing another thunderous sky behind Christ's waxy body – but with some colour on this one: on his thorn-crowned forehead, on his face, on his body, on his arms and legs and feet, shiny blobs of his blood like Very lights on cloud.

There were no other pictures. But at least this room had two sizeable windows. Visible through them was a back yard and a long outhouse built at right angles to the house, from which gushed great clouds of steam, droplets of which were condensing on the windows and running down like rain.

'The laundry,' the girl said, watching Carole and Bunty staring at it. 'That's where we gotta work all day. We all get stinking colds. Up to our ankles in water. That's why we have to wear these.' She stamped her clogs.

'Why is there so much washing?' Bunty asked.

'The home takes in laundry to keep this place going. We've all gotta work at doing it. Till we have our kids and for two months after.'

'What's the food like?'

'Horrible, and not much of it. Bread and a bit of dripping mostly, or—' She shut up suddenly, and covered her mouth with her hand as the formidable figure of Matron appeared.

Five minutes later, Bunty and Carole were outside and hurrying away into the town. Each was clutching a tract describing the work of the home and warning of the even deeper degradation into which fallen women could fall.

'You can't go there,' Carole said. 'It's awful. It's a prison.'

Bunty puffed breathlessly beside her, too full of despair to do more than sigh.

'Matron's as bad as Flight Sergeant Grimble. Bed by nine. No talking after lights out. No leaving the home without permission.'

'So where could I go?' Bunty wailed.

The question was unanswerable.

'I don't know. But we'll talk about it. There's a tea shop in the High Street.'

The tea shop in the High Street was closed, but there was a little notice to say that the British Restaurant further down was now open, and refreshments were being served at budget prices.

They found it in some sort of church hall. It was faintly warmed by oil stoves. A trestle table was laid out with plates of hefty sandwiches and solid scones and cake, some of which, however, had the indulgence of dribbles of white icing. There was a big urn of tea, and a cash register at the end of the table, where a very elderly man was taking the money.

Despair had made them both hungry. A plate loaded with

sandwiches, scones with margarine and a semi-iced cake cost less than a shilling. They sat at a folding table near one of the oil stoves, chewed their food and sought inspiration.

It eluded them.

'At least we know what to do with these.' Carole picked up her tract, tore it across twice and dropped the pieces in the large white ashtray. She reached over to do the same with Bunty's, but Bunty put her plump hand over it. Having today faced up to the fact that Chris was dead, she must now face up to the fact that the home for fallen women might be her lot.

Now their roles were reversed. 'You can't go there,' Carole said.

'I might have to.' Bunty pushed back her chair. 'Anyway, don't let's talk about it any more. It's been nice to get out. But it's time you got back or you'll have Chiefie after you.'

'I suppose so.' Carole got reluctantly to her feet, put on her cap and slung her respirator. 'But we'll still keep thinking. You never know, something will turn up.'

They said the same as they stood at the crossroads on the edge of Lincoln with their thumbs up, waiting for a vehicle heading towards Holmfirth. A Humber preferably, Carole was thinking, with the Wingco at the wheel. Then she would ask him if he had ever got around to writing to Chris's mother about Bunty, but she suspected he hadn't. He would have been too busy, too preoccupied with his squadron. She was learning the lesson that men rarely kept their promises or meant what they said, and that aircrew were faithful only to each other. The vehicle that finally stopped for them was a petrol bowser, itself bound for RAF Holmfirth to top up their hundred-octane tanks.

Bunty and Carole both squashed into the cab beside the driver. He told them the roads were chock-a-block with Army vehicles, tanks, gun carriages, armoured cars, you name it, they were all out there clogging up the main roads. He entertained them with predictions about the Second Front, where it would open and when, told them he regularly listened to Lord Haw-Haw's broadcasts – 'Jairmany calling!' – and gave them a fair imitation of the renegade Englishman's oily voice. He dropped Bunty at the gate of the Burford cottage.

As the bowser continued up to the camp, Bunty stood for a moment on the doorstep, cheerfully waving them away.

She felt anything but cheerful. When she went inside, Mrs Burford was chopping some windfall apples her sister had given her. She eyed Bunty frostily, brought the knife down more vigorously on the chopping board, and told Bunty sharply that Mr Burford and she would like a word with Bunty as soon as he'd had his tea.

Shortly after she had climbed upstairs to her room, Bunty heard the coal lorry draw up outside, and then Mr Burford stamping into the kitchen; Mrs Burford calling that he hadn't wiped his feet properly, followed by the sound of raised voices and the rattling of kitchen utensils.

Bunty tried to concentrate on the form she had to fill in for admission to the fallen women's home, but somehow she couldn't get her mind round it. About twenty minutes later, she heard another vehicle draw up outside the gate. After a few minutes, the front doorbell rang.

Bunty tiptoed on to the little landing and peered over the rail. She saw Mrs Burford emerge from the kitchen, hasten to open the door, wiping her hands on her apron as she went.

The door opened unwillingly.

'Good afternoon, madam,' Mrs Burford said cautiously in a very unnatural voice.

Then whoever stood on the doorstep must have said something, her name perhaps, which Bunty couldn't catch.

'You'd best come in, I suppose,' Mrs Burford murmured in a voice that became stranger and more unlike her by the second – very subdued, grovelling almost, and yet resentful. She opened the door a little wider and took a pace back.

Into Bunty's vision miraculously stepped the lady from the photograph in Chris's room. Bunty couldn't believe her eyes. She thought she must be going bananas. And when the lady spoke, her words were even more miraculous.

'May I see Bunty please?' the lady asked in her beautiful voice. 'I have come to take my daughter home.'

Fifteen

Through the grimy window of the MT section, Chiefie Tordoff watched Carole dismount from the cab of the petrol bowser. He affected a cynical expression.

'Jeezus!' he exclaimed, as soon as she came through the doorway. 'Can't trust you out of my sight!' He sighed heavily. 'Still, I suppose tanker blokes are better than Brylcreems.'

'He was married with three kids.'

'When has that ever stopped a WAAF?'

'And bald.'

Chiefie ran his hand through his shock of black hair and said, 'You're right! Forget him.'

Carole hung up her cap and respirator and waved to the two drivers, Kevin and Fenella, warming themselves by the stove. Chiefie became immersed in scrutinizing the duty blackboard, tossing the chalk in his hand, frowning. Everyone seemed restless, impatient for the stand-down to be over. Maybe that feeling was replicated all over Britain; everyone wanting that vital step to be taken which would bring the end of hostilities, and, at the same time, dreading that step. But Carole was aware of another deeper, more personal feeling, that something cataclysmic, something life-changing was about to happen. Not something to do with the war or the raids or the Allied invasion, something personal to her that would for ever change her life.

It was all imagination of course. Everything was much as usual. Fenella was sloshing tea from the tin pot into a chipped mug. Kevin had the *Daily Mirror* spread out and was goggling at the antics of the near-nude Jane.

Chiefie was cheerfully calling over his shoulder to Kevin, 'Want to bet they'll put on an op as soon as the stand-down finishes?'

'I bet they will.'

'And you'd be right, laddie!'

'Wanna bet where to, Chiefie?'

'I'll have two bob on Dortmund, laddie.'

'I fancy the big one, Berlin.'

'Two bob?'

'Two bob it is.'

'You'll lose, kid.'

In the end, they both lost. When the op was laid down for next day, the target was Nuremberg. Chiefie reckoned it was certainly part of the softening-up for the invasion, and who wanted to bet on the exact date? Nobody did.

For Carole, that day had begun well. A note had been delivered for her at the guardroom from an ecstatic Bunty, saying she had left the Burfords' for ever and was now on her way home with Chris's mother.

Back on duty again, Carole watched Chiefie chalking up the drivers' duties. There were the usual grumbles, which Chiefie loftily ignored. Surprisingly, in a fit of generosity, he gave Carole one of the crew transports for tonight's op. Bladowski was captaining one of them and Bob Halliday was still acting as his W Op/AG.

The weather forecast was good, the night sky almost clear of cloud – just a few gauzy veils trailing over the now waning moon, as Carole drove round to the officers' mess to collect her crews.

They burst out through the glass wing doors as they always did, laughing and joking. They clambered into the back of the Bedford, leaving the front seat by the driver vacant for the Wingco.

He was the last to emerge. He took his time, sauntering out, smiling, still fastening up the buttons of his battledress. With strange mixed feelings, she watched him descend the steps. Despite Bunty's good news, despite sharing in the almost universal feeling that, with one good push, the war would be over, she couldn't shake off this elusive feeling of impending gloom.

Yet her gloom lifted as soon as the Wingco turned the handle of the door and jumped inside. It was not just his physical presence, his smile, his seemingly unshakeable optimism, it was the way he looked at her. The eyes told so much more than words. He was delighted to see her. He wanted her. Her spirits soared.

She drove with one hand on the wheel, the other holding his, squeezing it tightly. They were isolated in a little cocoon of happiness, an iridescent bubble, floating away from the war and its terrors. Behind them, the men kept up a continuous sparkle of quips and laughter. The sound somehow preserved their isolation.

When they finally reached O-Orange at dispersal, the Wingco turned, lifted the neb of her cap, put his arms round her and kissed her. One of his special, slow, expert kisses.

'See you in the morning, sweetie,' he whispered, reminding her of Cambridge. He sighed. 'It was fun, wasn't it?'

She nodded.

He said coaxingly, 'We'll do that again, won't we?'

'Oh, yes. We will. Soon.'

'Very soon!'

As his bulky, flying-suited figure began to merge into the darkness, she called after him, 'See you in the morning!'

By morning it had begun to go wrong. At four hundred hours, shortly after first light, Carole shivered in the cab of her Bedford truck and waited. In the intervening hours, she hadn't gone to the rest hut; she knew she was too anxious and excited to sleep. She had spent some time talking to Poppy and Beaky in flying control, but there was no news by the time she went out to her truck. She watched the tremulous paling of the sky in the south-east, and, as the sun began to rise, heard that low rumble of the returning fleet. Shortly afterwards she saw two of the Holmfirth Lancasters in the circuit overhead, the dawn light catching the perspex of their windscreens.

Those two were followed in quick succession by four more.

She counted them down. All but one had returned.

She sat twisting her fingers as the sun rose and flooded the empty runway with a pale lemon light. Everything was quiet. Birds twittered in the bushes on the scrubland between the runways. From a distance, she heard a lorry accelerating, the clanging of a fire bell. Still no one came.

Then she caught the faint sound of an aircraft's engines; she willed the sound to get louder, closer. She wound down her window, held her head on one side, like a dog listening.

The sound swelled. It was intermittent, harsh, laboured. From behind her, the quiet was broken by other sounds, the ambulance bell, the fire engines, the scream of their tyres. One of the fire engines began spreading white extinguisher foam on the runway.

Another minute and a Lancaster appeared, flying very low and uncertainly, at little more than treetop height. Almost immediately, a red Very light arced into the sky.

The Lancaster didn't attempt a circuit. It did a belly flop straight down on to the runway like a wounded elephant. It screeched and swivelled along, red sparks crackling up from the concrete behind it. Then it slewed and stopped.

The pursuing ambulances and fire engines caught up with it. Men spilled out of the vehicles, hoses were dragged. Carole put her hands over her ears. But there was no explosion.

Five minutes passed. A stretcher was taken out of the aircraft and slotted into the ambulance. The black Lancaster was now turning white with foam. Disaster seemingly had been averted.

An hour passed. The sun was climbing in the sky. There was a spring warmth in its rays. Carole turned her face upwards, drawing in the curious mixture of country scents and burned fuel. She began daydreaming about Cambridge.

The Wingco appeared first. Immediately behind him, his crew. A grim-faced Wingco ignored the front seat and climbed into the back with them. They were followed by PO Bladowski and four of his. They were like grey ghosts. All silent. Not even Bladowski spoke to her. And she knew better than to speak to them.

But she did part the flap that separated driver and rear passengers to ask of the crew in general. 'Anyone else to come? Or is that all?'

'All.' Bladowski said stonily.

Bob Halliday leaned forward. 'Chalky's been taken to hospital. He'll be OK.'

She still couldn't see any sign of Jumbo. But Bob didn't

mention him and she didn't ask. Maybe he'd stayed behind talking in ops. Maybe he'd decided to walk.

She started up the engine and pulled away. The gloom in the truck was palpable. For some reason, the Wingco seemed too angry to try to raise anyone's spirits. The silence held till after she had dropped the crews off at their messes. The Wingco was the last to jump down. He didn't even say goodbye or thanks. Nor did he seem to notice that PO Bladowski had stayed behind in the truck.

Neither did PO Bladowski seem to notice he had been left behind. He sat with his elbows on his knees, holding his head in his hands.

Carole started up the engine, but he didn't seem to notice that either.

After a moment, she asked, 'Where to, sir? Or shall I drop you here?' His response was an emphatic shaking of his head.

'We're at the mess, sir!'

'I know.'

He lifted his head. There were tears running down his cheeks. 'I fucked up!'

Then he began to speak. Disjointedly, his words punctuated with silences and sobs.

It had turned out to be a helluva raid. The flak and the Ju 88s with their cannon. Over the target they had taken heavy punishment. His port inner was hit, the starboard damaged. The rudder wasn't responding properly. He was leaking glycol. And Jumbo, good old Jumbo, always so keen to be accurate, he wouldn't press the tit till he was certain they were right on target. It had been hell. Chalky in the turret got shrapnel in his neck. He was OK, he'd live! But Jumbo, good old Jumbo . . .

'What?' Carole shrilled, when Blad's groaning voice came to an abrupt halt. 'What happened to Jumbo?'

Blad looked at her mournfully. 'Hit. He was hit.'

For a moment, he was too overcome to continue. Then he gulped. 'Lying in the bomb bay there is no protection from the cannon fire. The fighters get underneath. Fire upwards.'

Carole closed her eyes.

'His right arm was blown off.' Blad made fists of his hands and dug them into his eyes. He muttered something in Polish.

'He was in agony – agony!'

When the Lancaster staggered clear of the target, they tried to staunch the blood, put on a dressing, used up all the morphia they had on board. But Jumbo couldn't stop screaming.

'Christ!' Bladowski groaned. 'The screaming!'

He put his hands over his ears as if he could still hear Jumbo's agony.

'We had no heating. It was icy cold. We could scarcely keep airborne. We didn't know if we'd make it. And no way could he have lasted the long journey home. So . . .' Blad's voice trailed away. Though it was warm in the truck, his teeth chattered.

Carole sat in silence, waiting for him to go on. A gruesome possibility had sprung into her mind, which she hoped and prayed hadn't happened. She had heard the rumour of such a grisly event on a bombing raid before. The rumour was never substantiated, but neither was it denied.

'So?' Carole prompted after a while.

'So,' Blad said at last, speaking with a curious dignity, 'I did what I thought right.'

Clasping and unclasping his hands, his voice dropping at times to a hoarse whisper, at times failing altogether, he told her he had come to his decision as skipper of the aircraft. He had asked the navigator for a heading that took them just over into France. Then he had brought the aircraft down lower, to what he judged the best height. The navigator had clipped Jumbo's parachute on to his harness, and put Jumbo's left hand on the rip-cord. Jumbo had known what they were going to do. He had put up his thumb.

Suddenly, Bladowski looked up at her sharply, as if to surprise the horror on her face. But she had realized what was coming and stiffened her face to show no emotion.

More calmly, Blad went on, 'Then we pushed Jumbo through the escape hatch.' He sighed heavily, as if relieved to get those words out. 'His parachute opened. I saw it. I figured the French would find him. Even if the Germans did, he would get treatment as a POW. Be hospitalized. It was his only hope.' Blad, the flippant, the irreligious, crossed himself. 'May God help him.'

Carole reached out her hand and squeezed his arm. She nodded. She couldn't speak.

'But . . .' Bladowski drew in a long sobbing breath. 'The Wingco does not agree. He is very angry. Very much now my commanding officer and I the wrongdoer. Yet I ask him, what do I do? Let Jumbo bleed his life away? Freezing in a metal coffin? Or give him that one chance?'

Carole shook her head. How could anyone know? All she knew was that these were questions no human being should ever be told to answer. No wonder these young men were such a strange mixture of childishness and a terrible unnatural maturity.

'I didn't think we'd get back . . .' Blad muttered.

Then suddenly he stiffened. He was looking over her shoulder towards the mess entrance.

The Wingco had appeared at the top of the steps. Unhurriedly, he sauntered down the steps, walked up to the truck, bent down to peer in the side window, ignored Carole and caught Bladowski's eye.

He didn't speak. He just jerked his head.

Without another word, Bladowski scrambled out. The Wingco made some remark to him, and Bladowski actually smiled. Then the Wingco put his arm round his shoulders. Together they climbed the steps and disappeared through the swing doors. Neither of them had said another word to her. She was surplus to their present requirements.

However long I live, Carole thought, I will never understand them.

Nor for that matter could she understand Chiefie. When she reported for duty next day at fourteen hundred hours, she expected some stinging comments on Bladowski and Jumbo and the behaviour of the Brylcreems.

Eating her early lunch in the cookhouse, the airwomen's conversation had buzzed with it. Every event was known about in every section within minutes. Top-secret events took a little longer, but not much.

Comment that lunch time was evenly divided between those who reckoned Bladowski had done the only thing possible, and those who, equally vehemently, reckoned he hadn't.

But Chiefie simply gave Carole one of his penetrating looks, told her she looked shagged, said nothing about Bladowski or Jumbo, though he would have known every detail of what had happened, and discussed it with the experts in the sergeants' mess. She wondered if they would have given Jumbo a farewell thrash, or maybe not, bearing in mind that everyone hoped he was still alive.

At first she had been unable to get to sleep for thinking about him. And even when she had drifted off, her dreams turned into nightmares of a lonely figure dropping into a dark void, who was at first Jumbo and then her.

'Out on the razzle, were you?' Chiefie asked.

'Yes.'

'Who with?'

'I'm not telling.'

Then she relented. 'Edith.'

'Where did you go?'

'The Sally Ann. Dried egg and chips and a jam doughnut.'

'You girls live the life of Riley.'

Carole walked over to the duties board, and studied it. She was down for the officers' mess ration truck. A nice easy run.

She turned. 'Thanks, Chiefie.'

He grunted. 'Just the way the cookie crumbled.' He unhooked the keys of the Bedford and tossed them to her. 'Before you go, I warn you, there's been a bit of a barney in the mess.'

'When?'

'Last night.'

'Who with?'

'You'll soon find out.'

'Was it Bladowski?'

'You could say that.'

The telephone rang then. Chiefie answered it. He waved her to get cracking, turned his back on her and began listening intently to what he was being told.

Outside on the forecourt, she scrambled into the Bedford and started her up. Then first round to the airmen's mess to collect the bulk rations, then round to the back of the officers' mess.

When she backed the lorry level with the kitchen entrance ramp, it seemed to her that the whole place was swaddled in an unnatural quiet. And when she climbed up the ramp and pushed open the door to the big kitchen, she was received, not by the ubiquitous Corporal Butterworth, but by Sergeant Fisher himself, and a manifestly ruffled sergeant at that.

He cast only a hasty uninterested eye over the rations, scarcely glanced at the list and then signed it without a proper check. That was unusual.

'I'd like a word with you, dear,' he said. 'In my office. It won't take long.'

He led the way down the corridor, opened his office door for her, invited her to take a pew, and then closed the door tightly behind them. That too was unusual.

'Tell me, dear,' he said, seating himself behind his desk. 'Have you heard anything lately on the grapevine?'

Carole smiled faintly. 'Lots. Most of it duff gen. What about specially?'

'About here. This officers' mess.' He spoke reverently, as if of some sacred place.

'No. Not really. Except that there'd been a bit of a barney.'

'Who told you that?'

'Flight Sergeant Tordoff.'

'When?'

'Just before I came here.'

'And who told him?'

'I haven't a clue.'

Sergeant Fisher chewed his lip nervously. 'Well, listen, dear. This is for your ears only. There was an upset.' He shook his head at the memory of it.

'Was it to do with the Wingco and Bladowski?'

'Who told you that?'

'I drove the crew transport. There was something up then.'

'Yes, well. That's how it began. There was a difference of opinion among the crews. They were drinking like there was no tomorrow. Which there probably isn't.'

'Were they tight?'

'Blad was. As a tick. He got obstreperous.'

'Was there a fight?'

206

'Officers don't fight, dear. But it got rough.'

'Was that all?'

'Not quite. That's all I know for certain. But something else is supposed to have happened. To the Wingco. I thought I ought to tell you.'

Carole's expression froze.

'I must say, I don't think it's true. And if no one spreads it around, I reckon it'll all get forgotten.' Sergeant Fisher drew in a deep breath and went on at a rush. 'It seems the Wingco was found in bed.'

'So?'

'Found, I said. Found in bed! And not in his own bed! And not alone! With someone he didn't ought to have been with.'

It took Carole several seconds before she could breathe. When she could, her voice came out cracked and unrecognizable. 'I don't believe it! Who on earth was he supposed to be in bed with? Who? Who?'

'With your Queen Bee, dear. It seems he's fond of her too.'

'So, what was it all about, pussycat?' Chiefie asked her the following day. 'What was this barney?'

'Just the usual thrash. Chug-a-lug. Shooting glasses. Riding motorbikes in the corridors. Just the usual good clean fun.'

'Wasting my petrol, the silly clots. So, that's all it was?' Chiefie sounded disappointed. 'Let's hope they've slept it off for tonight.'

'Is something on?'

'Softening up for the Second Front, my spies tell me. You don't have to worry. I haven't got you on tonight.'

Carole's face fell. Then she volunteered, 'I don't mind doing an extra duty.'

'I hoped you'd say that, pussycat.'

'I don't mind doing the crew transport.'

'Kind of you, pet. But Kevin and Buster are doing those. However, I do have a run to the MU at Broadbridge. Spark plugs. The section's screaming for them. Means you won't be back till late. But it'll do you good to get off the station.'

It wasn't until Chiefie said it would do her good that she realized how much she needed to get away. She needed to think. To sort herself out. To come to terms with the happenings of the last few days.

He called after her as she climbed into the truck. 'I'll see the tea's hot when you get back. Watch out for brown jobs!'

The roads were full of brown jobs. Army trucks, Army motorcyclists, staff cars, gun carriages. American tanks and jeeps and personnel carriers. As the newspapers kept saying, Britain was becoming an armed camp as the allies prepared to invade and free Occupied Europe.

The spring weather was lasting. March had gone out like a lamb. April was soft and mild. The hedgerows whipped past like pale green ribbons, there were primroses in the ditches and in the woods just this side of the MU there was a haze of blue. She took off her cap, wound down the window and let the cool wind whip through her hair.

The MU runs were usually uncomplicated and unemotional. No one you had to talk to, no tight schedule, and above all no passengers you had to worry about or wonder if you would ever see again. The spark plugs were loaded, and signed for. They made no intrusive sound except a faint rattle, a background to her thoughts as she sped back to Holmfirth.

By the time she turned in through the guardroom gates, she was even more certain that the Wingco had done nothing wrong, that it was all gossip and rumour. Nothing, she swore to herself, would ever make her change her mind.

At the MT section, she found Chiefie standing by a glowing stove brandishing the tin teapot.

'Sit yourself down, pet. Thanks for doing that. Stores were breathing down my neck. Everyone's twitchy. Something moving towards something.'

'I enjoyed the trip,' she said, holding out her hands to the warmth of the stove. She could remember so little of it, going over and over what Sergeant Fisher had told her, and speculating on what he had withheld.

Chiefie began pouring the dark mahogany-coloured liquid into two enamel mugs.

'The kites have gone. No hold-ups. No snags.'

'How many went?'

'Eight. And, to save you asking, yes, the Wingco was one of them.'

He laced the brown liquid with a reluctant dribble of gooey white liquid from the ancient and encrusted condensed milk can.

'Always reminds me of my kid brother's nose,' Chiefie said as he handed the mug to her. 'Sorry! Just trying to make you smile.'

He sat himself down on the opposite side of the stove.

'I heard one good thing today. One of the NAAFI girls' mother always listens to Lord Haw-Haw. She told me last night's "Jairmany Calling" said they'd picked up an injured RAF airman, presumably Jumbo, and that they were treating him in hospital.'

'D'you believe it?'

'Yes. Can't see why not. Haw-Haw said his arm was severed.'

'But it means he's a POW.'

'A live POW. Better than a dead bomb aimer. Blad did the right thing.'

'The Wingco didn't think so.'

'So I heard. But he wasn't there. A skipper's got to judge when it happens. A split-second decision.' Chiefie squinted at her over the rim of his mug. 'Not still sweet on the guy, are you?'

'I don't know what you mean.' She flushed.

'So, you are still sweet on him! Oh, dear. Oh, dear.' He sighed hugely. 'Well, take it from me, you should cut your losses.'

'What are you getting at precisely?' she asked frostily.

'Don't come all hoity-toity with me, sprog. What I'm getting at is there's even more to this than meets the eye. There's a dreadful hush in the close tonight. They're keeping quiet. They will for as long as they can. Carry on regardless! Keep the scandal in the family. Sit on the story. But when the story breaks, one thing is certain, your dear Wing Commander is not going to come out smelling of roses.'

Those were the last words Chiefie spoke on the subject for most of the following week. A week in which the dreadful

209

hush held. The Wingco didn't contact Carole and no one spoke to her about him. Even among the drivers, his name was never mentioned.

In desperation, Carole left a note for the Wingco with Sergeant Fisher. When she handed it to him, he raised his tufty eyebrows and whispered, 'Is this wise, dearie?' But he promised to deliver the note in person. The Wingco didn't reply.

Carole's desperation sank to the depth where she agreed to consult Arnold on the Ouija board, with Edith and a reluctant Poppy. One couldn't get much more desperate than that.

The seance took place in the early evening, before a long-haul operation to Turin. Poppy was going on watch at 2000 hours and Carole had finally managed to wheedle a crew transport duty out of a suspicious Chiefie.

Arnold was never keen to materialize with merely three supplicants round his board, but this time he consented and made his entrance with a single loud thump. Poppy objected to the speed with which the glass flew round the table, because it threatened to damage her nails and she was growing them for a forty-eight-hour pass, when she would be spending a dirty weekend with a very special bod in ops.

Despite her protests, the glass went on whipping round to the letter C, where it rested decisively.

'Have you a message for Carole, Arnold dear?' Edith asked humbly.

He had.

'Can you spell it out for us, please?'

Immediately the glass began to move again. This time it didn't go round the board. It just made a little sideways move-ment and then positioned itself again in front of the letter C.

'We know it's for Carole, dear. Is this the start of the message?'

A hefty thump confirmed they had guessed right.

'Go on then, dear.'

'C . . .' Edith began chanting as off the glass flew. 'O . . . U . . . R . . .

When the loud thumping started again, they thought at first that it was Arnold, seriously displeased. But the banging came from the front door of the married quarter. It was followed by the unmistakable bellow of F/Sgt Grimble. 'You're showing a light! Your blackout isn't up properly!'

The voice was accompanied by the woman herself, striding in on a great gust of cold air over the threshold and through into the kitchen. She made straight for the window, pulled at a corner of the blackout which was showing about an inch of light, tweaked it into place, and swivelled round to survey the guilty-looking group round the table.

'What the bloody hell d'you think you're doing, airwomen?'

Edith had had the presence of mind to whip the Ouija board under the table.

Poppy the innovative piped up virtuously, 'We were practising . . .' Then, after racking her brains for what they were practising, she extemporized. 'Practising the rhymes about poison gases. For next week's fire drill, Flight Sergeant. You know . . . Phosgene smells like musty hay . . .

'I know them all by heart, stupid bitch! And upside down! Well, I suppose you could've bin getting up to worse. Heh!' She suddenly spied the glass. 'Were you drinking alcohol?' She lifted the glass hopefully to her nose, sniffed deeply, then grunted with disappointment.

Determined to find something, she snarled, 'That glass is not issue for married quarters. You've no right to it. Nothing on any married quarter inventory about glasses, drinking, airwomen for the use of . . .'

'It's mine,' Edith said. 'I brought it from home.'

'Or you won it from your section . . . or our sergeants' mess. You equipment types are all light-fingered.' She turned her pebbly eyes to heaven and scowled. 'I could put you on a charge!' she threatened.

But by now they had all got used to that being her way of saying goodnight.

No one felt like resuming the seance and anyway it was almost time for Poppy and Carole to get on shift.

In a mixture of excitement and apprehension, laced with a tiny dash of hope, Carole watched the crews emerging from the officers' mess. They clattered down the steps, smiling, patting their stomachs, replete with bacon and eggs, stuffing

211

wakey-wakey pills into their pockets, as they waited for the Wingco, the last one to board.

Politely, they left the front seat by the driver vacant for him. She fastened up the tailboard, and tried to rehearse what she would say.

But when he appeared, he ignored the vacant seat, ignored her, vaulted over the tailboard and sat with the boys at the back, maintaining a lively buzz of conversation as they picked up the sergeants and sped along to the operations block.

The only words he spoke to her were when she had finally driven them from briefing to their aircraft. Then he came round to the front of the vehicle, and, like a polite stranger, called, 'Thank you, driver.'

His face was a pale rigid mask, not even a recognizable expression in his eyes.

Boldly, desperately, she called after him, 'Sir?'

He turned, paused, then took a couple of swift and angry paces back. He shoved his head through her open window, grabbed her by her tie, pulled her close and kissed her lips, furiously, passionately, painfully. Not a loving kiss, a brutal goodbye kiss.

She managed to gasp, 'I'll see you in the morning . . .'

But if that touched him, or revived a memory for him, he didn't show it. He didn't reply. He simply turned and went striding away after his crew. He must have cracked some joke to them. Their laughter floated back to her.

She watched his aircraft until it was safely airborne and the low cloud had gathered it in.

Bad weather was forecast en route. A warm front swaddled Northern Europe and the moon was hidden.

But the bad weather served others who were fighting that night in the Allied cause. In the damp darkness, some miles to the south-east and far below the track of the Lancasters, Gabby's Resistance group was grateful for the shelter of the misty darkness as they tried to carry out their orders from London.

Her small wireless set had picked up the message for French speakers at the end of the BBC News: '*Une ligne claire a l'horizon promet un ciel dégagé.*'

That was a prearranged signal for Resistance groups to carry out their tasks – in her case, to disrupt the railway line by blowing up the tunnel, which now carried heavy armaments to defend the Normandy coast.

The war was moving to its climax, every piece of information, every act of sabotage was vital to the opening up of the Second Front and the liberation of Europe.

Last week, their group had been instrumental in discovering a flying-bomb site near Alluay, and before that she had transmitted on to London a coded message that had come through the network from anti-Hitler plotters in Berlin.

Gabby had arrived as their network, 'Gauguin', had been hit by a series of disastrous arrests. Their previous radio operator was in the dreaded d'Orages Gestapo prison. They all knew their lives hung on a thread, their only hope of survival that the Allies invaded in time.

Now, as Gabby scrambled over the sodden moss towards the ventilation shaft of the tunnel, she heard the distant rumbling thunder of the bomber stream. She glanced momentarily upwards. But the clouds were too low and dense for her to catch a glimpse of the Lancasters. She crept closer to the lip of the tunnel. The acrid smoke from the last train down the line caught at her throat. Now everything was silent except for the squelch of her feet and her own breathing. There was no signal from her watchers on the road above.

Gabby crept forward, reached the ventilation shaft. She pulled out the detonator pin.

As she did so, there was an owl's hoot from the road above, the signal of imminent danger. Gabby froze. The signal was repeated, and almost immediately she felt the vibration of approaching vehicles, then heard the trundle of a military patrol rapidly closing in on them. Gabby prayed it wasn't the Abwehr, or worse still, Himmler's Sicherheitsdienst.

Then she gritted her teeth, raised her arm and flung the bomb into the steamy mouth of the shaft, drew her revolver and ran.

Behind her, the shaft erupted in a huge billow of orange flame. It lit the sky, silhouetted the bare trees, glowed on the army vehicles now drawn up on the road. Almost immediately after the flames, a great rumble, the breaking up of the soft ground around the shaft and then an enormous gust of exploding air.

It hit her like a tidal wave, lifted her off her feet, hurled her across the marsh, scraped her against a tree trunk and dropped her, bruised and breathless, on the wet road beside an armed Abwehr posse.

There was no sign of the other two members of her group and she had lost her revolver.

The same wet weather front was straddling the Channel and drifting over eastern England. Two hours after Gabby's arrest, sea fog began rolling in over the Lincolnshire coast. Visibility at Holmfirth was down to fifty yards. The decision was taken to divert the returning bombers and their exhausted crews to Linton-on-Ouse.

When the 777 Squadron Lancasters returned from Linton, Carole was not on duty. And twenty-four hours after that, the balloon went up.

Sixteen

It was a strange, alien balloon. Rumours about it spread around the camp as swiftly and as lethally as any of the Nazi poison gases. Just at this most important moment, when the Allied invasion of Occupied Europe could not be far distant, when Bomber Command was the only weapon capable of striking at the heart of Nazi Germany and 777 Squadron was one of its most successful squadrons, their much admired wing commander had been placed under house arrest. So the rumour went. He was confined to his room awaiting court martial under the escort of an officer of his own rank who had to be flown in from group.

Totally unbelievable, everyone said at first. The wing commander, of all unlikely people. Of all essential people. And why? Why should he be arrested? What was the charge? It would have to be something serious. Treason? Spying? Sabotage? Murder?

Rumours as to the charge proliferated, each rumour swelling until it was more unlikely than its predecessor. And then, all rumours were dominated by what was surely the most unlikely. Rape.

'Holy bloody mackerel!' Flight Sergeant Tordoff whistled. 'Jesus wept! What the hell got into him? Him of all people! Her of all people! He didn't have to rape anyone! Let alone her! Rape's a terrible thing. D'you know, sprog, if he was a Yank or a Jerry, they'd shoot him for rape. Maybe we do that too. Tie him up. White handkerchief over his eyes. Firing squad. Christ! Don't look at me like that, sprog!'

'Then shut up. You make me sick! You know it isn't true!'
'Do I?'

215

'Everyone else on the camp does!'

'Well, I'm not so bloody sure. I think you're one helluva lucky girl! Had a lucky escape!'

'You don't know what you're talking about! He isn't like that! He wouldn't rape anyone!'

'You might know him a bit, pet. But not enough. You see, our well-beloved and soon to be lamented Wingco can probably keep it in his trousers with Miss Innocents like you! But nice little innocents build up quite a head of steam inside lusty young men. It will out! And there's always some woman around who will let it out!'

'So, if it happened, which it didn't, it's my fault?'

'I'm not saying that. I'm saying he may have been the perfect little gent to you. He knows your sexual experience wouldn't cover a threepenny bit. But when he's feeling horny, if you'll pardon my French, he might try to have it off with someone who wanted ditto.'

'That wouldn't be rape.'

'Ah, you're learning! No, it wouldn't. But it would be if he was mistaken. If he was so pissed he mistook the signals. Thought she was giving him the green light when she was flashing on red. Then it would be.'

Carole shook her head wordlessly.

'You might well shake your head! Either way, he's a shit! A big shit and up shit creek if he raped her, or a little shit for getting into bed with her when he's sweet on you. So you make your choice, sprog. Big shit or little shit.'

'He isn't either!'

'Well, don't say you weren't warned. Let it be a lesson. Luckily there's more fish in the sea.' He stretched. Then his tone became businesslike. 'And there's work to be done. You're on the Humber this afternoon, pussycat.'

'Not the Wingco's?'

'No! Would I be so tactless? The section Humber to Lincoln station. You're to pick up two gentlemen from the Judge Advocate's deptartment. Arriving from the big city.'

'Oh, Lord!' she wailed. 'For the court martial?'

'To take preliminary statements, I reckon. Anyway, they're legal eagles in blue uniform. The worst of both worlds. Not my favourite fruit. Real bastards, I'd say. But don't you dare land them in the ditch.'

'I might be tempted.'

'Or take them to the wrong airfield.'

'It's an idea!'

'Don't try anything, pussycat. They could well be on his side. And don't you dare breathe a word to them about the court martial.'

'Of course I wouldn't. I'd probably make it worse.'

'Knowing you, so you would. Anyway, they wouldn't answer. They're a tight-lipped bunch. So keep your pretty mouth shut, or I'll put you on a charge. Just answer yes sir, or no sir, and don't even give them three bags full.' He laughed heartily at his little joke.

'Have you been at Holmfirth long, driver?' The younger and plumper of the two officers leaned forward as Carole drove down the incline from Lincoln railway station.

'No, sir.'

'How long?'

'Six months.'

'Getting the feel of the place, are you?'

'Yes, sir.'

'Has it gone quickly?'

'Yes and no, sir. In a way it feels longer than that . . . Like . . .' Like a lifetime, she thought, but didn't say aloud. It was as if she had been an infant when she arrived and was now fast accelerating into adulthood. She gave up trying to sort out what she meant. In any case, the lawyer gentlemen weren't interested to find out. They had done with exchanging pleasantries. Each opened a briefcase, extracted a typed document and pored over it. They looked up only as they began to skirt the estuary. 'How far now, driver?' the older, more gaunt-faced one asked.

'Another mile and a half, sir.'

'It looks very pleasant countryside.'

'Yes, sir.'

'Those look like Brent geese rising.'

'Yes, sir. I think they are.'

217

'Commendable mess, I understand.' The younger, plumper one turned to his companions. 'Local produce, they tell me. And good cooks.'

He rubbed the beginnings of his pot belly.

'Just as well. We're likely to be here for some time.'

They stopped at the guardroom, where their passes were examined with extra diligence, bearing in mind their rank and muster. The SP saluted the officers crisply, winked at Carole and raised the red and white pole.

'We're coming to the officers' mess now, sir.' Carole looked at them in her driving mirror.

'Ah, yes. I see! I like these pre-war, neo-Georgian messes. It looks reassuringly comfortable.' The older one snapped his briefcase shut.

'Pity,' he added, sighing, 'that the case is so unsavoury. Give me a straightforward mess fraud or cowardice in the face of the enemy any time.'

Carole got out, slammed her door and opened theirs, stood rigidly to attention and saluted.

Then, loud and clear, she said, 'He didn't do it. He's not guilty. You're wasting your time.'

They stared at her in blank astonishment, as if the Humber itself had found a voice. Then they returned her salute wordlessly, climbed the steps and disappeared inside the swing doors.

'I hope you give those bastards two broken beds with springs sticking through. And if there's a treat on the menu, tell them it's off!' Carole said to Sergeant Fisher vehemently.

'That's not possible.' Sergeant Fisher drained his coffee cup and pursed his lips severely. 'I have a high reputation to maintain. This officers' mess is known throughout Bomber Command. And besides, one of those bastards, one of those Judge Advocate's men, will be on the Wingco's side.'

'How d'you know?'

'I just do. I know my *King's Regulations*. The RAF upholds British justice and all that. The Nazis haven't got here yet.'

'You could fool me!'

'Now, you don't mean that. Have another bun. Have the one with the icing. Cheer up. It'll all get sorted in the wash, as my mum used to say.'

'Do you know what's to be sorted?'

'I know the basics.'

'Which are?'

'Simple really. Your Queen Bee says the Wingco forced himself into her room when he was drunk and raped her.'

'He couldn't have!'

'My very words, dear! The Wingco would never do that!'

'And he wouldn't need to!' Carole exclaimed in fury and misery. 'Not with her!'

'Oh, meow, meow! But you're right, dear. As I said to the doc, the Wingco might lose his rag, knock a man down in a fight. But rape a woman? Never! It's not in the character of the man. But the doc said, show me the man whose character it isn't in, and I'll show you . . .'

'What?'

'Well, he's very rude, the doc. A pouf, he said. I'll show you a pouf. And then he said, and I'm not sure about them either!'

'The bastard!' Carole exclaimed.

'Yes, a bit uncalled for. Just his nasty way of saying all men are capable of rape.'

'But why, if it happened, wasn't she screaming her head off. And why has it taken so long to come out?'

'Wheels within wheels. There's a war on. We live in dangerous times. The war effort needs Holmfirth. Holmfirth needs the Wingco. Mata Hari couldn't have done more damage than this. So they've been trying to contain it. Keep it within the family as it were.'

'Do you think they were found together?'

'Well, yes. That much I do believe. Now, don't cry, please. But yes. In flagrante delicto as the GC calls it. Caught redhanded to you and me.'

'Who caught them?'

'Olive Spinks. Intelligence officer.'

Section Officer Spinks, now in her late thirties, was one of the older and less nubile officers; clever, unobtrusive, rarely joining in the social side of the mess. The men had nicknamed her Olive Oil, for her supposed physical similarity to Popeye's girlfriend.

Carole had only exchanged a few words on duty with her, but the IO seemed kindly enough, a decent type. 'She's not the type to make things up,' Carole said, 'or spread them around.'

'Far from it. She knows how to keep her mouth shut.'

'Why didn't she?'

'To be fair, I think she may have tried. But . . .'

'But?'

'But only she and the GC know that.'

In fact, as Olive Spinks had reflected ever since, her knowledge of the affair, though first hand, was very limited and inconclusive.

True, she had, to her own chagrin, surprised the Wing Commander and Hermione Caldbeck tangled on the bed in the midst of what looked like a rather desperate struggle.

Olive had gone to the Queen Bee's room when she came off shift, to ask if she could change her orderly officer duty. Now she could kick herself for ever having done that. Her reason was so unimportant to have started such a chain reaction. An American penfriend from her library days had turned up among the invasion forces gathering in Lincoln, and asked her out to dinner.

His company was moving on the following day, so it was no use suggesting an alternative evening. It would have been nice to meet him, to be with someone of her own age, who shared her interests, nice to get off the camp, where tension was building almost unbearably. But she knew she was no beauty and he would probably have turned out to be a brash American who would have classified her as a boring old fart.

And now all this.

She had done her very best at damage limitation. After standing a moment transfixed, she had apologized, stepped back out of the room and softly closed the door behind her. That, as far as she was concerned, would have been the end of it.

But it was then that Hermione let out a piercing scream and called loudly, 'Don't leave me!'

As Olive stood in the corridor hesitating, wondering what in the world to do, the Wing Commander rushed out past her. His face was flushed and furious and he glowered at Olive as

it if were all her fault. 'Go back in!' He told Olive peremp-
torily, grabbing the handle, turning it, flinging the door open,
then putting his hand in the small of Olive's back and bundling
her roughly inside. 'She needs help!' Help. Olive had been
turning that word over in her mind ever since. Why did
Hermione need help? Was it an admission that he in some
way had hurt her? And if so, why had he? Was he drunk?

That was one of the first questions the CO asked, when
somehow, but not through her, word had reached him.

'He'd had a few,' she had answered. 'But drunk? I don't know.'

'Did he slur his words?'

Now, of that she could be certain. 'No.' Far from it. His
words had come out sharp and crackling, and said with bitter
anger rather than remorse. He had hurried off down the corridor, almost cannoning into Corporal Butterworth, who was
collecting dirty glasses from the hall bar.

'Oh, Olive!' Hermione had sighed as Olive went back in.

Hermione was wearing her uniform skirt. The side placket
was unfastened. Her shirt was also unbuttoned, showing her
breasts cupped in a lacy black bra. 'Come and sit down.' She
patted a corner of the rumpled white coverlet. 'Pour us both
a drink, for God's sake! The bloody man tried to rape me!
Well, you saw, didn't you?' She began to cry. Then she dabbed
her eyes and repeated tersely, 'Didn't you?'

Olive had shrugged. 'I don't think so. Anyway, he didn't
rape you.'

'Because I didn't let him. I fought him off. He might have
raped me. If you hadn't come in.'

'What was he doing here?'

'How does that help?'

'Clearly it makes it worse if he rushed in on you.'

Hermione had thought about that for a moment and then
said reluctantly, 'No.' She stopped and wiped her eyes. 'I said
he could come in for a drink. He was upset. He'd had another
argument with that bloody Pole. I was drinking with the boys
in the bar when the argument started.'

'About Jumbo, I suppose. And this latest Lord Haw-Haw
broadcast?'

'That's it. Haw-Haw saying the honourable Germans had

221

found the wretched airman thrown out of his bomber by the dishonourable RAF, and were now giving him medical care. The ghastly Pole reckoned it justified him, and the Wingco took the opposite view.'

'Understandable,' Olive murmured. 'Group weren't best pleased.'

'So I said to the Wingco, very diplomatically, to stop things getting worse, let's take a walk. The Wingco and I are very fond of each other, as you all know. I know how to get him in a good mood. So we strolled round in the starlight and he seemed better. Then he said he needed another drink, so instead of letting him go back into the bar and start the row up again, I said I had a bottle of my father's best brandy in my room and offered him a dram.'

'I see.'

'No, you don't see! You're looking po-faced! You're thinking even that is a court-martial offence! But, as you well know, if everyone was court-martialled who'd been in a WAAF officer's bedroom, or every WAAF officer who'd had a man in her bedroom, they'd have few officers left.'

Section Officer Spinks said nothing.

'Aren't I right, Olive?'

Olive shrugged.

'These men need a woman's comfort and understanding.'

'And you were offering that?' Section Officer Spinks tried to keep the dryness out of her voice.

'Exactly. But he wanted more. He's highly sexed. He finds me attractive. He got carried away.'

After a long silence, Olive asked soberly, 'So, what are you going to do, Hermione?'

'More importantly, Olive, what are you going to do?'

'I? Nothing!'

'Really? Honestly? You'll keep your mouth shut?'

'Yes. It serves no purpose to do otherwise.'

'If the GC hears, the Wingco and I would be in trouble.'

'He would certainly be court-martialled,' Olive said soberly.

'He's much too valuable.'

'Don't be so sure. If the GC hears about it, he'll have no alternative.'

'But he's not going to hear about it, is he?'

'I sincerely hope not!'

'Certainly not from you?'

'No. Not from me. Not unless he asks me!'

'Oh, God! Are you telling me if the GC heard something, and asked you about it, you'd do a bloody George Washington? You wouldn't tell a lie?'

'That's right!'

'God, what a pious bitch you are.' Hermione bit a corner of her nail thoughtfully, her brain working in double-quick time. 'And if the GC heard the Wingco had been invited into my room, I might get court-martialled.'

'Possibly. Or you'd be moved. Posted.'

'To the back of beyond?'

'More than likely.'

'And this time not as acting flight officer.'

'I really don't know.'

Hermione thought hard again. 'Was anyone else outside in the corridor? Did anyone see him leave?'

'Just Corporal Butterworth.'

'Just! Just! Just Corporal Butterworth! Are you mad? She's the bitchiest gossip on the station. Half the mess will have heard by now!' Hermione bit her lip. 'What if she tells someone who tells someone else, like the S Ad. O? Or the group captain himself?'

'Hermione, I really don't know! I do advise you, though, to think carefully and say nothing. And if anything does get out, stick to the absolute truth. Attempted rape is a very serious crime.'

To give Flight Officer Caldbeck her due, saying nothing had been her first choice. But some whisper got out, and travelled along the grapevine until it reached the GC's ears. And although he tried to close his ears, because, as he told Beaky, it could not have come at a worse or more sensitive time, the GC knew he had to act. Otherwise his own job might be on the line.

One week after the occurrence and two days after the arrival of the Judge Advocate's men, Beaky and the GC were sitting in the tiny box of a controller's sanctum.

223

The squadron had been stood down for the night. Apart from its listening brief, Holmfirth was quiet.

The staff had lowered their heads in feigned concentration as the group captain had swept in and, with an imperious jerk of his head, bellowed, 'A word if you please, Beaky.'

Portentously, he preceded Beaky into the sanctum, then, like a collapsed barrage balloon, subsided into an inadequate chair, put his feet on the table and silently held out his hand for a mug of aircrew rum.

'God! Talk about up shit creek without a paddle! What the hell was the stupid bastard playing at?'

Beaky spread his hands wordlessly.

'Has he blown all his gaskets? Why fight for what is offered on a plate? Tell me Beaky? Why?'

'I don't know, sir!'

'Well, you ought to know. You see the aircrew more than I do. Besides, you're the schoolmaster. The intellectual. Use your brains. Think us all out of this one.'

Beaky rubbed his forehead and frowned. 'Could it be downplayed, sir? The whole incident?'

'Downplayed? How the hell does one downplay rape?'

'But it wasn't, was it?'

'Near as dammit.'

'But she doesn't say it's actual rape. Attempted. That's entirely different.'

'Really? I'm not a woman and I'm not a raping man, so I don't know. What I do know is she's making the most of it! Anyway, for even coming into her room and trying it on, I'd still have to court-martial him. He doesn't have to go the whole hog.'

'Has she seen the doc?'

'No. It wasn't deemed necessary.'

'Why ever not?'

'Because it wasn't actual rape. So, no medical. I took advice. But what a bloody thing to happen! Good squadron commanders are scarce as hen's teeth. You expect them to be killed. We get used to that. All in the day's work! But grounded for rape!'

'Near rape!'

'What gets me is why did he have to when she fancies him? He only has to crook his finger. And we need him. The next few weeks are going to be hell. We have to have him. We have to think of a way.'

'I know, sir. I sympathize.'

'Sympathy is not enough! Think! Get your head round it.'

'My advice, sir, would be, just don't proceed. Turn a Nelsonian eye. Lose the file. Release him for lack of evidence.'

'That's the whole point! He won't have that! He says she either withdraws the accusation or he asks for a court martial!'

'Gee whizz!' Beaky turned his eyes to the ceiling. 'Shit creek it surely is!'

'And don't forget, Beaky, Hermione has friends at court, high up among the air officers.'

'Get her to withdraw the charge herself then. Do the decent thing. Work on her. Get her to say she mistook his intentions. Appeal to her better nature.'

'She hasn't got one. But you're on the right lines. I shall proceed in that direction. It may take time to unravel, the S Ad.O having got the bloodhounds on to the scent. We may not get things sorted out –' the group captain frowned – 'in time for . . .'

Mr Birdsall nodded gravely. 'For what may be on the cards.'

'Yes, Beaky! If that comes up and he misses it, he'll spit blood!'

Beaky sighed heavily. 'I'll say he will. An op like that! He'd be the one to do it! And just when it happens . . .' Beaky's voice trailed away regretfully.

The group captain finished his sentence for him. 'The stupid clot's under arrest for getting his cock out of line.'

Seventeen

Chiefie Tordoff used much the same words, but not in Carole's hearing. This last week, he had been treating her with the mournful respect one used towards the bereaved. It was unnerving. He actually asked her if she wanted to drive the crew transport for what the grapevine had informed the station was to be a raid of special skill and significance.

'Do I have a choice?'

'Of course, pussycat. You might be feeling . . . well . . .'

'I don't feel anything. If you've got me on the crew truck, that's fine. If you haven't, that's fine too.'

'Right! You're on! Only three crews going. Quick turn-round apparently. In and out like a dose of salts.'

'Daylight?'

'Last light.'

'Risky.'

'It's all risky, pussycat. Anyway, why should you worry? You can come to the sergeants' mess dance as a treat tomorrow. Be my guest.'

'I'll think about it. Thank you.'

'I've given you the Commer. You'll have just the one crew. Squadron Leader Barlow's.'

'The acting wing commander?'

'Yep. He's a good type, for a Brylcreem. You'll like him. Jim's driving the other two in the Fordson.'

All the sections had been put on top line. Punctuality was to be the order of the day. There were to be no delays, no scrubbings. Clockwork precision from beginning to end.

Squadron Leader Barlow and his crew appeared punctually as soon as she drove round to the front of the mess. They didn't seem nervous or concerned, and the only thing that was

226

slightly different was that the crew had been joined by the navigation leader, which gave considerable credence to the rumour that this was to be a raid requiring considerable skill.

Bob Halliday was the W/Op air gunner. She didn't get the opportunity to ask him if he had heard from Gabby. But he looked confident, pleased to have been included in Barlow's crew in the absence of the Wingco. She wished him luck. This was how he coped, she thought, throwing himself into his work.

When she drove the truck round to operations, the group captain's car was already parked outside. As soon as Squadron Leader Barlow joined him on the dais and the crews had settled in, the group captain began to speak.

'Good afternoon, gentlemen. Make yourselves comfortable. Light up if you want to. Listen carefully. This is a very tricky and unusual operation. But of the kind we've trained for.'

Yet when the curtain that covered the blackboard was pulled back, disclosing the target, it seemed more puzzling than tricky. It showed the small French town of d'Orages and its mediaeval square. The large target letters caused a ripple of surprise rather than apprehension to stir the assembled crews.

'D'Orages!' one of the sergeants called out. 'What the hell is there?'

'Good wine, for a start. Mind, that's no excuse for bailing out.' Squadron Leader Barlow laughed, taking up his pointer and indicating a tall harmless-looking building in the medieval square.

'That is your target, gentlemen. To minimize civilian casualties, our ETA is last light, when the square isn't busy. We go in low. Drop four-hundred-pounders and then incendiaries and smoke bombs. In that order. Not the other way round. The front of the building is to be destroyed by HEs; panic will be caused by the smoke bombs. I shall be leading. The rest of you follow and then get the hell out.'

Then, after they had been given the co-ordinates, it was Section Officer Spinks' turn to give the crews their Intelligence briefing.

Neat as a pin, reassuringly unemotional, she stepped forward, lifted the long billiard-cue pointer, drew a deep breath and outlined the tall building. It had been impressed on Olive Spinks by group that she must tell the crews as little as possible; only that which they needed to know.

'This fortified building,' she said, 'is the area headquarters of the Gestapo. This headquarters has acquired the most infamous reputation in France.'

Good-humouredly, the aircrew hissed as if at a pantomime.

Olive Spinks smiled faintly and continued. 'Because of the imminence of the Second Front, the Gestapo have been very active. We know they are holding several important prisoners who will certainly be tortured. Some of these prisoners possess valuable knowledge from which the enemy might deduce something of the invasion plans. They must not stay in enemy hands. They must be released.'

Someone asked hollowly, 'How?'

'The object is to destroy the front of the building, burst it open, then, in the panic caused by the smoke, the prisoners can escape.'

'And I'm to be Queen of the May!' a voice called derisively.

The group captain rose to his feet and took his place in the centre of the platform.

'At least with this plan they have a chance. If we do nothing, they have no chance whatever. They're dead men, painfully dead. And on top of that, war plans might be jeopardized. Thousands of lives lost. I need hardly say I would give my eye teeth to be coming with you.'

As he sat down, he exchanged a look with Olive Spinks. They were the only two who knew something of the torture in that tall house; that some of the prisoners were newly arrested Resistance workers, and that one of them might be Gabby. Olive and the station commander also knew that command wanted the prisoners to escape, but if they couldn't escape, then command wanted them dead.

The station commander rubbed his eyes wearily. Who would be a bomber station commander? He watched the eager concentration on the young faces, allowed himself to speculate on how successful the operation might be, and how many of these lads would return unharmed.

What he didn't allow himself to speculate upon was how much better a chance of success this raid would have if the Wingco could have led it.

Then, when the navigation leader and the bombing leader had given their twopenn'orth, the group captain got to his feet, strode outside, jumped into his car and drove at a vicious pace around the perimeter to station headquarters. People were at work in their offices. He strode past his own, down the corridor to the door marked Flight Officer Caldbeck, Officer i/c WAAF.

With a brief knock, he threw open the door of what he privately called The Cattery. He lifted his fingers perfunctorily to his cap, then took it off as a sign that this was off the record, and announced grimly to an exaggeratedly surprised-looking Hermione, 'You and I, my girl, are going to have a very serious talk.'

What took place at this talk was never revealed. In fact, the GC denied that it had ever taken place. And even if it had taken place, its effect on the events that followed was difficult to quantify. What did affect subsequent events was much more tragic. Squadron Leader Barlow's Lancaster failed to return from the d'Orages raid. His aircraft was hit by flak and crashed close to the target.

Debriefing of the surviving crews indicated that the raid had been a success, the mission accomplished. Photographs showed the bombing had been of surgical accuracy. The front of the building was totally collapsed, rubble strewn halfway across the square; and figures were seen fleeing out of it in the midst of fire and billowing smoke.

For three days the squadron was stood down. There was a wild drunken thrash in the officers' mess to commemorate Barlow. Another squadron leader was posted in to replace him. Bob Halliday was given a riotous wake in the sergeants' mess. The ground crews drowned their sorrows in the pubs within striking distance of Holmfirth, coming back to grumble that the lanes were clogged with the Brown Jobs' lorries and armoured cars, and tanks chewing up the road surfaces. And from time to time overhead the sky shook to aircraft flying south, and other quieter, less common birds, gliders. In the

MT section, Kevin proposed taking bets on what would be the actual D-Day, but it was too immediate, too alarming, and there were no takers.

Then, after that brief respite, two things happened. A signal came through that all operational aircrew were confined to camp. And even more importantly for 777 Squadron, the Wingco was released from close arrest.

According to the grapevine, Flight Officer Caldbeck had sent a formal letter to the group captain, withdrawing all charges, apologizing for the concern she had caused, and pleading nervous exhaustion, almost a breakdown; a plea in which Doc Malone supported her wholeheartedly, recommending sick leave.

With the Wingco totally exonerated, the JA's men grudgingly and reluctantly departed. Within hours of being freed, the Wingco was at the top of the battle order for the night's operation.

The date was June 4th.

D-Day. The Invasion of Europe waited only for a favourable wind and tide and weather.

'I'm putting all you girls on camp duties. No outside runs,' Chiefie Tordoff announced. 'I have a six-five-eight to take our beloved stationmaster to SHAEF, but it will need a man. There's a lot of rude soldiery out there. You wouldn't last five minutes.'

'What on earth does he think they would do to us?' Fenella asked Carole as she sat in the MT office filling in her duty log.

'God knows!'

'Oh, you can afford to snigger, you girls. Because you bloody well get looked after by me. Mind, you're probably in more danger on camp than you are off it. You've heard the news? The rapist is released!'

'That's a bloody awful thing to say! He did not do it!'

'Only kidding! Keep your hair on! Mind your language, sprog! We all know the Wingco didn't do it. Wouldn't have to. She's even made a pass at Wright in name and Right in nature!'

230

'She's a bitch!' Fenella said equably. 'But then most Queen Bees are. It's the genus.'

'Seeing he's on ops tonight –' Chiefie glanced at Carole placatingly – 'would you like the crew transport, pussycat?'

'No, thanks.'

'Oh, be like that!'

'I'm not being anything. I'd prefer something else.'

'Righty-ho! Coal truck to dispersals?'

'If you say so.'

Anything, she thought, rather than crew transport. Anything rather than seeing him for the first time after all this in front of other people, especially his crew. When they got together again, as they surely would, in Cambridge perhaps, as he'd promised, it had to be without anyone else there. Just the two of them. Alone. To sort it out together.

Already she found that most difficult to bear were the exciting little tremors of hope that kept spiralling up inside her. The episode with the Queen Bee had obviously been a terrible misunderstanding on his part, and mischief perhaps on hers. Flight Officer Caldbeck was, as Fenella said, a bitch.

The Wingco didn't even like her, let alone fancy her. She had probably made the whole thing up. Or most of it. He must have felt gutted.

But suddenly, miraculously, it was over. He was totally cleared. All that he needed now was her love and understanding. Everything was beginning to fall into place. Even his apparent rejection of her was understandable. While he was under arrest and under suspicion, he was doing the decent thing to her as he saw it.

Flying Officer Wright had wandered in from his office and was standing by the noticeboard talking to Chiefie about tonight's operation. The grapevine had it, Flying Officer Wright said with relish, that it was going to be a really dicey do. The Hun was on his toes, determined to defend the Fatherland. It was the Battle of Britain in reverse. He would throw up everything he had.

Mr Wright was well known for his colourful exaggerations, but suddenly Carole had a vision of the Wingco going off into acute danger, with this unresolved shadow, this strange coldness, still between them.

When F/O Wright finally returned to his office, she went over and stood beside Chiefie. He was staring ahead at the notice board. He affected not to see her.

'Chiefie?' she said humbly.

'Oh, we are speaking, are we, pussycat?'

'Yes.' She paused. 'Can I ask you something?'

'Sure. I suspected that would be the object of the exercise. Fire away!'

'May I change my mind?'

He screwed his head round, stared down at her, black eyebrows raised. 'Change it how?'

'May I do the crew transport?'

'Jeezus wept! What d'you think I'm running here? An escort agency? No, you cannot! I've detailed Buster.'

'Please?'

'Oh, for Chrissake! You silly clot! Ask Buster if he'll swap. He'll probably prefer a load of nutty slack to a load of Brylcreem boys.'

Buster did. He also preferred, he said, not to wait up half the night for the buggers to return. Or not, as the case might be.

Despite the dicey-do rumours, they were two cheerful crews whom Carole picked up from the sergeants' and officers' messes. Everyone now was touched, electrified, by the certainty that the Allied invasion of Europe was imminent. Everyone had heard of the massed armies all along the south coast of England. Everyone knew the invasion was going to take place today, tomorrow or the day after, when winds and tides were favourable. But where? That was the one uncertainty.

As on the last time she had picked up the Wingco and his crew, he was the last to emerge from the officers' mess, and as before, the passenger seat beside her in the truck remained empty.

When he appeared in the doorway of the mess, his helmet and goggles dangling from his hand, she felt an overpowering urge to get out and rush forward to meet him. She half

232

expected him to hold his arms wide for her as he had done when he escaped from France. But she restrained herself, simply leaning out of the open driver's window and smiling at him.

His unsmiling eyes met hers. Then he walked to the back of the truck, vaulted over the tailgate, and banged imperiously on the side for her to get going.

She could hear the boys laughing and singing all the way to ops. Which, of course, was why he had no time for her yet. The morale of the aircrew was rightly of greater importance. They were a long time in ops. She wondered if that was of any particular significance. She searched their faces when they emerged, but they all seemed equally cheerful. When she finally drove them to dispersal, as before, the Wingco called out tersely, 'Thank you, driver,' over his shoulder without turning. This time she didn't call after him.

Time passed slowly. After a while, on the pretext of cadging a cup of tea, she went up to flying control. She hadn't been up there since Bob Halliday had been lost and she had not had the opportunity to ask Mr Birdsall about Gabby. Carole knew that Gabby and Bob had invented a simple code for letting each other know they were all right. Carole suspected the messages came via the Holmfirth frequencies and that Beaky was well aware of them, but kept his mouth prudently shut.

When Carole climbed the steps up to control, it was the last bit of their time of quiet before the bombers' return. Poppy was manicuring her nails, her earphones pushed a little to one side. Beaky was writing, as usual, to his wife.

He looked up as Carole came in, and smiled warmly and yet sadly. It was simply not done on an operational station to discuss or enquire after individual casualties. A pint might be raised to the poor sod who'd gone for a burton or into the drink or just simply had it. But to discuss his finer points or mourn his death was bad taste, worthy of the favourite gesture of pulling an imaginary lavatory chain and holding one's nose.

Mr Birdsall watched approvingly as Jan put a mug of tea in Carole's hand, then he beckoned her over. 'You might like to read what I have just written in my letter to my wife.' He turned the notepad round for her to see. In his neat hand he had written,

I particularly mourn Bob Halliday. I had got to know him so well when he worked here. My first reaction to his death was naturally for Gabby, how distressed she would be, when word got through to her. Yet after that night when he died, her signals died too. There have been none since.

Mr Birdsall looked up at her. 'Is that any consolation?'

'I'm not sure.'

'Nor I. It might just be that . . . she was there. In that Gestapo headquarters. That she was killed. They died together.' He turned the pad around again.

'It's possible.'

'I think that's what happened.'

'In a way, I hope you're right. In a way, I don't.'

When he resumed his letter, Carole walked over and stood beside Poppy.

'Any returns?' Carole asked her.

Poppy shook her head.

'Where have they gone?'

Mr Birdsall replied for her. 'Four of our crews went on combined ops with the Yanks. A diversionary raid to make the enemy think we're landing where we aren't. The others are on a pinpoint raid to take out a certain site. Peenemunde. Intelligence has it they're making another secret weapon to attack London.'

'Is the Wingco on that one?'

'That's right.'

'Dicey?' Carole asked.

Beaky didn't reply.

'If your name's on the bullet,' Poppy said comfortably, shaking a bottle of bright pink nail varnish and beginning to paint carefully.

'You'll get the bullet,' Beaky frowned, 'if your Queen Bee sees you wearing that.'

'She's not too fussed about us at the moment. She has other fish to fry.'

'How many went with the Wingco?'

'Five.'

'Isn't the Pas de Calais a very heavily defended area?'

'Naturally.'

Carole looked at her watch. 'Aren't they due back?'

'Not yet awhile. Have another cuppa.'

'No thanks.'

After a few minutes, Mr Birdsall checked his own watch with that on the wall, sighed, folded his letter and slid it into an envelope and pushed it into his desk drawer. Poppy clamped her earphones back into position and waved her hands to dry her nails.

'Why don't you go on to the balcony, Carole?' Beaky suggested. 'You'll be able to hear them in a moment.' He smiled to soften his reproof. 'You make me nervous pacing up and down.'

'Sorry. I didn't know I was.' She pulled aside the blackout curtain and stepped out into the sweet-smelling early summer darkness. The weather had cleared. An almost cloudless sky arched above. The moon was low in the sky, flooding the airfield with its soft pale light.

She could pick out all the buildings on the other side of the perimeter, the chequerboard of the ground control hut, dispersals, baffled headlights moving around the perimeter track.

As she watched and listened, the runway lights blossomed, and a few seconds later, she heard the rattle and shriek of the fire engines moving to the end of the runway. Almost at the same time, from the south-east, came the first faint throb of engines, swelling in seconds to a deep, deafening bombination that shook the sky, vibrated through the soles of her feet, and lifted her hopes. A flock of black shadows swept in over the horizon. Three peeled away, the rest flew northwards.

Just before she turned to go back inside, a red Very light arced from the lead Holmfirth aircraft. Ambulances followed the fire engines round the perimeter track. Now, as the Lancaster began its clumsy descent, she saw the moonlight gleaming through the holes in its fuselage, thin swords of silvery light that made the great damaged bomber look like a huge black injured bull lumbering down to its knees in the ring.

She couldn't read the letters on its side, but she knew it was the Wingco's. Not bearing to watch, she went back inside. Beaky was on the R/T. She heard the Wingco's voice over the speaker. 'I'm coming in. Permission to pancake.'

Poppy crooked her finger for Carole to go and stand beside her. Poppy whispered, 'Undercarriage shot away. No rudder control. Put your fingers in your ears.'

Instead, Carole took a deep breath and forced herself out on to the balcony.

Another ambulance was streaking to the runway head. Down the Lancaster came, swaying drunkenly, over the hedge, over the dispersal huts, infinitely slowly, close to stalling, then gliding, then screeching like dozens of stuck pigs as its fragile belly ground against the tarmac. Sparks flew up, clouds of dust, a trail of smoke. A wing dipped, threatening to scrape the ground, straightened. On the Lancaster lumbered, pursued now by the fire engines and ambulances.

Then, amazingly, it slewed off on to the grass and stopped. Firemen tumbled off the engine. Medics jumped out of the ambulances. The aircraft door opened.

A stretcher had just been carried off into the ambulance, when there shot out a vicious tongue of bright yellow flame, followed almost immediately by an explosion that seemed to rock the whole earth.

Eighteen

Carole drove an empty crew truck back to the MT section. The stretcher cases and the Wingco had been taken to sick quarters. Yes, the Wingco had got out, Beaky had assured her. The rest of the crew the Wingco had ordered to bale out over France. It was a miracle he had made it home. The two other Lancasters who were with him, and the rest of the squadron, had been diverted to Driffield until the fire was brought under control.

When she pushed open the door of the MT section office. Chiefie was standing beside the stove pouring tea into a mug. Without looking directly at her, he sloshed some Nestlé's milk in and handed it to her.

'I didn't think you'd still be up,' she said, accepting it gratefully.

'Want a drop of something stronger in it?'

He dragged a flask from his hip pocket.

'Yes, please.' She held out her mug.

'I'll make a boozer of you yet.' He poured in a generous slug of whisky. 'I've already made you grow up.'

'Have you?'

'Well, me and the WAAF and the odd Brylcreem boy have.' He drank deeply from his mug. 'Put on a bloody good show tonight, his nibs, I hear. Bloody good. No one knows how he managed to struggle home. A gong will be the order of the day.'

'It was awful to watch.' For a moment she shook uncontrollably.

'Heh! None of that! Drink up! I know! I saw it! The Lanc looked liked a colander. I was talking to my friend in the hangar. The Wingco should have baled out himself, apparently. But one of his crew was injured. So he stuck with him.'

In an almost hysterical somersault of mood, Carole felt a

237

sentimental smile creep over her face. 'No wonder the squadron are so loyal to him.'

'Don't give me that shit, pussycat! Any of them would have done the same. They stick together like glue. Birds of a bloody feather all right. But they're all bastards. Bloody two-timing bastards.'

He looked at her so piercingly for a moment that she wondered if he knew something that she didn't, but when she asked nervously, 'Why are you staring at me like that?' he answered, 'Just wondering if I should give you another drink or drive you round to your billet.'

'I'm half drunk already.'

'The billet it is then. And I'm going to use the Wingco's Humber. They'll either keep him in sick quarters overnight or drop him off at the mess by ambulance.'

This time she didn't mind. Stress had given way to euphoria. The Wingco was safely back. The charge against him had been denied and withdrawn. He had distinguished himself, reinforced his reputation again, wiped the slate clean. All would be well. Wouldn't it?

As she got out of the car at number five married quarter and thanked Chiefie, he said quietly, 'I aim to be around when you need me.'

'You always are,' she said, the whisky making her magnanimous.

Magnanimity was the order of the following day and the day after that. Everyone was euphorically happy. The group captain, back from the important high-level conference held at St Paul's School in London, had an important message to relay to the whole station.

'Under constant patrol by RAF Coastal Command, the Allies' invasion of Europe is under way. The Second Front has opened up. The RAF and USAAF are strafing German positions. Paratroopers of the Airborne Division have landed in France, and Royal Marines have gone ashore. An artificial port known as the Mulberry Harbour is in place. The Americans have landed at Omaha beach and, despite stiff resistance, are advancing on.'

The group captain finished his speech by saying, 'The padre has suggested to me that it would be appropriate if we were to hold an informal, voluntary church parade of prayer and thankfulness at eighteen hundred hours this evening.'

'Right, you lot!' Flight Sergeant Grimble bellowed, banging on all the doors in the married quarters and yelling in through the doorways of the WAAF Nissen huts. 'Volunteers for church parade! All you lot inside are volunteering! And that's an order! Get yourselves into your best blues and polish your buttons. Ma'am wants us all there! And we're not going to let her or the GC down! Everyone off duty, form up at seventeen thirty on the parade ground to march to the chapel.'

'By the right, qui-ick march! Left, right, left, right. Swing those arms. Heads up!'

It was another beautiful early summer evening, the sky clear blue except for a few fluffy fine-weather cumulus. The ash trees beyond the perimeter track were in full leaf and, despite the losses, spirits were high. This surely would be the last summer of the war. Peace was just around the corner. Everyone said so.

Carole found herself marching between Edith and a girl from the PBX. Poppy had managed to get out of this church parade by persuading Beaky to put her on duty. Though she would never replace Gabby in his estimation, he was, as he wrote to his wife, quite fond of her in a fatherly way, and she was becoming a good and conscientious operator. There was still no word from Gabby. He had made up his mind what had happened. He no longer expected to hear.

Outside the chapel, the squad halted, right dressed, then re-formed to march two by two into the chapel.

The first row of chairs was taken up by the station top brass – the group captain, the S Ad. O, the adjutant, the medical officer, the squadron leader engineering and the chief equipment officer. Usually the Queen Bee would have been there too, but she wasn't.

'Been sent on sick leave,' Edith whispered, as they filed into the chairs behind the squadron. 'Should've sent her to the glass house.'

Carole looked around the squadron, but she couldn't see any sign of the Wingco. Maybe he was still in sick quarters.

The first hymn was 'Eternal Father, Strong to Save'. The young corporal who was the padre's assistant had just played the first few bars on the piano, and the congregation had risen to its feet, when quietly, in through the open door, came the Wingco. He had his arm in a sling, but he was otherwise unhurt, almost his old self. But not quite: deathly pale.

Carole smiled her relief and raised her hand just an inch or so. But he didn't notice. His eyes were turned to someone behind him. Another figure was following him in, a figure holding his arm solicitously, helping him unnecessarily down the aisle and to his seat. She opened his hymn book for him and stood so close their arms touched.

Flight Officer Caldbeck.

Carole's mouth, open to sing, remained open in massive disbelief. Her throat constricted. She felt she would never sing again. Now everyone seemed to be looking towards the Wingco and the Queen Bee. From time to time, as the congregation sang and prayed and listened to the padre giving thanks for blessings so far manifested, and hopefully for more to come, people's eyes were inexorably drawn to the unlikely couple sitting close together.

Finally, mercifully, the service came towards its end. The padre, with a foolish smile on his handsome face, held his hands wide. 'Before I pronounce the final blessing,' he said, 'I have a happy announcement to make on this already auspicious day: the engagement of our wing commander and Hermione Caldbeck, our WAAF commanding officer. Let us give thanks for that and ask the Lord's blessing on their union.'

'Which I hope you didn't do, pussycat.'

'No fear!'

'Toe of newt, more like. Or toe of boot up his backside.'

'Something like that! Anyway, they don't need my blessing. She looked like the cat that's swallowed the cream.'

'So she has. I hope it chokes her.'

'But how did you hear about it? You weren't at the service.'

'Grapevine. And what I suspected.'

'You didn't warn me.'

'I nearly did. Thought you needed your sleep first.' He sighed. 'What bastards they are!'

Once again she and Chiefie were by the stove in the MT section. She had retreated there straight after the service. 'I'm beginning to think of this place as my burrow.' She smiled shakily. 'The place I go when life's a shit.'

'Life is nearly always a shit, pussycat. But I'm glad you think like that. Shows I'm not all bad to you.'

You're not. You're my rock, she began to say, then instead she asked, 'What did you mean by what you suspected?'

'I suspected the GC brokered a deal. I suspect Hermione would drive a hard bargain. Maybe she would only withdraw her accusation if he married her.'

'The GC wouldn't do that!'

'Wanna bet?'

'Besides, the Wingco would never agree. Never! Never! He isn't a bastard.'

'He's a Brylcreem bastard! They're totally different. They've their own rules. Their own morals. They live and die by them. The Wingco wouldn't let himself be put off ops. Miss all this! Let the squadron down! No fear! And let himself be discharged with ignominy. It would have been that, if not worse.'

'You can't mean you think he did it! We're not back to that, are we?'

'Keep your hair on! I don't think he did it. But some of what she said would stick. Being who she is, they'd take her word for it. Or some of it. They could do no less. He'd have had it. Really had it. But the squadron would suffer most. The squadron desperately needs him. He knows that.'

'But that's diabolical.'

'Life's diabolical, pussycat. I don't suppose she planned it. She just seized an opportunity. He was steamed up about Jumbo and Blad. He cares about them. He cares about all of them. He thought she was a sympathetic ear. He might have thought all women were like you, sprog. Sweet and virginal. You've got a lot to answer for. No.' he held up his hands. 'I didn't mean that! Only kidding. Oh, now don't go and cry on me.'

'I can't help it. I love him. And he loves me.'

241

'Sure he does. Always knew he fancied you. It just so happens he loves his squadron, so he's marrying someone else. A real marriage of convenience. Now dry your eyes. There are more fish in the sea, remember. One of those fish is quite good at looking after you: he cleans up well and he's very tasty.'

'I'd sooner be a vegetarian!' she said. But smiled.

'That's it! Smile, pussycat. You'll get over it. That's what life is about, getting over things. And this war won't last for ever. Roll on Civvy Street. Then those Brylcreem boys won't be Lords of the Air any more. One of these days, when it's over, I'll look you up, and you'll tell me I was right.'

She shook her head. 'I won't.'

'You will, I promise you. You'll see. You'll wonder why you shed all those tears for him. Meanwhile, I've got a dandy little trip to group to pick up some documents. No passengers. You don't have to talk to anyone. SHQ Humber. Cry all the way if you want. Get away from the station for a while. Get all this out of your system.'

She had gone back to the billet, and changed into battle-dress. Edith had already gone on duty, but she had left a little note on Carole's bed. 'If you want a session with Arnold later on, you only have to say.' But Carole didn't. She swore to herself that she didn't trust any man, even a dead one like Arnold.

The trip to group, however, was therapeutic. The roads were less choked now that the Second Front was under way. The weather was still sunny. She wound down the window, took off her cap and let the wind blow through her hair, heard the summer birdsong, smelled the sweet scents of the fields and hedgerows. The hum of the engine, the smooth steady speed, the sound of the tyres on the road, the feeling of going somewhere soothed her spirit.

And though the same question, should she or shouldn't she write to the Wingco, remained unresolved when she returned, she felt calm, even accepting.

Before she went to bed that night, she detached the little Victorian ring the Wingco had bought her in Cambridge from its silver chain, and dropped it down the lavatory. But despite flushing the lavatory several times, the ring wouldn't be flushed. Wouldn't disappear – so, fearful of leaving it there for some inspecting officer or NCO to find, she had to roll up her sleeves, retrieve it by hand and thread it back on its chain again.

And, like the ring, the question she kept asking herself refused to disappear. Should she write just one last time to the Wingco, take the note round to the mess and ask Sergeant Fisher to deliver it? She must have dozed off later, because some time about first light, she was awakened, as she had been on the night of her arrival, by the voice of the tannoy, this time ordering all squadron personnel to report to their sections.

She sat up quickly. Edith was fast asleep. Poppy, she knew, was on duty. She got up, washed and dressed. Walking towards the MT section, she heard the roar of aircraft engines being started up, and, as she reached the yard, the first of the Lancasters took off into the beginnings of a bright gold dawn.

'Whole squadron is posted to Sussex. To take part in support-ing our gallant invasion troops,' Chiefie told her. 'Matter of some importance.'

Momentarily, she was aghast. 'So, we won't see any of them again!'

'Mebbe not.'

She subsided into a chair and held her head in her hands. Then she asked, 'Have you been here all night?'

'Off and on. It's been a busy night. six-five-eights for all the squadron ground staff pouring in. Kevin and Buster are off on the road. Nearly had to take a transport myself to Lincoln station. So I thought I'd write you a letter.'

'Why?'

'In case I missed you, pussycat. I wanted to tell you before you went that I meant what I said.'

'Before I went where?'

'You're posted too! The orderly room rang just after you left! Don't look so pleased. Not to Sussex.'

'Where then?'

'Turnhouse.'

'Where's that?'

'Edinburgh.'

'That's the other end of the country.'

'From where, pussycat?'

'From . . . I don't know.'

From where the Wingco and the squadron have gone, she was thinking. But that of course didn't matter any more. 'You're a big girl now,' Chiefie said gently. 'You'll be OK.'

'Of course I will.' And then, though she hadn't meant to say it: 'I'll miss you.' She suddenly realized how true that was. 'I won't know who to go to when life's a shit.'

'I'll be around, sprog. I might even look you up some time. Turnhouse isn't all that far north of Newcastle. When this bloody war's over, I'm going to make my way! I'm not a Brylcreem boy but I've got brains. And I've got a burning ambition.'

'To make money?'

'Hell, no!'

'To do what then, Chiefie?'

'I reckon you know.' He drew a deep breath. 'To be around when you need me, sprog. To take care of you.'

Last Light

2004

He had done that. Tom had always been there when she needed him. Her eyes filled with tears. The Messerschmitt bullet in its cage, that memento of the air raid on Holmfirth, rattled as she braked sharply in front of the signpost to d'Orages and swung right. When she had been posted to Turnhouse, Tom had come up to see her every week, either driving there or thumbing a lift. She had learned to stop calling him Chiefie and use his proper name. She had not so much learned to love him as discovered she loved him.

They had been married by her father in the little village of Austwick the following year, in the general rejoicing shortly after V-J Day.

It had been a loving, contented marriage. They were a loving happy family. Tom was a dutiful, caring son-in-law to her parents and a devoted, delighting father to their two sons – James, named after her father, and Harry, named after his. Both boys were mad about flying. Both of them got their private pilot's licence before they joined the RAF. They went to Cranwell, then to their squadrons. Tom had been immensely proud of them. He never called them Brylcreem boys.

Tom had once said that he didn't want to make money, just to be around when she needed him. But he had made money too, firstly buying up the scrap metal that littered so many old airfields and the land around them, then shrewdly investing in a garage, then another, then a whole chain of them. She ran the office. Tom was reliable. He knew his job inside out. He treated his staff well. The customers trusted him. The garages acquired a first-class reputation. They were a good team. Life was comfortable and steady. No great highs or lows.

Then out of the blue came the low; a double whammy.

247

James was killed during action in the Gulf War, and a few months afterwards, Tom, always so strong and healthy, suddenly died of a heart attack. Harry was now out of the RAF and flying for Qantas, married to an Australian girl, and living north of Brisbane; a long way away.

Like a hypnotist's glittering pendant, the bright afternoon sun flickered through the tree branches, summoning sharp memories back into her mind. Her hands on the wheel felt clammy. She eased her foot off the accelerator, opened the windows wider. She was too old, too alone for this confrontation with the past.

None of her friends from number five married quarter at Holmfirth would be here to honour Gabby. Bunty was dead. She had stayed with Chris's mother after her son was born. They had brought him up together. Carole was his godmother. He was blond and handsome, the image of Chris. Polly had married a theatre director and only recently died. Edith was in America. She had developed her psychic powers, become a well-known medium. She had never remarried, but remained faithful to Arnold, her trustworthy spirit guide. In America, she was hailed as a worthy successor to the famous Elizabeth Garrett.

Several miles from d'Orages, she heard the distant beat of the brass bands. Now she was even less in the mood for a celebration. She looked out for a suitable place to reverse in and go home. She spied a wooden gate giving on to a field of sprouting spring vegetables, further along past a beam and plaster farmhouse another gateway leading to a meadow full of white geese.

But the car seemed to keep up its own steady momentum. The music of the brass bands swelled. Houses and trees in blossom now lined the road. The sweet scent of cherry mingled with the smell of wine casks and resin and paraffin.

There was more traffic on the road, the beginnings of the town, a proliferation of signs to the square. She drove over an old stone bridge spanning a swirling stream, past the remnants of the old town wall, past a paper mill, under red, white and blue streamers stretched high over the road, tethered to chestnut trees.

248

She passed a large covered market, more signs to the square, to the refreshments, to the parking. The music of the bands was deafening. The town square loomed. At the south end, in front of the Hotel de Ville gushed a large ornamental fountain surrounded by newly cast bronze statues. At the north end stood the flag-bedecked crimson-canopied dais, above roped-off rows of little gilt chairs reserved for invited guests. The square was already filling up. Crowds wandered from the ropes to the fountain at the far end of the square.

She was going to be late. Hastily, she followed the sign to the car park. But when she found it, the park was full. She had dawdled too long. Having not wanted to come, now she was determined not to be late. She didn't know the town, or where to find alternative parking. Her invitation had merely said that seating would be reserved in the front two rows.

She heard the band strike up the Marseillaise, so the dignitaries must be mounting the dais. In a panic, she hastily slotted the car between two lorries parked on a side street, hurried back to the square, pushed her way to the front of the crowd, lifted the rope and slid into a seat in the second row.

The last of the dignitaries were taking their places on the dais, among them three senior RAF officers with their medals and their gold-acorned caps. They looked very young; 777 Squadron had been disbanded decades ago. Holmfirth-on-the-Moor ceased to be an RAF station in the 1970s. It was turned into one of HM prisons, and now into a detention centre for unsuccessful asylum seekers.

There was hardly anyone in the enclosure, and when she looked around her, no one she recognized. Eventually, she spotted a large woman wearing a big black hat at the end of the front row who might just be Corporal Butterworth, and an old, old man in a wheelchair who could have been Flying Officer Wright. Neither of them responded to her tentative smile. She had probably changed beyond recognition. Time was airbrushing them all out.

A tall, officious-looking man in black tie and breeches rapped with his gavel for silence, and the mayor rose to his feet. He spoke in French. She knew just enough to gather he was welcoming them all, then paying tribute to the courage of the Resistance and the British bomber crew who had gone to their rescue.

As the mayor sat down, the Bishop of Lincoln took over. Pink and smooth-faced, with a melodious voice, he looked even younger than the senior RAF officers. He would certainly not have been born, maybe even his parents would not have been born when the bombers flew over his predecessor's cathedral. He prayed for the Resistance workers and the crew of the Lancaster, and gave a short sanitized version of that raid at last light. He stressed the importance of ensuring that the plans for the invasion of Europe were not jeopardized. He had not of course been told that Bomber Command had wanted the prisoners dead if they couldn't be rescued. He gave thanks for the prisoners who had escaped, and mourned those, including Gabby, who had died. Some official had briefed him about Bob Halliday's marriage to Gabby. He ended with a biblical text – that in death they were not divided . . .

Finally, the German padre was invited to pull the gold tassel so that the crimson curtain slid back and revealed the ornate plaque inscribed with all their names. It was the same colour as the curtain in operations, which was pulled back to reveal the target for the bombers that night. Overcome by a sense of futility and loss, tears ran down Carole's cheeks. But at least there was no one there to see them.

As the service reached its end and dusk began to fall, they all stood for the national anthems. Immediately the last notes died away, Carole rushed to the exit. She ignored the sign which pointed to the refreshment marquee, and hurried to the side street where she had left her car. She found it eventually. But another larger lorry had replaced the one immediately in front of her, squeezing itself right up against her bumper.

She opened the car door and then sat for several minutes in a curious and atypical despair. She bit her lip and tried to rouse herself. Being boxed in between two lorries in a little French street was surely not such a problem to an experienced driver. But it was not just that. Today had been too much. There had been too much emotion, too many sharp, fragmented memories. She felt unnaturally weak, at the end of her tether, and so very, very old. Next year she would be eighty. Life for her was over.

She tossed the keyring in her hand, then slid the key into the ignition and began the laborious business of easing her car out. Finally, she managed it. Age had not quite succeeded in robbing her hands of their skill. It was just that today had made her realize that she had reached the end.

The street was full of home-going traffic. As she steered the car out into a gap, she revved the engine too desperately. The Jaguar shot out into the road, and immediately clipped the bumper of an approaching MG. There came the squeal of rubber, the screech of metal on metal, the derisive shouts of onlookers.

Carole stopped. She sat frozen. This clumsy act was the final straw. The last light in her life had faded. She felt too drained, too tired, to contemplate even the simple effort of getting out of the car.

As if it were all happening in a distant dream, she saw the driver's door of the MG being thrust open. A tall, vigorous, still handsome old man with springy grey hair sprang out to take charge of the situation. He strode over belligerently, and wrenched open the door of her car.

She saw his grey hair was streaked with an almost vanished but still familiar red. Vivid blue eyes glared at her angrily. Then the anger was quenched in a sudden delighted shock of recognition. The blue eyes melted.

'You don't change, sprog,' he breathed. 'Thank God you don't.'

He put her hand on his arm, and very gently drew her out of the car. They stood for a moment simply looking at each other, too moved, too delighted, too awed that this had happened, to speak. Then slowly he put his arms round her, and held her tightly. Her head pressed against his chest, she heard his heart beating as wildly as her own.

She felt a strange mixture of homecoming and wild excitement. She was suddenly invigorated, full of life. Her world had turned upside down. Time was unravelling. The terrible accelerator which had made them all grow up much too fast was spinning her backwards to her youth again . . . Last light had faded, but now, in what had seemed darkness, a miraculous first light glimmered again.